KAIJU WINTER

JAKE BIBLE

ONE

"Jesus, this suit is roasting," Dr. Allison Hartness snaps as she suffers yet another drop of sweat falling into her eye. "Couldn't Bartolli have sprung for the cooled versions?"

"He did," Dr. Robert Tomlinson replies as the two volcanologists make their awkward way across the ash covered earth a few miles from the epicenter of the Yellowstone caldera. "But the bastard kept those suits for himself. Like the ass is ever going to come out here in the field."

Ash falls about the two scientists, adding to the six inches that already coat the dry and cracked earth underneath. There to recalibrate the eastern sensors in Zone Two of the supervolcano, Dr. Hartness and Dr. Tomlinson are ready to get the final task finished and head back to the "comfort" of Bozeman, Montana a few miles away. Not that Bozeman is either comfortable or safe since the entire population has been evacuated in response to the imminent eruption of the Yellowstone supervolcano. Neither of them is happy they have to fetch their own towels and bed sheets at the abandoned motel they are staying in. Especially since they have to wrap the towels and linens in plastic to walk the breezeway from the office to their rooms in order to keep the ash from soiling everything.

"You two know the radio is on, right?" Dr. Cheryl Probst of the United States Geological Survey says in their ears.

"Yeah, but we know you are the only one back in Virginia listening," Dr. Hartness responds. "Bartolli hasn't once done radio duty."

"Would you want him to?" Dr. Probst laughs. "Half the reason you go into the field is to get away from that ass."

"Says the woman that gets to sleep in a bed without having to wear a respirator," Dr. Tomlinson grumbles. "Want to trade places? You are welcome to come out into the field in my place. I don't mind."

"Just fix the sensors and get back to the motel," Dr. Probst says. "You can have a few drinks and sleep the night away knowing you only have two more days of repairs."

"Cram that bright side up your ass, Cheryl," Dr. Hartness laughs. "You can also cram anything else up there you want. Be my guest."

"There it is," Dr. Tomlinson says as he points to the top of a black box that sticks up from the ash. "Last one, then I'm taking Dr. Probst's advice and heading back to get drunk."

"I didn't say get drunk. I said have some drinks," Dr. Probst replies.

The scientists kneel down by the box and get to work, each systematically going over the machine to double check each other's work so they can make sure they don't have to come back out and repair the sensor any time soon.

"That should do it," Dr. Tomlinson says. "Is it working?"

"Hold on," Dr. Probst says.

The two doctors wait not so patiently as their colleague back in Reston, Virginia goes over the signal and readings being sent to the USGS headquarters. Dr. Tomlinson looks up at the dreary winter sky, ignoring the small flakes of ash that begin to coat the plastic face mask he wears. It's almost impossible to tell what are actual clouds and what are the never ending ash clouds that puff up from various points close to the Yellowstone caldera. The man shakes his head and then looks down, watching the grey flakes softly land on the unseen ground.

"Anything?" Dr. Hartness asks.

"Yeah," Dr. Probst replies. "But it isn't making sense. Is there a vehicle close by?"

"A vehicle?" Dr. Hartness asks. 'What kind of question is that?"

"I'm getting readings, but they are uniform, almost rhythmic," Dr. Probst replies. "That's why I wanted to know if a vehicle was close by. Maybe some redneck that didn't evacuate and is out in his bubba truck with the stereo on."

Dr. Hartness turns awkwardly in her environment suit, the thick plastic crinkling and bending as she looks at Dr. Tomlinson. The man looks back at her and shrugs his shoulders, which looks more like a twitch in his identically bulky and awkward suit.

"We don't see anything," Dr. Hartness says. "It would have to be some stereo system for the sensor to pick it up."

"Do you feel anything?" Dr. Probst asks. "Because whatever it is should be right about...huh. Never mind. It stopped."

"Does that mean we can go now?" Dr. Tomlinson asks Allison

"I just mentioned a weird anomaly the sensor is picking up and you think you can go?" Dr. Probst laughs mockingly. "Nice try, Bob."

"I hate you, Cheryl," Dr. Tomlinson replies. "We'll take it apart and start over."

"Joy," Dr. Hartness sighs.

Dr. Tomlinson kneels next to the box again and pulls his tools back out from his bag. He gets the sensor open, and then stops, one hand resting on the ground.

"Hey...I do feel something," Dr. Tomlinson says. "It's getting stronger. Allison, check this out. This doesn't feel-"

Dr. Tomlinson is yanked down flat and a large cloud of ash explodes up around him. He's jammed hard against the ground, his arm lost from sight and the rest of him shaking as he starts screaming bloody murder.

"Bob!" Dr. Hartness yells as she rushes forward. "Bob! What is it?"

"Jesus Christ!" Dr. Tomlinson screams. "It has my arm! IT HAS MY ARM!"

Then the man is suddenly free and rolling across the ground, his right arm torn right from his body. Blood sprays everywhere, turning the grey ash black. Instead of continuing forward, Dr. Hartness stumbles back, turns, and throws up. The vomit fills her suit which makes her vomit even harder as her colleague lies on the ground screeching.

"Allison! Bob!" Dr. Probst shouts over the radio. "What's going on? What happened?"

3

Dr. Hartness rips the hood off her suit and wriggles out of the whole thing as fast as possible, her chest coated in her own sickness. She keeps her eyes averted from the man crying for help just feet from her, afraid she'll never stop vomiting. Unfortunately, what she sees instead doesn't comfort her any.

"What the hell…?" she rasps as ash begins to coat her throat.

The ground before her starts to crack and split, and then something comes shooting out; something long and bright blue. It wraps around Dr. Hartness' body and yanks her down into the newly formed hole, folding her in half in order to make her fit. Blood spurts up from the hole like a small geyser. Geysers are common around the Yellowstone area, just not ones made of human blood.

"Bob!" Dr. Probst yells. "Tell me what is happening!"

But Dr. Tomlinson is too busy screaming to give her an answer. Then he's too busy being yanked into the hole after Dr. Hartness by the same long, bright blue thing. His screams are cut off suddenly and all that can be heard is the buzzing of the radio earpiece in Dr. Hartness' suit that is slowly being covered over in ash as it lies empty on the ground.

"Bob! Allison! Someone talk to me!" Dr. Probst yells from the earpiece. "Hello? Hello? Tell me you're okay! Let me hear your voices! Please!"

***

The sounds of Hank Williams' "Lonesome Whistle" play quietly as the late model sedan makes its way down the ash coated Montana highway. Special Agent Tobias Linder watches out the windshield as tiny flakes of ash float down from the sky, adding to the three plus inches that have accumulated just in the past 48 hours alone. He's lost count of what the actual total is now. His attention drifts from Highway 37 to his dashboard and the small device that continually flashes red numbers at him.

He sighs as the number climbs from 36% to 38% in seconds. Another two miles and the number hits 40%, telling him he can just make it to his destination before he has to change the air filters. Otherwise, the car's engine will be choked with ash and turned into a useless hunk of metal.

His phone chimes for the seventeenth time that morning, but he ignores it, knowing exactly what the voicemail will say. As much as he'd like to do his duty, as ordered by the Office of the President of the United States, Linder has a wholly different agenda than helping with the evacuation of the Southwest United States. There's business waiting for him in Champion, Montana, a small town just a few miles ahead on the edge of Lake Koocanusa.

Or so he hopes. It's taken him well over a decade, and hundreds of dead end clues, to track down this place, and supervolcano or no supervolcano, Linder has zero intention of letting his one chance slip away. He's been so close in the past, but come up short every time. This time, he knows in his gut he's right, that the person he's been hunting is only a couple miles ahead. And it all came down to one monitored phone call.

The last refrains of Hank Williams fade away, but Linder ignores the lack of music as he comes around a bend and finds himself facing two sheriff's patrol cars parked across the road. He comes to a stop and rolls his window down as a puzzled looking deputy walks up to the side of his car, a light blue medical mask across his mouth and nose.

"Sorry, sir, but the highway is closed," the deputy says, pulling the mask down. "Champion is being evacuated today and this stretch of road is one way only."

"I understand, Deputy...?"

"Mikellson," the man replies. Tall, square shouldered, and young, Deputy Eric Mikellson leans forward, his eyes studying the interior of the car. "You have business in Champion, Special Agent...?"

Linder grins and pulls his badge from his pocket, flipping it open for Mikellson to see.

"Special Agent Linder," Linder says. "How'd you know I was FBI?"

"Good guess," Mikellson shrugs. "You look federal and your car sure looks federal." He nods at the air filter gauge stuck to the dashboard. "I just watched the webinar on those things and know they're only handing them out to agencies assisting with evacuations." He nods his head towards the patrol cars. "Guess they forgot to ship us ours."

"The ash shut down your engines yet?" Linder asks.

"Not yet," Mikellson replies, "but just a matter of time."

"That's the saying of the day, isn't it?" Linder laughs, looking towards the patrol cars. "Think I can get through? I have some business to take care of in Champion."

"I doubt that," Mikellson laughs. "Only business in Champion is fishing, hunting, and camping." He peers up into the early winter sky and the constant fall of ash. "And ain't none of that happening around here anymore."

"Right, right," Linder nods, grabbing a manila folder from the passenger's seat. He opens it and pulls out a photo of a young boy. "You ever seen this boy before?"

Mikellson reaches for the photo and Linder reluctantly lets it go. The deputy studies the picture for a few seconds, and then shakes his head.

"Can't say that I have, Special Agent," Mikellson says.

"Linder," Linder smiles, "you can call me Linder."

"Well, Linder, he doesn't ring a bell," Mikellson says, "but we get so many kids up here in the summer it's hard to keep track of them all. Come winter, my mind usually wipes the slate clean and makes room for the new faces that show up in the late spring."

"Of course, totally understand," Linder nods, tapping the photo. "But this is an old picture taken when he was six. The boy would be about seventeen now. I've been looking for him since he was born and I got a lead that pointed me this way. He'd probably be a lot taller and might even have facial hair. And he's staying with an older woman, I believe. Red hair, green eyes, looks like a mature model for L.L. Bean. Or she used to, at least."

Mikellson hands the picture back to Linder and shakes his head. "Sorry, Linder. Wish I could help you, but I can't. Haven't seen this boy, and to be honest, there's a lot of fine looking older women up around here. Just the way the land breeds 'em."

Mikellson gives a short laugh and smacks his hand on the car door.

"Sorry you wasted your time coming all this way," Mikellson says. "I'm sure you're needed down with the major evacs to the south."

Linder watches the deputy for a long, hard second then smiles wide. "Oh, I don't think I wasted my time," he says, then points at the patrol cars. "You mind if I move through and have a chat with your sheriff? Since I'm already here. I promise not to waste any of his time."

"Her," Mikellson says. "Sheriff Stieglitz is a woman."

"Really?" Linder asks. "Didn't know Montana was so enlightened."

"We are in Lincoln County," Mikellson says. "You fit the job and it's yours. That's how we do things around here. And it's the 21st century."

"Then may I proceed to Sheriff Stieglitz? I won't be a bother to her at all," Linder says. "Scouts honor."

Mikellson watches Linder for a couple of seconds then nods. He backs away from the car and pulls his mask up over his nose and mouth.

"Go ahead," Mikellson says, then he turns and waves at the other deputy standing by the cars.

The man cocks his head, shrugs his shoulders and gets into one of the patrol cars. The engine sputters as its starts up, but it catches and the deputy reverses enough to make space for Linder's sedan.

"I appreciate it," Linder says as he puts the car into drive. "I'll only be a few minutes, then on my way and out of your hair. I know you have more important things to think about than some stupid fed coming around right when you're all trying to get your friends and neighbors to safety."

"We sure ain't bored these days, that's for sure," Mikellson says as he waves Linder along. "Drive safe and watch that filter gauge. The ash is getting heavier and heavier by the day."

"Thank you, Deputy Mikellson." Linder nods as he rolls up his window and slowly moves the car past the two patrol cars.

The second deputy waits a minute, and then puts the patrol car back in place, so both sides of highway 37 are blocked again.

"Who was that?" Deputy Shane Weaver asks as he pulls his soft bulk from his car and adjusts his face mask. "Stephie said no one gets through."

"FBI," Mikellson says. "Looking for someone."

"In this shit?" Weaver asks, spreading his arms as the ash continues to fall. "Who is he looking for?"

"Someone that doesn't want to be found," Mikellson says.

***

Sheriff Stephie Stieglitz stands on the curb outside Sheena's Diner, her brow smeared with soot and sweat as she watches a family board one of the school buses being used to evacuate the townsfolk of Champion. The father helps the youngest up the steps, while the mother holds the older one's hand, waiting their turn. The girl looks over her shoulder and her eyes crinkle, the smile hidden behind her medical mask.

Stephie lowers her own mask so the girl can see her reassuring smile. Champion is a very small town, and Stephie knows every single person being loaded onto the dirty yellow school bus. This little girl, Brita Hoverson, just turned seven last Monday, the day the Yellowstone supervolcano started to spew ash actively into the atmosphere.

Pretty crappy birthday present in Stephie's opinion.

"Hey, Stephie?" Deputy Mikellson's voice calls out from the radio on the sheriff's hip.

Stephie puts her mask back on and grabs the radio. "What's up, Eric? You and Shane holding down the fort?"

"You have a visitor coming your way," Mikellson replies, skipping the niceties. This gets Stephie's attention instantly. Eric Mikellson is known for his easy going charm and politeness, so when that disappears then things aren't good.

"What kind of visitor?" Stephie asks. "And why is this visitor coming my way when no one is allowed into Champion?"

"FBI," Mikellson responds. "He's looking for our friends."

"Shit! Now?" Stephie barks, causing little Brita's mother to turn and open her eyes wide in surprise. Stephie pulls down the mask, mouths, 'sorry' to her, pulls the mask back up and walks off down the sidewalk, careful of the slick ash that covers every inch of the pavement. "You're sure he's looking for our friends?"

"Positive," Mikellson replies. "He showed me a picture of Kyle when he was a kid, then described Terrie to a T."

"Shit," Stephie says again. "Shit, shit, shit!"

"You want me and Shane to head back there?" Mikellson asks. "You think you'll need backup?"

"No, I can handle this," Stephie says. "What I want you to do is track down Terrie and Kyle. They were supposed to have been here by now, but they haven't showed. You mind running out to the cabin and seeing if they're still there? We have to get a move on or we'll miss the federal convoy rendezvous in Coeur d'Alene. Lu did us a solid by getting us space in that line. I'd hate for her mother to be the one to screw it all up."

"What about the agent?"

"What's his name?"

"Linder," Mikellson responds. "He's probably getting close to town by now."

Linder. Shit.

Stephie turns and looks down the road, her eyes peering through the ash haze. She sees a black sedan come around the bend in the road, the backdrop of the Montana mountains barely seen as the ash keeps falling.

"I got him," Stephie says. "You find Terrie and Kyle. Once you have them, you let me know ASAP. No more names over the radio, though, got it?"

"You bet," Mikellson says. "Oh, and hey, Stephie?"

"Yeah, Eric?"

"Watch yourself," he warns. "The guy's smile don't meet his eyes. He's a predator."

"Oh, don't worry, I know all about Special Agent Tobias Linder," Stephie responds. "I'll stay on my toes."

She places her radio back on her belt and watches as the sedan drives around the line of school buses and parks a few yards from where she stands. Special Agent Tobias Linder steps from the car, pulls on a mask, and walks quickly over to Stephie.

"Sheriff Stieglitz?" Linder asks, holding up his badge. "I'm Special Agent Tobias Linder. You have a quick second?"

Stephie looks the man up and down. Tall, dark hair, dark eyes, muscular. She can see the outline of a pistol on his right hip under his suit jacket that's getting covered in ash. She catches the hint of a backup pistol on the inside of his left ankle. When she looks up again, Linder locks eyes with her and she knows everything she's heard about the man is right. This guy is a predator.

"A second is about all I have," Stephie says as she walks towards Linder. "What brings the FBI up this way? I thought all federal agencies were gearing up for the impending order of martial law?"

"Yes, well, I'm trying to tie up some loose ends before everything turns completely to chaos," Linder replies, putting his badge back into his pocket. He pulls out the photo of the boy and holds it out for the sheriff to see. "This boy went missing over ten years ago and new information just came in that he could be around this area."

"That so?" Stephie says. "I hate to burst your bubble, Agent Linder-"

"Just Linder, please," Linder says, his mask stretching as he grins.

"Well, Agent Linder," Stephie says and smiles inwardly as she watches the man's eyes narrow at the edges. "I know every face in this county, and probably the next two over, and I haven't seen that one."

"He'd be much older by now," Linder says. "More a young man than a boy."

"Strange time to be working a missing persons case," Stephie says. "I'm surprised the FBI authorized your trip here."

Linder doesn't reply, just stands there with the photo held out.

Stephie takes the photo and studies it closely, careful to keep her emotions in check and expression neutral.

"Handsome kid," Stephie says. "Bet he's a fine looking young man now." She hands the photo back. "Must have been hard for his parents when he went missing."

"It was," Linder says.

"You deal with that a lot, Agent Linder?" Stephie asks. "Breaking bad news to parents when their children go missing? I deal with lost hikers and hunters up around here and that's difficult enough. Couldn't imagine what it's like being in the Missing Persons Division of the FBI."

Again, Linder doesn't reply. He looks at the row of school buses. Stephie follows his gaze.

"Well, as you can see, I'm a little busy today. Have a deadline to meet so we can get down to Coeur d'Alene," Stephie says.

"Coeur d'Alene?" Linder asks. "I thought all civilians in this area were to head due south down to the gulf?"

"We're meeting the federal convoy," Stephie says, "then on to Seattle. We have space reserved on one of the carriers in Everett."

"That must have taken some string pulling," Linder laughs.

"I have a friend," Stephie replies. "Didn't take much, just a phone call."

"Yep," Linder nods. "That's all it takes. One single phone call."

Stephie's blood runs cold as she realizes why Linder is all of a sudden in Champion. So many years of being careful, then she picks up the phone and decides to call in a decade of favors.

"Listen, Agent Linder," Stephie says. "I hate to be rude, but I'm going to need to focus now. Wish I could have been more help. I'd offer to have you caravan with us, but I'm sure you're busy." She points at the six buses. "And you can see we're still filling up two buses, so you probably don't want to waste your time waiting on us. Better get that car of yours out of the ash fall before that engine gets gummed up."

"Actually, I think I'll stick around and talk with some of your fine citizens here," Linder says. "I came all this way and it would kill me if I didn't at least put in the leg work. You don't mind, do you Sheriff? I promise not to hold you up or get in your way. Like you said, you're still waiting to fill two buses."

"No, go right ahead," Stephie replies. "But try not to push too hard. Folks around here aren't always the most friendly to the federal government in the best of times. Put the threat of martial law on them and their tolerance level drops fast. You know what I mean?"

"Oh, I do," Linder nods. "I certainly do."

He holds out his hand and Stephie shakes it.

"A pleasure, Sheriff," he says as he walks towards the first bus. "Hope your trip is a safe one."

"Thank you, Mr. Linder," Stephie replies. "Good luck with your search."

Linder pauses and looks at Stephie for a few seconds then shakes his head. "Thank you, Sheriff. I can use that luck."

He moves quickly to the first bus and pulls out the photo of the boy as he takes the steps and stands by the driver's seat.

"Hello, folks, my name is Special Agent Tobias Linder of the FBI. I'm not here to hassle anyone, just need to know if you've seen this boy."

***

"Grandma!" Kyle Morgan shouts. "Eric's here! We need to go!"

Seventeen and still growing, Kyle stands six feet tall with a shock of pure blond hair peeking out from under his baseball cap. A medical mask covers a big toothed grin as he waves at the patrol car pulling up to the cabin he shares with his grandmother, Terrie Morgan.

Not that they've used those last names in a long time. Most folks know to refer to them as the "Holdens" when strangers are around. Their identities are a loose secret in Champion, but a secret everyone accepts. Northern Montana is a place where people go to escape pasts that they would rather forget, so Kyle and Terrie fit in just right and have for quite a few years.

"Hey, Kyle," Mikellson says as he gets out of the patrol car. "You and Terrie are supposed to be in town by now."

"Hey, Eric," Kyle says as he comes up and shakes the man's hand. "Biscuit took off after something and Grandma is chasing after him again."

"We can't wait for your dog to show up, Kyle," Mikellson responds. "You know that."

"Grandma won't leave without Biscuit," Kyle laughs, "and you know that. I think she loves that dog more than me half the time."

"Well, that's a crock of shit," Mikellson says. "Everyone in Champion knows how much Terrie Morgan loves her grandson."

"Terrie Holden, you mean," Kyle says.

"Well, that's what I'm here about," Eric says, nodding towards the two story log cabin. "Can we go inside and out of this ash? I'm getting sick of this shit."

"Watch your mouth, Eric Mikellson," Terrie Morgan snaps as she comes around the corner of the cabin, preceded by the massive half-husky, half-wolf named Biscuit. "What the heck you doing out here? Shouldn't you be watching the road?"

"We have a problem," Mikellson says. "Someone's come to town looking for you."

A handsome woman in her early sixties, Terrie Morgan stands almost as tall as her grandson. Her bright red hair is now mostly white and it is twisted up into a bun under her ash covered black cowboy hat. Her face is weathered from a life out in the elements, but still holds a glow of youth and strength common to the people of northern Montana. Some of that strength drains away at Mikellson's words.

"Get your butt inside," Terrie says. "Tell me all about it."

She turns and smacks her leg and Biscuit heels instantly, the 100 plus pound canine falling in step as they all walk inside the cabin.

Terrie shakes off her hat and sets it on a rack by the door. They strip off their ashy coats and hang them up as Biscuit runs to the huge deer hide couch and jumps up, spins around four times, then lies down in a puff of ash.

Animal heads of all types and sizes adorn the cabin's walls, side by side with pictures small and large of Kyle with Terrie, as well as Terrie and Kyle with a woman younger than Terrie, who looks just like the two of them. There are also quite a few pictures of Terrie standing arm in arm with Stephie, some with Kyle, some without, but it's obvious the cabin is home to the sheriff as well.

"You aren't boxing everything up?" Mikellson asks as he looks around the cabin, seeing only a few duffel bags and suitcases stacked by the door while the rest of the cabin's contents remain where they've been for years.

"No point," Terrie says. "That supervolcano blows and this cabin will be buried under several feet of ash. Won't make a difference if this stuff is packed in boxes or sitting out. We won't be coming back for it anytime soon, if at all."

"True," Mikellson nods and takes a seat at the breakfast table next to the open kitchen.

"This is a sitting visit?" Terrie asks, her hands on her hips. "Better just come out and say it."

"Special Agent Tobias Linder just rolled into town," Mikellson says. "Sure you don't want to sit down?"

"Shit," Terrie says, surprising both Kyle and Mikellson. "Pardon my French."

She takes a seat and gestures for Kyle to do the same.

"Where is he now?" Terrie asks.

"Talking with Stephie, last I heard," Mikellson replies. "She'll get rid of him, but I don't know how long that will take."

"Who's Special Agent Tobias Linder?" Kyle asks.

Mikellson gives Terrie a surprised look, but the woman just shakes her head and the deputy drops it.

"FBI," Terrie says to Kyle. "He's one of the reasons we live here."

"I thought the FBI helped with witness protection?" Kyle asks. "Why are we afraid of him?"

"I'm not afraid of that man," Terrie snaps. "Not ever."

Kyle looks from his grandmother to Mikellson then sighs and crosses his arms.

"So, who is he?" Kyle asks.

"Trouble," Terrie says.

"And a delay," Mikellson says. "If he stays in town, then that means you can't get on a bus."

"I'd rather drive the Bronco anyway," Terrie says. "The thought of being cramped in one of those school buses gives me the creeps. And Biscuit won't like it none either."

At the mention of his name, the huge hybrid looks up and gives a low woof, then settles back down and closes his eyes.

"See?" Terrie says. "He's completely stressed out."

"You two still haven't told me why we are hiding from this Linder guy?" Kyle says. "Maybe Mom sent him. The US Marshals and FBI work together all the time. Maybe he's here to help escort the buses to the convoy?"

"He's not," Mikellson says. "He's here for you two."

"I'm confused," Kyle says. "Mom's a US Marshall, Stephie is the sheriff of Lincoln County, and you pretty much live here." Kyle points at Mikellson. "Or at least you always eat here. It's not like we're hiding from the law. Why are we worried about an FBI agent? Isn't he one of the good guys too?"

"No, he's not," Terrie says. "And I don't have time to explain it all to you."

"Probably should have done that a while ago," Mikellson says quietly.

"Shut your meat hole," Terrie says, jabbing a finger towards Mikellson. "You have no idea what it's taken to keep us hidden here."

"I have a pretty good idea, thank you," Mikellson replies. "Don't think I don't, Terrie Morgan."

"Yeah, yeah, you do," Terrie nods. "Sorry, Eric."

"So no one is going to tell me who this guy is?" Kyle snaps. "Just gonna leave me in the dark like usual."

"Oh, stop being such a drama queen," Terrie says. "Finish packing the Bronco while I talk with Eric. You do that and maybe I'll fill you in once we get on the road."

The sarcastic reply dies on Kyle's lips as he sees the look in his grandma's eyes. Not the time to be a shit.

"Fine," Kyle says as he stands up quickly, knocking over his chair.

Biscuit jumps from the couch barking, his massive jaws open wide.

"Biscuit!" Kyle shouts. "Shut up! It's just me!"

The hybrid gives a last bark, then looks over at Kyle and whines.

"Come on, boy," Kyle says as he walks over and grabs his coat. "You can help me pack."

"Keep an eye on him," Terrie says. "We're leaving as soon as the Bronco is ready. We won't have time to chase him down if he takes off after another darn squirrel."

"Yeah, yeah," Kyle says, sounding just like his grandma. "Come on, B."

The boy opens the door and Biscuit rushes out, straight for the firs and pines that surround the cabin.

"Biscuit! Dammit! Get back here!" Kyle yells as he closes the door behind him.

Mikellson looks at Terrie, but she holds up a finger. "Don't say it."

"You still haven't told him who Linder is?" Mikellson asks.

"I said not to say it," Terrie replies. "And, honestly, it wasn't my choice. Lu is the one that said she'd tell him when she thought the boy was ready."

"But, Terrie, knowing who the man is, is important to keeping you safe!" Mikellson exclaims. "You know better!"

"And so does my daughter!" Terrie snaps. "But no matter how many times I bring it up, she just says she'll do it later."

"Why do you think he's here now?" Mikellson asks. "There's a freaking volcano about to fully erupt and cover most of this country in feet of ash. Strange time to all of a sudden pick up the trail."

"It's not strange at all," Terrie says. "He must have gotten a hold of Lu's call logs."

"Why would that matter?" Mikellson asks. "Lu uses burners when she talks to you. You never call her work number. Did she screw up and call here with a damn federal phone?"

"She didn't screw up, Stephie and I did," Terrie says. "When the evacuation information came in, and we found out it was going to be a lottery system for all civilians to get on the ships leaving Galveston, New Orleans, and Mobile, Stephie called Lu directly to see if we could get the folks here in Champion on one of the military carriers."

"I know all of that," Mikellson says. "Why would that lead Linder here?"

"Lu didn't have a chance to get a new burner when this all happened," Terrie explains. "The only way to get a hold of her was to call her on her official cell phone. It was one call and only lasted five minutes." Terrie spreads her arms to indicate the cabin. "It has taken Stephie a lot of work to make a home for us and keep us safe. To say Lu owes the woman a favor or two is an understatement. Stephie took a risk to cash in on those favors. We thought that even if Linder was snooping on Lu's phone logs there'd be no way he could come up here now, not with the chaos of everything."

"I guess you were wrong there," Mikellson says.

"Yeah, we were," Terrie says. "Don't rub it in."

"What's the plan?" Mikellson asks. "How do we get you two out of here without Linder knowing?"

"I'll take Kyle with me in the Bronco and we'll head over to Bonners Ferry," Terrie explains. "We'll wait for you there."

"But you have to go right through town to get to 37," Mikellson says. "If he's still there he'll see you. I can tell this guy doesn't miss much."

"He doesn't know my Bronco," Terrie says. "And I won't be driving."

"Who will?" Mikellson asks then pauses. "No...Kyle? You think he won't recognize him?"

"It's been years," Terrie says. "Lu barely recognizes the boy each time she sees him and that's every three months or so. It'll be enough to get us through town and onto the highway."

"I hope so," Mikellson sighs. "For that boy's sake, I really do."

***

"Just stay right there," Kyle growls at Biscuit as he drags the hybrid over by the Bronco. "Don't move. No more chasing squirrels."

The hybrid woofs, and then lies down in the ash by the rear wheel of the big SUV. A classic 1984 full size Bronco, the vehicle has been outfitted with heavy duty suspension, a turbo charged V-8 multi-fuel engine, oversized tires, and reinforced front and rear bumpers. Kyle calls it the Tank.

He lowers the back and tosses in two duffel bags, then turns to go back to the porch for the suitcases. Biscuit watches him go, then his hackles rise and he jumps up barking.

"Jesus, B!" Kyle yells, leaping a foot into the air. "You scared the shit out of me!"

Biscuit keeps barking and barking and Kyle is about to stomp over there and whack him on his massive snout, but he stops as he feels his legs start to tremor.

No, not his legs, but the ground. The ground is tremoring. Then it's shaking and after two or three seconds, it's full on quaking.

"Grandma!" Kyle yells. "Grandma!"

Terrie and Mikellson burst from the cabin and stare at the swaying trees around the cabin.

"This can't be good!" Mikellson shouts over the sound of the earthquake.

TWO

"We have to send someone out there!" Dr. Probst shouts as she stands in front of Dr. Alexander Bartolli's desk. Short, thin, with dark hair and hazel eyes, Dr. Probst's physicality is far from intimidating, but the tone in her voice puts her immediate superior on edge in seconds. "We haven't heard from Coral or Bob in a full day!"

"The interference from the volcano is the problem," Dr. Bartolli says, trying to dismiss her with a casual wave of his hand, but all it does is stoke a fire in the woman's eyes. "Are the sensors working?"

"No," Dr. Probst replies quickly. "But-"

"Have you tried the local authorities?"

"There are no local authorities and you know that!" Dr. Probst snaps. "The whole area has been evacuated down to Mobile or Galveston or one of those places. Coral and Bob are on their own out there and it didn't sound like the radio went out because of interference. I heard…"

"Screaming, yes you said that," Dr. Bartolli sighs. "I'm going to have to default to interference again. It was probably a static squeal you heard. The stress we are all under, it's no wonder, really."

Dr. Probst has to use all of her willpower not to reach across the desk and smack the man.

"If we don't hear from them by tomorrow, you make a call and get someone to go look for them," Dr. Probst says. "Or I go looking myself."

"In what? Your secret spy plane?" Dr. Bartolli laughs. "Just do your job, Cheryl. Let the military worry about people out in the field. I'll file a report as I'm required to, but I'm not making any special calls. I can bet we'll hear from them soon, once they get to a working phone."

"Fine," Dr. Probst says, turns abruptly, and storms out of the office.

Dr. Bartolli watches her go, and then shakes his head as he goes back to the work on his desktop. He makes a mental note to file the report later. Or in the morning. Well, sometime tomorrow.

***

US Marshal Lucinda "Lu" Morgan reaches out and puts her hand against the side of the bus as the world around her shakes. Her sunglass-shaded eyes search the area, finding the other US Marshals bracing themselves against the four other buses with "Federal Bureau of Prisons" stenciled on the sides. The ground continues to shake for a good couple of minutes before slowly becoming steady once more.

"Hal! You good?" Lu shouts to a short, heavily muscled man on the other side of the gas station.

"Fine here!" US Marshal Hal Stacks shouts back. "You?"

"Just a little wobbly," Lu replies. "Talley?"

"Cool," US Marshall James Talley replies from the bus behind Hal's. Tall and lanky with deep black skin, Talley adjusts his sunglasses, then pulls the gas hose from the bus and sets it into the pump. "Ready to go."

"Good," Lu nods. "Stevie?"

"Five by five, Lu," US Marshall Steven LeDeaux replies from the bus right behind Lu's. Skinny legs with a great big beer belly, Stevie looks like he's about to fall over at any second from his top heavy body. Many a fugitive have made the mistake of underestimating the speed of those skinny legs.

"Do you even know what that means, Stevie?" Lu laughs.

"Not a clue," Stevie laughs back. "Just something my Aunt Jessie always said."

Lu turns and looks at the bus up ahead of hers. "Tony? All good?"

"All good, boss," US Marshal Anthony Whipple responds. The youngest of the marshals present, Tony has the look of a star quarterback with blond hair, blue eyes, perfect complexion. He lowers his sunglasses and gives Lu a wink.

She lowers her sunglasses and glares as the winter wind whips about the gas station, kicking up ash and snow that covers the whole city of Salt Lake. Tony winks again and raises his glasses, then pulls the gas hose from the bus and sets it back into the pump. Lu hears a loud click and does the same with her hose before pulling her jacket tight about her and walking towards the station's small market.

"Bathroom?" Lu asks.

The cashier points towards the back, his eyes angrily studying the street outside his station. Dozens of cars are lined up along the road as National Guard soldiers pace back and forth at the gas station's entrances, with M-16s in hand, blocking any access to the station's precious gas.

"You folks about done out there?" the cashier asks. "I gotta let those folks fill up so I can get out of here."

"We just dropped nearly a thousand dollars on gas," Lu says. "That should make up for it."

"It's not about the money, lady," the cashier grumbles. "It's about living."

Lu rolls her eyes, heads to the women's bathroom and flips on the dim light. She locks the door and undoes her jeans, carefully taking her sidearm from her belt and placing it on the small sink next to the toilet. She takes care of business, and then stands before the mirror as she washes her hands.

Tall like her mother, red haired like her mother, a natural beauty that could have been a model just like her mother, except for the obviously broken nose that healed crooked, Lu has had to fight her way up the ladder to her post in the US Marshal's Denver office. No one takes a woman that looks like her seriously in law enforcement. They instantly think she's a lipstick lesbian and only there to fill a quota. So she was glad she could handpick her crew when she was given the assignment to move fifty of the most dangerous federal prisoners from the Florence, Colorado maximum security penitentiary across the West and up to Seattle.

Knowing the other marshals respect and trust her goes a long way when she has to deal with the fact that the fifty men spread out in the five buses would have zero problem cutting off her head and shitting down her neck.

She redoes the ponytail her hair is tied up in and then takes a deep breath, ready to get back out there and get on the road to Coeur d'Alene.

"Speaking of," she laughs as her cell phone rings just as she walks out of the bathroom. She pulls it from her belt and her heart leaps into her throat when she sees the number. "Mom? Mom, what's wrong? Is it Kyle? Is he hurt? Why are you calling me directly?"

"Calm down, sweetheart," Terrie replies. "Kyle is fine. We're a little shaken up by an earthquake that just hit us, but we're both okay."

"You felt that too?" Lu asks. "Jesus, if it's coming from Yellowstone, then we are fucked."

Lu hears her mom take a deep breath at the use of language, but she doesn't get a reprimand; they are long past that argument.

"Listen, Lu, there's been a change of plans," Terrie says. "Kyle and I will be driving the Bronco until we meet up with you all. We're in the car now and about to head through Champion on our way to Bonners Ferry."

"You're driving?" Lu asks as she nods to the cashier and steps out of the market and into the brisk winter air. "Is something wrong with one of the buses? Did they fill up too fast?"

"No, it's not the buses," Terrie says. "Everything is running on time and smooth with those plans."

"Okay, then what is it. Mom?" Lu asks. "You're starting to freak me out."

Lu raises a hand and twirls her finger in the air. Hal sees it, turns and gives a loud whistle. All of the prison corrections officers that are accompanying the buses as backup hustle to their vehicles followed by the US Marshal assigned to each bus.

"I don't want you to freak out, okay?" Terrie says. "Can you promise me that? No freaking out."

Lu hears Kyle say something in the background, but Terrie tells him to be quiet and drive.

"Goddammit, Mom! Spit it the fuck out now!" Lu snaps.

Talley looks over and frowns, but Lu shakes her head and points at his bus. He hops on with two corrections officers and the bus doors close and locks behind him. Lu waits for her two officers to board the bus, and then she follows right behind. Inside sits the driver, safe in a steel mesh cage around the driver's seat, two more corrections officers in a steel cage at the back of the bus, and ten federal prisoners shackled to their seats in the middle of the bus. Lu takes her seat next to the two officers that boarded with her and looks through the steel mesh a foot from her face.

All eyes are on her and she has to fight not to shiver.

"He found Champion," Terrie states, her voice calm and cool. "He hasn't found us, but he's here."

Lu loses against the shiver and her body shudders. One of the prisoners meets her eye and smiles. She lowers her sunglasses, glares, and then flips him off. His smile widens.

There are several honks and the driver looks over his shoulder at Lu.

"We set to leave, Marshal?" the driver asks.

"Yeah," Lu replies. "We're set. Move out." She turns her attention back to the phone. "Listen, Mom, I'll need to call you back. Fifteen minutes tops. I just need to make sure we get back onto I-15 and are headed your way."

"I understand, sweetheart," Terrie replies. "I know the drill. You do your job and just know I'm doing mine. There's no way I'll let that man get our boy, you hear me?"

"I hear you," Lu says. "Thank you, Mom."

"Never thank me for protecting this family," Terrie says. "It's a mother's duty and why God put me on this earth."

"Call you in fifteen," Lu says and hangs up.

It takes all of her will to keep the tears and screams at bay. She can't risk showing any weakness in front of the prisoners. Men like this can smell it, and even shackled, they will find a way to exploit that weakness to their own ends.

The convoy of buses moves out into the street, pausing only so the National Guard soldiers can move to let them pass, then they are off to the I-15 onramp and on their way north to I-90 and Coeur d'Alene.

He found them, Lu thinks. *How the holy fucking hell did he...? Shit...*

She looks down at her phone and realizes that the one and only time they've ever broken protocol must be the reason. Lu just hopes that the fact a supervolcano is weeks, days, minutes from erupting will slow the man down.

She hopes, but she doesn't kid herself. She knows the man too well.

***

Linder steps from the last bus just as the Bronco cruises down Main Street. He turns and glances at the vehicle, giving the driver only a cursory glance; a teenage boy with his dog (a huge dog) in the passenger seat. Probably a common sight in Montana. He's about to mentally wish the kid good luck making it out there when he catches the sheriff watching the Bronco closely.

Then she turns and looks right at him.

Linder forces himself to keep walking towards his car and not to look over his shoulder at the Bronco. If the situation was a game of poker, then the sheriff would have already lost, as she gave her entire bluff away.

"Thank you for your time, Sheriff," Linder says as he casually wipes ash off the driver's side window then opens the door and hops in. "Travel safe."

"You too, Agent Linder," Stephie says. "Hope you make it back to Sacramento without any trouble."

This makes Linder pause, but only for a split second. He nods and hops into the sedan, starts up the engine, and pulls away from the sidewalk. He turns the car in the direction he came, which is the same direction as the Bronco was going, waves to the sheriff, and drives off.

His first thought is of how the sheriff knew he was from the Sacramento field office when he clearly hadn't told her. He pulls his cell phone from his pocket and sees he now has thirty plus voicemails, most of them coming in within the last half hour.

"The bitch checked up on me," Linder laughs. "What does she think she's going to accomplish with that? Get me reprimanded? Fired? Too late for any of that now."

He turns the stereo on and begins to sing along to Hank Williams's "Cold, Cold Heart."

***

"He's following you," Stephie says the second Terrie answers her phone.

Terrie pauses, about to sit up in the backseat of the Bronco where she's been hiding.

"How do you know?" Terrie asks.

"Everything okay?" Kyle asks from the driver's seat.

"Just keep your eyes on the road," Terrie says. "Don't worry about anything else."

"The man is super paranoid like you said," Stephie replies. "I glanced your way for a split second and he caught it. I could be wrong, but my gut says I'm not."

"Okay," Terrie sighs. "We'll have to take some back roads and get to Bonners Ferry the long way. We may miss you guys. Just keep going if we aren't there. We'll catch up to you in Coeur d'Alene."

"What if he tries to stop you? You prepared?" Stephie asks.

Terrie looks at the .45 in her hand and laughs. "If I'm not ready after ten years with ICE and another twenty with the marshals, then the man deserves to win."

"Don't say shit like that," Stephie says.

"Don't cuss," Terrie replies.

"Oh, shut up," Stephie chuckles. "I love you."

"Love you too," Terrie responds. "Now hang up and do your job. You have a whole town to move."

Terrie waits for the click, and then puts her cell phone back into her pocket.

"Take Cedar Ridge Trail," Terrie says.

"What? Why?" Kyle asks. "That road dead ends."

"I know," Terrie says. "It's also not on any GPS maps. We're going to drive to the end and wait. Once I know the coast is clear, we'll get back on 37 and head to Bonners Ferry."

"Are we really going to miss connecting with the Champion buses?" Kyle asks.

"Not if I can help it," Terrie says. "But even if we do, there's enough extra gas in the reserve tank to get us to Coeur d'Alene so we can meet up with your mom."

***

The sedan shakes and starts to swerve and it takes all of Linder's control to keep the car from skidding off the road. Another tremor; a bad one.

He switches from Hank Williams to the local AM news station, but all he gets is a few words and mostly static. Linder turns the radio off completely and focuses on the road. He comes around a long bend, and then narrows his eyes. Ahead is a straight stretch of road that goes on for a mile at least. There's a couple dips and rises, but even with those, he should be able to see the Bronco.

But he doesn't.

"Wiley bitch," Linder says, struggling to keep his temper in check.

After more than a decade of hunting, he's so close to his prey he can taste it. Yet the woman has slipped from his grasp. He knows she's good, he'd be a fool not to know that, but there's no way they could have spotted his tail. They must have been given a heads up.

And Linder knows exactly who gave them that heads up.

***

"That's everyone that's coming," Mikellson says as watches the doors close on the last bus. "Time to go."

"Shane waiting for us?" Stephie asks as she walks to her patrol car.

"Yeah," Mikellson nods, stepping to his own car. "He's gassed up and ready to hit the road. You taking lead?"

"No, you can," Stephie says. "I'll follow. Shane can pull in behind me once we get to him."

"Works for me," Mikellson says.

He starts up his car and cringes as it sputters slightly. Even with new air filters, the ash is playing havoc with the engine. The diesel engines of the school buses handle the issue better than the gasoline engines of the patrol cars, but Mikellson wonders for how long. If any of the buses break down before they get to Idaho, they are screwed.

He shoves the worry from his mind and pulls out into the street, honks at the buses to follow, then takes off down the road, ready to get as far away from the source of the ash as possible.

***

The southbound lanes of I-15 are choked with cars, buses, RVs, tractor trailers, and National Guard trucks and Humvees. Everyone is heading south to the hundreds of ships in the Gulf of Mexico waiting to take them to gracious countries willing to offer the Americans sanctuary from the supervolcano that scientists believe will destroy most of North America when it erupts.

But the northbound lanes of I-15 are pretty much empty as far as the eye can see. There's the occasional local or state law enforcement vehicle, but mostly, the convoy has the interstate to itself.

"We getting our own cruise ship?" a prisoner asks.

"No talking," one of the corrections officers next to Lu snaps.

"Just wondering if I'll finally get to learn shuffleboard or not," the prisoner laughs.

A few others chuckle with him and the officer stands up and whacks the steel mesh with the butt of his pump action shotgun.

"I said shut up!" he shouts. "Don't make me say it again!"

"Or what, Muldoon?" the prisoner asks. "You'll come back here and shut me up?"

"No," Muldoon replies, his beady eyes glaring between the gaps in the steel. He pats his belt. "You all get a healthy stream of vitamin P."

"You're going to pee on us?" the prisoner asks. "I thought chicks like you had to sit down to piss, Muldoon?"

Muldoon scrunches up his face in anger and reaches for the pepper spray on his belt.

"Knock it off, Officer," Lu says, grabbing the man's arm. "You let them get to you now and it's going to be a long drive. Just sit down."

"Yeah, Muldoon, just sit down," the prisoner echoes.

Muldoon looks at Lu's hand and then at the marshal's face. Lu still wears her sunglasses, so the officer can't get a read on her. Finally, he shakes her hand off and takes his seat.

"That's a good girl," the prisoner smiles.

"You," Lu barks. "Shut the fuck up."

It's the same prisoner that was eyeing her earlier when she was talking to her mother on the phone. Head shaved, face covered in three day old black stubble, eyes like dark pits, the man just smiles at her, his eyes seemingly able to pierce the darkness of Lu's sunglasses and see right into her.

"Give me the list," Lu says to Muldoon. The officer hesitates. "Now."

The man reluctantly reaches for a clipboard hanging above him and hands it over to Lu. She flips past the first few pages until she comes to the seating chart.

"Anson Lowell?" Lu asks, looking up from the clipboard so she can meet the man's eyes. "That's you?"

"That's me," Lowell replies. "And you would be?"

"The person in charge," Lu replies. "You'll want to remember that."

"Hard to forget," Lowell says. "Hot piece like you with a gun? You have no idea how much my type you are."

Lu reaches under her seat and pulls out a tablet. She opens the case and scrolls the screens until she finds the file she wants. After a few minutes of reading, she lets out a low whistle.

"You are quite the badass, Mr. Lowell," Lu says.

"Just Lowell," Lowell grins. "Only people that ever call me mister are judges. It doesn't turn out well for them."

"No, no, I can see it doesn't," Lu says, reading through Lowell's file. She finally looks up and gives Lowell a grin to match his. "You killed two county judges before you were eighteen. Something they did must have irritated you."

The grin on Lowell's face falters slightly. Lu's grin widens.

"Oh, what? You thought those records were sealed? Seriously? A teenager kills two judges and there's no way to hide that, Lowell," Lu says as she turns back to the tablet and keeps reading. "Juvy until eighteen then transferred to the Oregon State Penitentiary. Another three years there and you actually figured out how to escape."

"Wasn't hard," Lowell shrugs. "Not exactly built by rocket scientists."

"On the run for three months before a state trooper spots you in Enterprise," Lu says. She pauses and looks at Lowell. "Why'd you stay in Oregon, Lowell? Three months and you only get from Salem to Enterprise? Doesn't take three months to get across the mountains to eastern Oregon."

"I'm a slow walker," Lowell shrugs again.

"But quick to kill," Lu responds.

She can see the other prisoners are listening intently. Most of the men in the convoy have been in solitary confinement for most of their stays at the Federal facility in Colorado. Getting to listen to something other than their own bodily functions must be quite the treat.

"You stabbed that trooper eighty four times," Lu continues. "Eighty three wasn't enough?"

A few prisoners laugh.

"Show some respect," Muldoon grumbles. Lu glares at him and he turns away.

"Killed that trooper, then you waited around for his backup to show before killing them, taking a hostage and heading north for the Washington border," Lu says.

She keeps reading, and then looks at Lowell for a long time. The man doesn't flinch under her gaze, but some of his cockiness is gone. Lu shakes her head and sets the tablet aside.

"Who was she?" Lu asks. "The little girl you took hostage? You made it across the border and into Washington, kept going until you hit Lewiston, Idaho. Then you dumped her at a Denny's and headed for Canada."

Lowell says nothing.

"Crossing state lines brought in the FBI and all of a sudden, you are the manhunt du jour," Lu says. "That's French for-"

"I know what du jour means," Lowell says.

"Yes, you do," Lu responds. "You taught yourself Spanish, French, Italian, Chinese, and German while in prison. You have an IQ in the 160s." Lu waves her hands at the other prisoners. "Most of these guys are barely smart enough to remember to wipe their asses after taking a shit, but not you. You are as smart as a rocket scientist. Yet, you get rid of your one bargaining chip. Why?"

Lowell doesn't respond.

"Yeah, that's the answer you gave the FBI," Lu states. "They checked through your past and couldn't find a single connection between you and the girl. Couldn't have been your kid since she was what, four?"

"Five," Lowell says.

"Five, right," Lu nods. "You would have been in prison when she was born. The parents weren't even from Oregon, just some tourists on vacation with their little girl. Violent man like you and you let her go. You could have kept her with you all the way to the border. Might even have gotten across if you had. The Canadians are a little easier to negotiate with than the FBI."

Lowell only stares at Lu.

"Kill two judges, stab a state trooper to death, kill a couple more," Lu says. "But you let a little girl go. Unharmed and untouched. A little hungry and dehydrated, but not a mark on her." Lu looks at the other prisoners. "Treated her better than some of the guys here would have."

A few of the prisoners look away from Lu while others meet her gaze head on, their eyes filled with violence and desire. She looks back at the tablet.

"Within the month, you killed four other inmates," Lu says, looking back up at Lowell. "One after the other. Just went down the line in the cafeteria and executed them. The first body hadn't dropped by the time you'd killed the fourth. Guards had no idea what was happening until inmates started shouting."

Lowell shrugs. "Weren't enough fish sticks to go around," Lowell says. "Had to thin the herd."

"Checkpoint, Marshal," the driver says as the convoy begins to slow. "Looks like they're blocking the connection to I-90."

"We knew this was coming," Lu says as she stands up. She picks up the clipboard once again and moves to the bus doors as it comes to a stop.

All along the convoy, the US Marshals stand outside their buses, clipboards in hand, as they wait for a checkpoint guard to come to them. Slowly, as if he has all the time in the world, a soldier casually walks from marshal to marshal, looks the paperwork over, walks up into each bus, comes back out, and looks the paperwork over again. Then he nods and moves to the next one.

"You having fun?" Lu asks when the soldier gets to her.

"Just doing my job," the soldier replies.

"Your job pay by the hour? Because mine doesn't and I have a time schedule to keep," Lu snaps. "Let's move it along, Sergeant."

The sergeant stops just as he's about to board Lu's bus and turns to look at her. "I think you should get your boss and follow me to the checkpoint. I'm not liking how this bus looks."

Lu stares at the man for a couple seconds, and then struggles to keep from bursting out laughing. "You're a fucking asshole, Bolton."

"Takes one to know one, Lu," the sergeant grins then lets it fall away quickly. "Your crew know who I am?"

"Not a clue," Lu says. "How many guys you got?"

"Four," Bolton replies. "Want me to give your folks a scare?"

"Nah," Lu says. "But maybe a nice demonstration is in order." She looks the man up and down. "I like the National Guard uniform."

"Easier to blend in," Bolton shrugs. "What kind of demonstration you thinking of?"

"Over the top?" Lu replies.

"You got it," Bolton smiles.

The man is a good six and a half feet tall with a broad chest and arms almost as thick as his legs, but he moves with a hidden grace that Lu knows very well. He presses two fingers to a flesh colored wire around his neck and speaks in a low voice.

"Hey, boys? Let's give our rides a nice welcome," Bolton whispers. "Maybe a wave from above?"

Bolton nods at Lu and they stand there, nose to neck, looking like they're ready to throw down and fight. The other marshals watch them closely, puzzled by the aggression. Hal tosses his clipboard onto the bus steps and moves his hand towards his sidearm. He watches Lu and Bolton for another couple of seconds, and then begins to step towards them.

"Best you stay where you are, Marshal," a voice says from above.

Hal looks up and the first thing he sees is an M-4 pointed at him. The second thing he sees is a smiling soldier. Then the soldier lets the carbine dip and he gives Hal a wink.

"Boo."

"What the fuck?" Hal says and turns and looks at the other buses. Soldiers have appeared on top of all the buses but Lu's. "LU!"

Lu turns and looks at Hal and starts to laugh. "Sorry, Hal. I couldn't help it."

She waves at the marshals and they all jog towards her, the looks on their faces ranging from pissed to confused. Hal's is pissed.

"Guys, this is Sergeant Connor Bolton," Lu says. "Bolton, this is Hal Stacks, James Talley, Steven LeDeaux, and Tony Whipple. Bolton and I go back a long way."

"High school prom," Bolton nods. "I was her first."

"Shut the fuck up!" Lu snaps and punches Bolton in the shoulder. "You were not!"

"I wasn't?" Bolton asks, honestly surprised. "Jesus, Lu, when did you start fucking?"

"None of your damn business," Lu says, and then looks at the other marshals. "Bolton and his men need a ride to Seattle."

"You guys SpecOps?" Tony asks.

"If I answer that I'll have to kill you," Bolton replies. "Just fucking with ya. I'll only wound you."

The other marshals don't smile at the joke.

"We have to get moving," Lu says. "Do we need to actually check in with the real checkpoint guards?"

"Nope, all covered," Bolton says. "You want a man per bus or do you have room for all of us on one?"

"Gonna have to be a man per," Lu answers. "Space is tight."

"Fair enough," Bolton nods and gives the orders to his men.

The other four soldiers climb down from the tops of their respective buses, sling their carbines, and climb inside.

"My guys will stay out of your hair the whole ride," Bolton says. "It'll be like they aren't even there. But you need any help, do not hesitate to ask."

The marshals look at Lu.

"What?" she says. "Let's get rolling."

They move off to their buses, climb aboard, and soon the convoy is up the onramp and onto I-90, headed for Coeur d'Alene.

"Who's this guy?" Muldoon asks as Bolton takes a seat next to Lu on the bus. "Marshals can't handle the work and have to call in the Guard?"

"Yep, that's it, Muldoon," Lu replies. "You're so smart."

Lowell snickers from the back, as do a few other prisoners.

"I'm guessing there's history here," Bolton says.

"Just some friendly ribbing," Lu smiles. "Right, Muldoon?"

"Yeah, right," Muldoon grumbles.

The bus shakes and rattles and everyone grabs onto anything they can to stay steady.

"Tremors are coming closer together," Bolton says. "Hope we make it to Seattle before it all falls apart."

"Don't you mean before it erupts?" Muldoon sneers. "That's what volcanoes do, they erupt."

"He *is* a smart one," Bolton nods at Muldoon. "Yes, Officer, that's exactly what volcanoes do. I was talking about our country. Things are going to get a lot worse before they get better."

Lu looks at Bolton for an explanation, but the sergeant only shakes his head.

***

"Jesus," Stephie cries out as she watches a small crack appear in the road ahead. The bus in front of her hits its brakes and the whole Champion convoy comes to a screeching halt.

"Talk to me, Eric," Stephie says into her radio. "The road damaged up ahead? That why we stopped?"

"No, Sheriff, the road is fine," Mikellson's voice replies. "But you'll never guess whose car is broken down and blocking the highway."

"You have to be kidding me," Stephie growls as she turns the wheel and drives her patrol car around the buses and up to Mikellson's.

The deputy gets out of his car, his hand on his sidearm, and slowly walks up to the sedan that blocks the road. The hood is open and Linder is standing there staring at the engine as ash continues to fall around them.

"Forget to change the air filters?" Mikellson asks.

"No, Deputy, I didn't," Linder says. "The new ones I put in must have been defective."

"That so?" Stephie asks as she comes up behind Mikellson, her hand on her sidearm as well.

Linder looks at the two and frowns.

"There a problem, Sheriff?" he asks. "Kind of aggressive body language there."

"How about we cut the shit and speak plain?" Stephie says. "I know who you are, Agent Linder. And after my conversation with your supervisor, now he knows who you are and why you abandoned your post to come all the way to Champion. It's over, Tobias."

Linder watches the woman for a couple of seconds, and then shakes his head.

"You shouldn't have done that," Linder says. "We're both in law enforcement and you should have shown me more respect."

His tone of voice changes and his body language shifts in the blink of an eye. The slick FBI agent he'd been presenting is gone and the predator that Mikellson spotted right away comes out.

"Respect is how things work," Linder says. "Respect for authority, respect for your elders, respect for your family, respect for your blood, respect for God. Respect. Without it, we're just animals fucking in the mud."

"Sheriff?" Mikellson says. "What's the call?"

"Stay cool, Eric," Stephie says as she takes a step past the deputy towards Linder. "I'm really not sure what you are babbling about, Tobias, but I think you need to show me your hands. You can ride with me in the back of my patrol car the rest of the way."

Linder laughs and looks up into the winter clouds. He blinks against the falling ash, and then closes his eyes.

"She's been with you this whole time, hasn't she?" Linder says, his eyes still closed. "Hiding the boy in your dyke love nest, that it? You two abominations make him watch? You force him to sit there as you lick each other's pussies?"

"Jesus Christ," Mikellson whispers. "You're crazier than they said."

Linder opens his eyes and glances over at the deputy, but keeps his head tilted towards the sky.

"You a faggot, Deputy Mikellson?" Linder asks. "That why you work for this bull dyke? You take it up the ass and suck cock? I'll bet you do."

Before either the sheriff or deputy can move, Linder spins and fires, a 9mm suddenly appearing in his hand. The back of Stephie's head rips open as the slug tears through her skull. Mikellson lets out a yell as he's spun around by a shot to the right shoulder, causing him to drop his pistol just as he gets it out of the holster. The deputy falls to the ground, blood pouring from the wound.

There's screaming from the lead bus and the driver floors it. Linder is barely able to dive out of the way as the bus rams into his sedan, shoving it from the road, and speeds off down the highway. The other buses follow and Linder lets them go, unconcerned with the townsfolk of Champion. He only cares about two people at the moment.

"How about you and me have a nice chat, Deputy," Linder says as he puts a bullet each into the backs of Mikellson's thighs as the man tries to stand up. Mikellson screams and Linder just shakes his head. "I bet this isn't how you expected the day to go, is it?"

"They're already gone," Mikellson gasps as he lays back on the pavement, Linder nothing but a shadow against the winter sky. "You won't catch them."

"Oh, I don't think that's true," Linder says. "I think they were tipped off that I was following them and they're somewhere close, just waiting for enough time to go by so they think I'm long gone."

"Fuck...you," Mikellson says and spits at Linder.

"Now that's not respectful," Linder says and slams a fist into Mikellson's right thigh.

The man's screams echo up and down the highway.

Linder places the muzzle of his pistol against Mikellson's head, then the thumb of his other hand against the gunshot wound on Mikellson's left thigh.

"How about you tell me which side roads they may have taken?" Linder says. "You know the ones I'm talking about. The local roads that aren't on GPS."

"How about you fuck off?" Mikellson snarls then screams as Linder's thumb slips inside his thigh.

"I don't have all day, but what time I do have, I can use to make your last moments excruciating in ways you can't imagine," Linder smiles. "So...those roads?"

***

"You have to be joking," Kyle states, his eyes wide as he stares at his grandma. "There's no way that guy can be my-"

He's cut off as the whole ridge shakes and Biscuit lets out a long howl followed by several sharp, loud barks from the backseat. Kyle watches his grandma's face get tighter and tighter with worry and frustration.

"We need to go, Grandma," Kyle says. "Whoever you say he is, he has to be gone by now."

"Stephie's not answering her phone," Terrie says as she dials the number again, letting their previous conversation drop.

"Maybe the cell tower fell," Kyle says. "These earthquakes are getting stronger."

"Maybe," Terrie says as she puts her phone back in her pocket. "Try the radio."

Kyle switches on the CB bolted to the Bronco's dash and grabs the handset. An ear piercing squeal of static forces him to shut it off quickly.

"Too much interference," Kyle says. "They said this might happen once the volcano gets more active. Do you think that means it's about to erupt?"

"I don't know," Terrie says as she looks out the windshield and watches the ash come down. "But those flakes look thicker."

"So what do we do?" Kyle asks. "We staying or going? Mom can't wait for us forever. We get too far behind and she'll have to leave us."

"I know," Terrie says. "She has a job to do and I raised her to always see a job through." She sighs and rubs her face. "Drive."

"What?"

"Drive, boy," Terrie says. "We'll catch up to the buses and deal with this man when we have to." The ridge shakes again, this time even harder and Terrie laughs. "God's telling us that our hiding is done. Time to come out into the light and let His path for us be revealed."

"So that means we head to Bonners Ferry?" Kyle grins.

"Yes, smart alec," Terrie says. "We head to Bonners Ferry."

THREE

"Where are we with sanctuary?" President Charles Nance asks as he walks into the situation room buried far below the White House and takes a seat. He looks around at his security council as well as the Joint Chiefs of Staff and the dozens of staff members busily hurrying about everyone with laptops, tablets, and cell phones. "Well?"

National Security Advisor Joan Milligan stands and clears her throat.

"As of right now, we have commitments from 38 countries willing to take in a total of close to two hundred million refugees, Mr. President," she says. "We're still in talks with China, Brazil, India, and many of the African nations."

"China hasn't agreed yet?" President Nance frowns. "When was the last time we heard from Ambassador Billings?"

"An hour ago, sir," Joan replies. "He's supposed to have an answer to us by this evening."

"Guess they don't give a crap now that their investment is about to be buried under a pile of ash," President Nance growls. No one replies. He shakes his head and looks over at Admiral Malcom Quigley, Head of the Joint Chiefs of Staff. "Admiral, what's the latest on the evacuation?"

"Everything is moving as fast as possible, Mr. President," Admiral Quigley replies. "But, as we guessed, not everyone wants to leave."

"What are the estimated numbers staying behind?" President Nance asks.

"Several million," Admiral Quigley responds. "I've received reports of some groups ranging in the hundreds actually taking up arms against the National Guard troops trying to move them to safety."

"Please tell me shots haven't been fired," President Nance sighs.

"I wish I could, sir," Admiral Quigley frowns. "But we know of at least one hundred dead because of various skirmishes."

"What the hell is wrong with these people?" President Nance barks. "Don't they know that they could die if they stay?"

"Some are seeing the supervolcano as God's judgment and refuse to leave on religious grounds," Joan says. "The Christian Right isn't helping and is actually fueling the notion that to leave would be to go against God's will."

"I'm a Christian born and breed," President Nance snaps. "And I sure as hell am not buying into the Rapture crap being spewed. Why can't people just be sensible and get to safety? They can debate God's plan all they want once they get to Japan or Australia or Egypt or wherever!"

"The good news is the AM radio stations are going dead because of the atmospheric interference," Deputy National Security Advisor John Jensen says. "Most of the fire and brimstone talk is now silenced by the supervolcano activity. I'm sure most of the nutjobs won't get the irony in that, Mr. President."

"How about we refrain from calling our fellow citizens nutjobs, John," President Nance says, "even if they are."

"Yes, sir. My apologies, sir," John nods. "I didn't mean any disrespect."

President Nance lets out a long sigh and loosens his tie. "Okay, someone get me some science types to explain why we're feeling these earthquakes all the way here in DC. And a cup of coffee. Someone get me some coffee while they find the eggheads."

***

Dr. Probst stares at her laptop, her eyes not even registering the readings the program is streaming across the screen. The level of exhaustion that has overtaken her is almost too much for her to comprehend. Her body feels like it's floating where she sits while her mind is filled with cotton and rocks.

"You just going to sit there?" Dr. Bartolli asks. "Or are you going to tell me what you've found?"

"Huh? What?" Dr. Probst mutters, then sits up and shakes her head. She taps on her laptop and the images on the screen are duplicated on the large monitor bolted to the wall. "Right. Sorry. I haven't slept in days."

"None of us have slept in days," Dr. Kevin Day snaps. "And you don't see us falling asleep at the job."

Dr. Probst looks around the room at the other members of the newly formed Yellowstone Scientific Advisory Board. Most of them are ranking scientists in the United States Geological Survey, while some are prominent geologists from various universities across the country. They all turn and look at the graph Dr. Probst has put up on the monitor.

"Seismic activity has increased a hundred fold within the last twenty-four hours," she states. "Tremors are being felt within an almost two thousand mile radius. That kind of activity is unprecedented."

"And scientifically impossible," Dr. Day sneers. "Not without major fault lines splitting wide open and other volcanoes, the Cascades for instance, being triggered to erupt. How do you explain this, Dr. Probst?"

"I can't," Dr. Probst replies. "All I can do is report what I've found. You put me in charge of this data and I'm telling you what is happening. The behavior of the Yellowstone supervolcano is not behavior typical of any other volcano that's been observed in modern times or even history. By all indications, this thing should have blown sky high weeks ago."

"And we have no indication as to why it hasn't?" Dr. Bartolli asks. "Every single government agency is focused on this thing. We have equipment at our disposal that many of us didn't know existed. For the first time I can remember, funds are unlimited and we can do whatever we want. Why? So we can get some sort of answer to the president." He holds up his cell phone to show a text message. "We have a videoconference with him in less than five minutes. Let's see if we can't get something pieced together that doesn't make us look like complete idiots, okay?"

"We'd have more information if we'd heard from Bob and Coral," Dr. Probst says, her eyes locking onto Bartolli's.

"We've been through this, Cheryl," Dr. Bartolli snaps.

"No, we haven't," Dr. Probst replies, looking at the other scientists. "Two of our colleagues are lost out there. Their job was to keep the sensors active. Now, one by one, the sensors are going down. We are losing valuable information and may have already lost two valuable members of this board. We need to send a new team out there to repair the sensors and to find Dr. Hartness and Tomlinson."

She waits for the others to speak, but none do.

"Our focus needs to be on what we tell the president," Dr. Bartolli says. "Bob and Coral knew the risks. We all do. And I won't sanction sending another team out there. I can't, in all good conscious, order men and women to their deaths. This is not the Army, Doctor."

"You don't need to order them," Dr. Probst responds. "I already have a team of volunteers ready. Some folks actually have guts and are willing to risk everything for their friends and for the safety of this country. Those traits aren't just for the Army, either."

Dr. Bartolli watches her for a second, then glances away dismissively. "Collin? What do you have for us?"

Dr. Probst begins to argue then just sighs. She leans her head back in her chair and closes her eyes, wanting nothing more than to shut out the idiocy she is surrounded by.

***

President Nance grips the sides of the conference table as the entire situation room shakes. A couple of the advisors and techs cry out, their bottled fear finally getting free. President Nance says a quick prayer under his breath then smacks his hand down on the table.

41

"We will not lose this country!" he shouts. "We are Americans and this land was destined to be our home for all of eternity! I want answers, I want solutions, and I want to know how we will come back from this catastrophe!"

The huge monitor that covers the main wall across from the conference table shows the scared and exhausted faces of Dr. Bartolli, Day and Probst with the remaining scientists tasked with getting those answers and solutions to the president seated in the background.

"Mr. President, you have to understand that a natural phenomenon like this has never occurred in modern history," Dr. Bartolli frowns. "This is unprecedented and we are doing our best to sort out any and all solutions to salvaging this country."

"I don't want this country salvaged!" President Nance yells. "I want it saved!"

"It can't be, sir," Dr. Day speaks up. "Not until we know what damage the main eruption will cause. At this point, we will have to wait and see."

Dr. Probst openly snorts at the comment.

"Wait and see?" President Nance laughs. "I don't wait and see anything! If I'd accepted 'wait and see' as an option in my life then I never would have become president! You figure out how we contain this disaster now!"

"Sir, as much as I'd like to agree with you and not with my colleagues, we can't contain it," Dr. Probst says. "What is happening has the full power of nature behind it."

"Then get me something more powerful than nature!" President Nance orders. "I've heard of fires being put out by explosions. Get me an explosion that puts out a volcano!"

"Sir, that's an interesting idea. Unfortunately, we have lost so many sensors that-" Dr. Probst begins, but is quickly cut off.

"We will do everything we can, sir," Dr. Bartolli says. "We are conferencing with scientists from across the world in the next few minutes. The best minds from all fields of science will be on this, sir. We won't let you down."

"You won't let the American people down, is what you mean," President Nance replies. "I want a full report by the end of the day. It had better be a good report, Dr. Bartolli. Once we are forced to scatter with the wind, it will be hard to put this country back together. Do you understand me?"

"Yes, Mr. President," Dr. Bartolli nods. "Thank you, sir."

The transmission is cut and President Nance looks over at Joan. He sees the look on her face and rolls his eyes.

"Oh, don't start going soft on me now, Joan," he barks. "Sometimes you have to get rough to motivate people, especially scientists used to living in their safe little academic labs."

"Yes, sir," Joan nods. "Of course."

***

The three geologists sit there, the bags under their eyes drooping even lower as they digest the president's orders. One by one, they turn and look at the rest of the men and women that stand around them, all looking like they've been punched in the gut.

"We're all in agreement that what he's asking for isn't possible, right?" one of the scientists says. "There's no way we can just blow up a volcano."

"It isn't completely unprecedented," a woman says. "But certainly not on this scale."

"It could make things a million times worse," Dr. Day says.

"Or it could work," Dr. Probst replies. "We have to be open to the idea, at least."

Most of the room stares at her like she's lost her mind while the rest just seem to deflate under the weight of their assigned task.

"Please, Dr. Probst, go ahead and explain," Dr. Bartolli sighs. "You're going to anyway."

"Okay, bear with me," Dr. Probst says and types on her laptop.

A satellite image of the Yellowstone National Park comes up and she taps a couple more keys, changing the image from realistic to thermal, showing the whole room where the most activity is centered.

"We've all been watching these images," she states. "There is mostly hot mud below the surface and not as much magma as would be expected. This could be turned to our advantage. Magma would be a real problem, and that's not something we can stop. But hot mud? That is something we can stop."

"And how would we do that?" Dr. Bartolli asks.

"We solidify the mud," Dr. Probst says. "Or, more precisely, we harden it by removing the water. If we can dehydrate the mud, then we can stop up the volcano. I'm not saying we can keep it from erupting, but I think we could add a mile or so of hard earth between the magma and the surface."

"That would only increase the pressure," Dr. Day counters. "It would make things worse than they already are!"

"No, it wouldn't," Dr. Probst says. "Think of this mud like the earth on a desert floor. If we can dehydrate it fast enough it would be pocked with cracks and holes. This would allow gasses to escape and not build up, keeping the eruption to average disaster level and not cataclysm level."

"Average disaster level?" Dr. Bartolli laughs. "Like a hurricane or tsunami? Yes, those are so average."

"Better than the end of the world," Dr. Probst says, "which is a distinct possibility if we allow all of that mud and ash to reach the surface. It will be an ashen winter, just like a nuclear winter, but without the radiation."

The room fills with excited chatter, some of it angry, some of it hopeful, as everyone begins to speak at once. Dr. Bartolli holds up his hands for silence, but he is ignored as ideas are thrown back and forth between the many scientists.

"Quiet!" Dr. Bartolli shouts. "Be quiet!"

The room goes silent and all eyes turn to him.

"Let's say we can figure out a way to do it," Dr. Bartolli says. "If we can, we will need far better, and more accurate, data than we have now. Satellite imaging is one thing, but nothing compares to an on the ground scan."

There are gasps and murmurs at what he is suggesting. Dr. Probst just smiles.

"You see what she's doing, right?" Dr. Day asks, pointing at Dr. Probst. "False hope so she can send a team into Yellowstone."

"Sometimes false hope is all we have," someone mutters from down the table. There are a few nods of agreement.

"If our calculations are off by a single percent, not only could we set off the volcano right then, the results could be exponentially worse," Dr. Probst states. "The only way to make the calculations we need to make is to have the most accurate data possible." She pauses and then stands up. "So, yes, some of us will need to go into Yellowstone and get the data we need. I'll do it. It's my idea, so I should be the one to go."

"You understand the risk you're taking, Doctor?" Dr. Bartolli asks. "You don't have to do this. You can stay here in Virginia and be safe. Send in the Army Corps of Engineers. Let those soldiers handle it. That would be the prudent choice."

"Your problem, Alexander, is you don't understand that none of us have a choice," Dr. Probst laughs. "Either we find the solution or we just sit and wait for the end of the world as we know it. Sending in the Army Corps won't help us. They can't do a damn thing without red tape. They'd need to do their own surveys before placing a single new sensor. I designed the sensors, I trained Drs. Hartness and Tomlinson. I've trained the techs that will accompany me. Just get me in there and I'll get the job done."

Dr. Bartolli watches her for a second then nods. "I'll call the president. We will need to get you there as fast as possible. Hopefully the military has a way to do that. We don't have 30 hours for you to drive there."

"But all aircraft are grounded," Dr. Day says. "The engines can't handle the ash."

"I have a feeling there's a way around that," Dr. Bartolli says then looks at Dr. Probst. "Get a team together ASAP. I'll get your transportation arranged. If we are lucky, you can leave within the hour."

"Within the hour?" Dr. Probst exclaims. "But I need time to-"

"You *want* time, you mean," Dr. Bartolli says. "And that is something you can't have. I'm finally saying yes, Cheryl. Don't make me regret it. You get your team, you get your adventure, now get your ass moving."

***

"They came through here, alright," the man answers just before he spits a wad of tobacco out of the corner of his mouth and into the dead grass at his feet.

Terrie frowns at the man, but stays quiet.

"Can you say how long ago, Howie?" Terrie asks.

"Maybe a half an hour. Could be longer," Howie shrugs. A car horn honks and he looks over as an SUV pulls into the parking lot of the small country store.

"Why ain't you left yet, Howie?" a man asks as he rolls down the window. "I'm hearing they're going to close down the highways after nightfall. You don't leave now and you'll be stuck here."

"Ain't going nowhere, Bart," the Howie replies. "This store's been in my family for four generations."

"You'll die when that volcano erupts!" the SUV man exclaims.

"Then I die," Howie states. "It's as good a place as any."

Bart shakes his head, then rolls up his window and drives off without another word. Terrie looks back at the Bronco with Kyle and Biscuit seated inside.

"We have room, Howie," Terrie says. "You can come with us. We're headed to Seattle to catch a ship."

"That where those buses and patrol car are headed to?" Howie asks.

"Yes," Terrie nods. "We have most of Lincoln County heading down to Coeur d'Alene to meet up with my daughter and a federal convoy. You come with us and we-" She stops and tilts her head. "Wait...did you say patrol car? As in just one?"

"Yes, ma'am," Howie replies. "Six buses and a Lincoln County Sheriff's patrol car."

"Just the one? You're sure?" Terrie asks. "There should have been three patrol cars."

"I only saw one," Howie responds as he picks tobacco from between his teeth. "And they was moving fast. Didn't even stop at the intersection there, just barreled right through. Good thing most everyone has evacuated or they could have run someone over."

"Doesn't make sense," Terrie says. "Why only one patrol car?"

"Maybe the others broke down," Howie shrugs. "You didn't see them along your way here?"

"We took the back trails," Terrie says. "Had to make a detour and it was easier coming in the back way."

"Well, I don't know about easier, but I guess you have the equipment to handle the back trails," Howie says, nodding at the Bronco. "You got enough gas in that thing to get you down to Idaho? I have some stashed away for my generators if you need it."

"We have plenty," Terrie says. "But thank you. Did you see a black sedan following the buses?"

"Can't say that I did," Howie replies. "Just the one patrol car was with them. That's all."

"Okay, well that's good," Terrie says. "Thank you. You sure you won't come with?"

"I'm sure," Howie says. "Like I said, this store goes back generations. My uncle died of a heart attack right next to the pop cooler. I figure I may camp out next to the beer and go out the right way when it all ends."

"It's not like it's going to be a nuclear explosion, and flash, you're dead," Terrie says. "It could take days or weeks before it gets bad enough to kill you."

"That's why I'm gonna camp by the beer," Howie smiles. "The longer it takes, the more ready I'll be."

"Well, good luck, Howie," Terrie says. "It was good knowing you."

"You too, Ms. Holden," Howie says. "I'll miss you and that boy and his wolf dog coming for bait on your way to the Kootenai for those fishing trips you all would take."

"Gonna miss that too," Terrie says and turns and walks back to the Bronco. "Good luck!"

Howie gives a wave, then fishes out a pouch of tobacco and grabs a plug, jamming it deep into his cheek.

"How far behind are we?" Kyle asks as Terrie gets into the Bronco, this time behind the wheel.

"Howie said thirty minutes, but you know Howie," Terrie says. "It could have been an hour ago and he'd say thirty minutes."

"Is it safe for you to drive?" Kyle asks. "What if we run into that guy again?"

"I think he already knows the Bronco," Terrie says. "Seeing me isn't going to change that. And we need to make up some time, which means driving fast."

"I can drive fast," Kyle protests.

"That's true, but I can drive fast without killing us," Terrie smiles. "So buckle up."

Biscuit whines and lies down in the backseat as soon as Terrie starts up the Bronco and revs the engine.

***

"What do you mean only half my team can come?" Dr. Probst shouts, trying to be heard over the whine of the jet engines only a few meters from her. She stands on the tarmac, her hands on her hips, and her face red with anger as she confronts the man before her. "I need every single one of those people!"

"You see that aircraft, Doctor?" Lieutenant Jason Coletti asks. "It can only carry twelve passengers, not including the pilot and co-pilot. That means six of my people, including me, and six of your people, including you."

"I don't need a military escort!" Dr. Probst shouts. "This isn't a war!"

"Yes, ma'am, it is," Coletti replies. "And we're fighting time. My orders are to get you into Yellowstone as fast as possible. That means you aren't hiking in. That would take you days, which we don't have. Not to mention the fact you'd probably be killed by the whackadoos that have started showing up all around the park!"

"What whackadoos?" Dr. Probst asks.

"All kinds," Coletti says. "Religious fanatics, conspiracy theorists, end of the world groupies, heavily armed militias. You name it and they're there."

"If we aren't hiking in, then how are we getting where I need to go?" Dr. Probst asks. "Driving? Are there vehicles waiting for us?"

"No, ma'am," Coletti replies. "The ash is so thick even our best Humvees can't handle it that close." He points at the jet waiting for them. "Those engines are self-contained and won't get choked with ash. Problem is that aircraft only has enough fuel to get us over the drop site and then back here. It can't stop for a second."

Dr. Probst looks at the jet, then at the man in front of her. "What are you saying, Lieutenant?"

"I'm saying that the six of you will be strapped to the six of us when we jump out of that jet," Coletti says. "And at the speed we'll be going, it ain't gonna be fun."

"Are you insane? You can't parachute out of a jet!"

"*You* can't," Coletti smiles. "But me and my men can. You just let us worry about getting you on the ground safely and once we're down, I'll let you worry about how we stop that volcano. Now pick your five people."

Dr. Probst looks over at the group of ten scientists standing at the edge of the tarmac.

"Dear God, I think I'm going to be sick," Dr. Probst says and quickly turns away.

Coletti let her have her moment as he turns and gives a thumbs up to five men waiting by the jet. They nod and hurry over to the group of scientists.

"You done?" Coletti asks. "Because we need to go now. Tell your people and then my men will get them loaded up and set for take off."

"Okay, okay," Dr. Probst says and takes a deep breath as she wipes her mouth, then looks at Coletti. "And there's no other way?"

"Ma'am, this *is* the other way."

***

"You've been flooring it since we left Bonners Ferry," Kyle says. "We're gonna run out of gas if you don't ease up."

"We have to catch them, Kyle," Terrie says. "Your mother loves us, but she can't wait for us in Coeur d'Alene. If we aren't there with the buses, then she has to keep going."

"She wouldn't do that," Kyle says. "Would she? Just leave you and me behind?"

Terrie looks over at her grandson and gives him a look he's known all his life. His throat goes dry and he shakes his head.

"Jesus. She would."

"Don't take the Lord's name in vain," Terrie snaps. "And yes, she would. I would too if I was in her shoes. This convoy isn't just about our little family, it's about other families and her duty as a US Marshal. That's a duty she doesn't take lightly and we wouldn't want her to."

Kyle shakes his head some more, then turns and looks out the passenger window as the firs and pines whiz by. He rests his head against the glass for a second, and then narrows his eyes as he looks into the side mirror. The ash is coming down so hard now it's like a grey blizzard all around them and makes it difficult to see details.

But blue and red flashing lights aren't difficult to see.

"Grandma? Look behind us," Kyle says.

Terrie glances in the rear view mirror and sees the outline of a patrol car coming up on them fast, its lights flashing bright in the ashen gloom of the day.

"Lincoln County," Terrie smiles. "About time. Can you see who's driving? Is it Stephie?"

Kyle turns around in his seat and tries to make out who the driver is, but he can't get a good look.

"Jeez," Kyle says. "If that's Stephie, then she better slow down. She's going to ram right into the back of us at that speed."

Terrie looks down at the speedometer, and then into the rear view mirror again.

"Buckle up," she orders.

"I am," Kyle replies.

"Then turn around and hang on tight," Terrie replies as she pushes the accelerator all the way to the floor.

"Grandma! What are you doing?" Kyle cries.

"That's not Stephie," Terrie says. "And it's not Eric, either."

"Maybe it's Shane?"

"No, Shane was waiting ahead," Terrie says. "The patrol car Howie saw was Shane's car. I think I know why they were going so fast."

"Why?"

Terrie nods at the mirror, her eyes watching as the patrol car gains on them.

"Because he found them," Terrie says. "I don't think Stephie or Eric is alive."

"What? How do you know that?" Kyle asks, looking back over his shoulder as the patrol car comes roaring at them. "OH, SHIT!"

Terrie instinctively reaches out and puts a hand across Kyle's chest just as the patrol car rams them from behind. Not that her old arm can do any good in a rear end collision at sixty miles an hour, but there's no fighting instinct.

***

"How far are we?" Lu asks the driver.

"Maybe two hours," the driver replies. "GPS just went down so I can't say for sure."

"I don't have cell service," Muldoon says as he jams his phone back in his pocket. "Damn, stupid volcano."

"Yeah, you tell it, Officer," Bolton grins. "We all knew this was going to happen."

"The buses should be at the rendezvous point by now," Lu says. "They'll sit tight and wait for us."

"We stopping when we get there?" Bolton asks. "Or are they just going to fall in behind?"

"Ideally, they'd fall in behind," Lu says. "But with GPS and cell phones out, we're going to have to stop so I can fill them in on the route and exact parameters of the convoy. After that, they'll fall in line and had better stay in line. We only have one fuel stop between Idaho and Everett. Other than that, we stop for nothing, even if it means they get left behind."

Bolton raises his eyebrows and gives Lu a hard look.

"You never have been one to cut people slack, Lu," Bolton says.

"Yeah, well, I come by it naturally," Lu frowns.

***

Kyle's body hurts. That's all he knows as he slowly comes to.

"Get up."

Kyle opens his eyes, but he can barely see anything. The world around him is red.

"Wha...what?" he grunts.

"Kyle, get up," his grandma says as she wipes the blood from his face and pulls at him.

"Grandma...? What happened?" he asks as he's roughly yanked from the upside down Bronco. He sees the knife in her hand and gets to his feet as she whirls around. "What's going on?"

"I had to cut your seatbelt," Terrie says, her own face bloody and bruised. "I don't see Biscuit, but we can't look for him now. We have to go."

"Wait, what?" Kyle asks, his head a fuzzy mess. "We can't leave Biscuit."

"We can and we will!" Terrie hisses as she looks over at the patrol car that lies on its side at the shoulder of the road opposite them. The front wheel is still spinning, but that's all the movement she sees. The woman turns and shoves Kyle towards the woods behind them. "Go!"

"Grandma? Who are we running from?" Kyle asks. "Who is this man?"

"We can't get into that right now," Terrie snaps. "Just go!"

Kyle limps into the woods. His left leg is banged up, but he's had worse, so he knows it shouldn't slow him down for long. He turns to say something else, but his words are caught in his throat as he sees Linder sit up from a ditch across the road. Linder smiles at him, and then raises a pistol, firing twice.

"Go!" Terrie chokes. "Run, Kyle! Now!"

Then she falls forward onto her face and Kyle is left standing there, his eyes locked with the man that just shot his grandma.

"Hello, Kyle," Linder says as he stands up. He grunts and stumbles, falling back to one knee. Blood coats his right leg. "I should have worn my seatbelt."

"Who are you?" Kyle asks. "Why...why'd you shoot my grandma?"

"That bitch?" Linder laughs. "Forget her. She doesn't deserve your love. No one does." He tries to stand again, but his leg won't hold him. "Now come help me up, will ya? We should get you away from this backwoods hellhole. No place for a bright kid like you."

Kyle just stands there.

"Boy, come help me," Linder snaps. "You listen to me and do what I say! NOW!"

The rage in Linder's voice breaks Kyle's fear and he takes a few steps backwards, then turns and runs, ignoring the pain in his leg, ignoring the branches that whip at his face and arms. Kyle runs and keeps on running, leaving a screaming Linder far behind.

"COME BACK, YOU LITTLE SHIT!" Linder shouts. "YOU DO WHAT YOUR FATHER TELLS YOU! YOU DO IT RIGHT NOW!"

Kyle refuses to listen to the words as they fade into the background. He refuses to recognize what the man is shouting at him. He refuses to believe any of it, no matter what his grandma told him.

You do what your father tells you…

***

"Nearing the drop sight. ETA two minutes."

"You ready?" Coletti asks Dr. Probst, his voice ringing in her ears through the com system in her helmet.

"No," she replies.

"Well, at least you're honest about it," Coletti laughs.

"How fast are we going?" Dr. Probst asks.

"You don't want to know," Coletti says as he walks them towards the back of the jet's small passenger area.

"How high up are we?" Dr. Probst asks.

"You don't want to know that either," Coletti says. "Just trust that the suit you're wearing, the helmet you're wearing, and the oxygen being pumped into it will keep you alive. That's your job until we touch ground. Got it?"

"And what's your job? Freaking me out?"

"My job is to know when to deploy our parachute," Coletti says. "It's an important job."

Dr. Probst gives a small squeak as she looks over at the five other scientists strapped in front of the five other soldiers. They are all outfitted in thick full body suits with heavy duty hoses going from their backs and feeding into the black visor helmets they wear. Because of the reflective material of the visors, Dr. Probst can't see anyone's faces, but she's pretty sure her colleagues are just as terrified as she is.

"Drop will commence in thirty seconds," the pilot's voice announces through their helmets. "Please proceed to the- HOLY FUCK!"

The jet rocks to one side and alarms begin to blare. Then silence. Dr. Probst feels her stomach flip, when suddenly everyone is slammed up against the top of the jet's cabin.

"Lieutenant!" Dr. Probst shouts. "Lieutenant!"

There's no answer.

"Lieutenant! What's going on?" she screams.

She isn't answered by words, but by movement. Even though it feels like her body is being crushed, she can feel Coletti moving against her and sees his arms reach out for handholds recessed into the jet's ceiling. Handhold by handhold, he claws their way to the back of the jet then slams his hand against a large button.

Nothing.

Dr. Probst tries to turn her head to look back at the others, but the g-forces are too much and it feels like her neck will be ripped apart if she moves an inch. She has no idea how Coletti found the strength to get them several feet.

The man grabs her hands and wraps her fingers around two holds, patting them again and again until she understands she's supposed to hang on and keep them in place. Once he knows they are secure, he pops open a panel underneath the useless button, and grabs the black and yellow handle set inside. He pulls down, turns the handle 180 degrees, and then slams it back in place.

The entire rear of the jet falls away suddenly as Dr. Probst's grip is ripped free and she finds herself and Coletti tumbling through the air, end over end.

"What's happening?" she screams, but there is still no answer.

The world is a spinning kaleidoscope of bright blue then dark grey, bright blue then dark grey. Over and over until Coletti gets them under control and they even out, their bodies flat against the air that tears at them, their faces looking down at the hell below.

"Oh, my God," Dr. Probst whispers.

All that's underneath them is a thick, dark grey cloud of ash. It rolls and rumbles at them as they rocket down towards it. Before Dr. Probst even has a chance to comprehend what she's seeing, and the implications of it, they pierce the cloud, their bodies swallowed whole by the volcanic ash.

"Nononononononononono," she says over and over.

They're too late. The supervolcano has erupted and she is diving right towards it. She knows that, at any second, despite the suits she and Coletti wear, they'll be roasted alive from the heat of the eruption. Anything caught under a half mile above the caldera will be a crispy critter in seconds.

She feels her arms being pinned to her sides by Coletti's and their trajectory changes. He turns them slightly, and then angles them downward, sending them falling even faster than before. They are a two person missile lost in the ash, aimed who knows where.

Then they are out, clear of the ash, and the whole world below opens up before her.

Dr. Probst can't believe what she sees. There should be nothing but ash and hot mud erupting again and again. Yet there's nothing. The ash is above them, filling the Earth's atmosphere. There's no mud, no magma, no more ash.

All that she sees is a gigantic hole in the ground. Her mind doesn't want to believe it, but it can't help but calculate the size of the hole.

It must be 200 miles across, she thinks. *But how?*

She feels their trajectory change once more as Coletti aims them for the northwestern side of the hole. Her brain calculates again, now that she has reference points and can see the ground clearly. The jet had to have been in the upper reaches of the stratosphere when they were ejected from it. Again her brain calculates and she realizes what Coletti is trying to do. He has to get them far enough to the edge of the massive hole, but still high enough so they can deploy their parachute in time not to be crushed on impact.

She honestly doesn't think they will make it. There's only empty space below them; a dark, bottomless chasm. At the speed they are plummeting, they'll get close to the edge, but every fiber in her body says they will fall short of solid ground and end up in the nothing that was once part of Wyoming, Montana, and Idaho.

Except it isn't all nothing. Smoke and brief flashes of flame ring the edge of the chasm, highlighting something. Or, to be precise, *somethings*.

She wants to scream, she wants to cry out, she wants nothing to do with what her intellect is telling her can't exist.

That creatures, unimaginably large creatures, are clawing their way up out of the chasm. Dozens, if not a hundred of the creatures scrabble out of the burning darkness.

If her estimates are correct, and she hasn't completely lost her mind, the creatures have to be at least…

"A hundred feet tall," she whispers to herself.

She wants to close her eyes, and just shut out what she is watching. There is no way things like that can be. It's not scientifically possible.

Then the wind that rages around her, deafening even with the helmet on, is overpowered by roars that she can feel in her bones.

Down there, just below the already impossible creatures, are things far more impossible, far worse, far bigger. She doesn't have the strength to turn her head to see the edge of the chasm that is already behind them, but she doesn't have to. What she sees in front of her is enough to send her into madness.

As they rocket towards the Earth, she watches the smaller things make way, parting like a monstrous sea, as new beasts pull their bulk up out of the hole. Chunks of earth the size of whole counties fall away as the monsters' claws tear into the ground and heft their massively thick bodies onto the surface. The things stand and turn their heads this way and that, then roar as one, nearly bursting Dr. Probst's eardrums.

Her mind, spent and pushed to its limits, decides this is the moment it has had enough and Dr. Probst's eyes roll back into her head as sweet, merciful unconsciousness takes her away from the nightmare she is falling towards.

FOUR

"Lu. Lu, get up."

Lu's eyes pop open and she reaches for her pistol, but a strong hand grips her wrist and stops her.

"It's me," Bolton says, his face close to hers. "Stay calm. You don't need to draw your weapon. You just need to get up."

Lu looks about and realizes the bus doesn't look right. She can see the seats across from her, but gravity tells her she's on her back. Bolton's face is scratched and bleeding and a drop of blood falls from the tip of his nose and lands on her cheek. He casually wipes it away with his thumb, and then he pulls her to her feet.

"What the fuck happened?" Lu asks, seeing the bus is on its side. And most of the rear is submerged in water. "Where are we?"

"In a river," Bolton says. "Come on."

"Wait," she says and pulls her arm from his grip. "The transfers."

"Dead," Bolton says. "So's your man Muldoon and the other guards. I already pulled the driver out, but I don't think he's going to make it."

Lu looks around and sees the corpses shackled to their seats. There's barely any light coming in the windows and Lu wonders how long she was out.

"Ash," Bolton says. "Way up there. The air down here is surprisingly clear now, but we have to find you a mask soon. When that shit comes down, breathing is not going to be fun."

"The volcano?" she asks. "It erupted?"

"That's my guess," Bolton nods. "Come on, I'll show you."

He hoists himself up out of the door and reaches down for Lu. She grips his wrists and is about to clamber up, when a noise catches her attention.

"Hold on," she says and let go of his hands.

"Lu, we don't have time," Bolton says.

"Hold on!" she snaps and moves back towards the prisoners.

The steel mesh cage is completely warped and she easily squeezes through without having to unlock it. She moves carefully back towards the sound, crawling along the edges of the seats. Dead men lay broken and wet below her, their heads at odd angles, faces smashed in, and eyes bulged out. Most died on impact, it looks like, but some drowned as the water rose and they couldn't get free of their restraints.

"Who's alive?" Lu shouts. "Tell me where you are."

"Here," a voice rasps and Lu moves quickly to the source. Anson Lowell. "You."

"Hey, Marshal," Lowell grunts. "Think I'm a little stuck."

The man's seat is twisted and turned so he is wedged against the bloody corpse of the prisoner that was seated next to him. Not seated so much anymore as crumpled.

Lu grabs at the keys on her belt and reaches down, her face close to Lowell's. She knows this is inviting trouble, but she doesn't have a choice. Not if she wants to get the man out of the bus alive.

"No need to worry, Marshal," Lowell says. "I'll be good. Promise."

"Not sure good is a word you understand, Mr. Lowell," Lu says. "But I'm sure self-preservation will win out. You hurt or kill me, and my friend will make sure you die slowly and in agony."

"I bet he will," Lowell says, then sighs as the shackles around his wrists are finally free.

"Here," Lu says, handing him the keys. "I can't get to your ankles."

Lowell bends forward and unlocks the shackles from his ankles. Luckily, he is on the seat closest to the aisle; his crumpled buddy is next to the window and half submerged in water.

"Thanks," Lowell says and hands the keys back. "Lead the way."

"You first," Lu says and crawls out of the man's way, her hand on the butt of her pistol. "I don't feel the need to have you at my back."

Lowell shrugs and works his way past her and up to the front of the bus. He looks up and sees the frowning face of Bolton right above him.

"Can I get a little help?" Lowell asks. "Muscles are kinda woogidy after being chained to my seat all day."

"One twitch and I snap your neck," Bolton says as he reaches down to Lowell. "I am not joking."

"Yet you seem like such a kidder to me," Lowell says as he grabs onto Bolton and climbs out of the bus.

Lu hurries after and climbs out without Bolton's help. Her first instinct is to grab her cuffs from her belt and secure Lowell, but that thought quickly leaves her mind as she sees the destruction before her.

"Holy shit," she whispers.

"Yeah," Lowell nods. "I'll agree with the holy part. I think God is mad and just threw a tantrum."

The world around them is destroyed. The highway, the hills, the trees, everything. It's all been ripped apart. Lu turns in a slow circle and takes in everything she sees, unsure of even how to process it all. Cars and vehicles lie this way and that, warped and twisted. The ground is nothing but fissures and holes, jagged hunks of rock and spears of asphalt. Half the trees have fallen as if a giant blew on them.

There are quiet moans and weak cries as people call for help from their destroyed vehicles. Maybe twenty cars and trucks are visible and Lu wonders how many more were swallowed up by the earth.

"That's the only other bus I could get to," Bolton says, pointing to the tail end of a bus a few yards away sticking up out of a wide crevice. Sulfuric smoke curls around the bus and slowly drifts away. "No one is alive in there."

"You sure, soldier boy?" Lowell asks. "You thought everyone in this bus was dead. Yet here I am."

"I'm sure," Bolton nods. "But you are welcome to see for yourself."

"You're staying with me," Lu says to Lowell.

"No place I'd rather be," Lowell says.

"Yeah, I'm sure," Lu laughs.

"No, seriously," Lowell replies. "Look at this shit. You think I take off in this, I'll stay alive for long?" He shakes his head. "No way. Best place to be is with a US Marshal and Mr. Black Ops. If anyone can get out of this hell, it's you two. Feel free to call Uncle Sam for a ride anytime."

"I'd love to," Bolton says. "Only problem is we have no way to call. Not a single damn piece of electronic equipment works. What hit us first was a massive EMP. Then shit got torn apart."

Lu searches the area for signs of the other buses, but all she sees is the one they stand on and the other one lost in the crevice.

"Back there," Bolton says, watching her scan the area. "In the river."

The bus they are standing on is lying perpendicular with the river, three quarters of it in the water. But a hundred yards upstream Lu can just make out the outline of one of the other buses as the river rushes around it.

"This river isn't that deep," Lu says. "I know this area like the back of my hand and the deepest point is five feet tops."

"Nothing around here is what it used to be," Bolton says. "In a matter of minutes, this entire landscape has changed."

A far off screeching grabs their attention and they all turn towards the east.

"What is that?" Bolton asks. "Hurt cattle? Sheep?"

"I don't know," Lu replies. "Sounds like some kind of animal in distress."

The screeching is abruptly cut off and replaced by new sounds. Sounds that make all three of them shiver.

"That's a predator," Lowell says. "Doesn't matter if those other things were cows or sheep, because they're dead now. Whatever the fuck made those noises took care of that."

"Bear?" Bolton asks, looking over at Lu. "Not a wolf or coyote."

"Didn't sound like a bear," Lu says. "I don't know what it was, but it sounded..."

"Bigger?" Lowell suggests. "My nuts are telling me that whatever it is it's not petite."

"It's a bear, but it doesn't matter because we need to move," Bolton says. "Find shelter before that ash comes down."

They all look up at the dark sky above. All they can see for miles is a massive ash cloud and one thing everyone has learned over the past few months is that ash falls eventually.

"Welcome to the new ice age," Lowell says. "That volcano keeps erupting and this world is long gone."

"We'll see," Bolton says. "I'll let the climatologists debate that. Right now, we need to worry about getting somewhere we can breathe when that comes down."

Bolton lowers himself over the edge of the bus and reaches up to help Lu down, then Lowell. Lu stops and looks at the body of the bus driver.

"How'd you get him down?" Lu asks.

"Windshield," Bolton says, pointing to the front of the bus. "Couldn't get you out that way because of the security cage around the driver's seat."

"Hey!" Lu snaps and shoves Lowell away from the man. "Back off!"

"Just checking his pulse," Lowell says. "Want to know what I found?"

Lu kneels down and checks for herself. She doesn't find one.

"He's dead," Lu says.

"Yep," Lowell nods. "That's what I was gonna say."

"What's that?" Bolton asks, pointing towards a shattered and broken road a good quarter mile away. "You know that road?"

"Could be 135," Lu says. "Might even be 200. Everything is so messed up I can't really say.

"Well, we follow the interstate until we get to somewhere we can hole up in," Bolton says.

"What we do is help these people first," Lu says, pointing at a crushed Toyota Corolla. A bloody hand waves weakly from the shattered driver's side window. "We can't leave them to die."

"They're already dead," Bolton says. "There's only three of us and we're all suffering trauma. We're functioning now because of adrenaline. It's only a matter of time before one of you two crash hard and I'm stuck with helping you walk."

"And they locked me up for being a monster," Lowell laughs. "I like your style, soldier boy."

"Bolton," Bolton says. "Just call me Bolton."

"We can try," Lu says and hurries over to the Corolla.

Lowell looks at Bolton and raises his eyebrows. "She always been this way?"

"What? Thinking she can save the world by herself? Yeah," Bolton says. He looks at Lu then at Lowell. "Are you going to be a problem?"

"I'm way past being a problem," Lowell smiles.

"You know what I mean," Bolton says. "Shoot me straight, psycho. Am I going to have to kill you when you try to kill me or Lu?"

"There are so many loopholes in your question that I could answer no truthfully and still rip your eyes out at some point," Lowell says, his smile growing wider. "But, in the spirit of apocalyptic camaraderie, I'll be 100% honest with you and say that if you do your best to keep me alive, I'll make sure to try keeping you and the Girl Scout alive. Deal?"

"Deal," Bolton says and offers his hand.

Lowell takes the hand and the two men stare at each other for a second.

"Your dad military?" Bolton asks.

"Maybe," Lowell nods.

"I know a military handshake anywhere," Bolton says and lets go of Lowell's hand.

"Fuck!" Lu shouts and kicks the Corolla's door.

"I'm guessing that one didn't make it," Lowell says.

"Let's check the other vehicles," Bolton says. "If there aren't survivors, there may at least be supplies we can salvage."

"I'd go for some jeans and a coat," Lowell says, pulling at his wet and torn prison jumpsuit. "Boots would be good to."

"I'll keep an eye out," Bolton says.

The two men freeze as the mystery animal calls out again, this time a little closer. Then far off, other calls answer it.

"I think your bear has friends," Lowell says. "How's about we hurry with finding supplies and checking on the soon to be dead people?"

"Yeah. Good idea," Bolton says. "Bears are territorial. They are going to want to protect their food sources. They'll see us as competition. Our timetable has just been moved up."

"That's why I said we should hurry," Lowell replies.

***

The rock under Kyle's fingers is slick with mud and he tries to get a better grip, but no matter how he moves, he just keeps slipping. His toes scramble for purchase, but there's only a lip of about an inch before the ledge drops off to hundreds of feet of open air below.

"Help!" Kyle shouts, knowing it's useless since he's in the middle of nowhere. "Please! Help!"

He glances over his shoulder at the pit around him, but just that small movement causes his left hand to fall free and Kyle lets loose with a scream that hasn't escaped his throat since before puberty. His body twists away from the ledge and he only has a split second to decide what to do. He shoves his hands against the cliff face and pushes off with his legs, sending his body flying out into the air.

His arms pin wheeling, and throat still screaming, Kyle rushes towards another ledge lost in the gloom of the pit. He slams into the wall of the pit and nearly bounces off the ledge, but he's able to jam his left hand into a crack in the rock and keep himself from tumbling over the side.

Kyle's breath comes in harsh rasps as he struggles not to panic. All around him is nothing but slick rock and it's a hundred feet to the edge of the pit above. He stares up at the near black sky and the thick, rolling clouds of ash that stream by. He watches as the clouds expand and contract, then wonders how long he has before that ash settles down on him and ends his life.

Because that's all he can think of right now, how his life is going to end.

Then a sound above causes a sliver of hope to cut through the gloom.

"Biscuit?" he wonders aloud. "Biscuit!"

The barking gets louder and Kyle tries to stand up on the ledge, but the ground is so slick that he rejects that idea and stays planted on his ass.

"Biscuit! Here boy!"

Far above, a white and grey head appears. Biscuit gives a couple of loud barks and starts to pace back and forth, looking for a way down to his boy.

"Stay, Biscuit!" Kyle orders, fearing the hybrid will jump down to him. It's not outside the realm of possibility with the half-dog, half-wolf. Biscuit has proven time and again, he has no fear when it comes to protecting Kyle. "Find help, Biscuit! Go get help!"

Biscuit barks three more times, then stops as his hackles raise and he growls low. The hybrid spins around and is lost from Kyle's sight.

"Biscuit!" Kyle yells. "Find Grandma!"

Then a gunshot echoes down to Kyle and he hears the distinct yelp of Biscuit in pain. There are two more gunshots, then silence. No barks, nor growls, no more yelps.

Kyle waits on the ledge, his eyes struggling to see above as the light slowly starts to fade. He looks about to see if he can find a large rock or something to use as a weapon, but the ledge is clear of debris except for mud and small, useless bits of granite.

"Hello, Kyle," a voice calls from above.

The light of day is pretty much gone and all Kyle can see is the outline of a man's head and shoulders. But he knows the voice.

"You," Kyle snarls. "Did you just shoot my dog? I'll kill you if you hurt Biscuit!"

"I shot the thing," Linder replies. "But I don't think I killed it. The big coward took off running. I guess it would rather stay alive than stay here to protect you. Not that you need protecting from me."

"Get away from me!" Kyle shouts. "This is all your fault!"

"Oh, I think once I find a way to get you out of that hole, you'll see there is no way any of this is my fault," Linder responds. "You stay put and I'll see if I can find something to lower down to you."

"Fuck you!" Kyle screams. "You killed my grandma and shot my fucking dog! I'd rather die down here!"

"I doubt that," Linder says. "No one would rather die. I'll be right back."

Kyle presses up against the side of the pit and tucks his knees up to his chest. He wants to be tough, to show the man he means what he says, but he knows in his heart that he doesn't want to die down in the dark all alone.

Several minutes go by before something heavy smacks into Kyle's head, causing him to cry out.

"What the hell?" Kyle shouts as he grabs onto a thick, black cable. "What is this?"

"Underground power line," Linder yells down. "They put them in a few years ago so the views wouldn't be ruined by power poles."

Kyle lets go of the cable and scrambles away.

"Are you trying to electrocute me?" Kyle snaps. "Jesus!"

"Don't worry," Linder says. "It isn't live. Pretty sure the eruption sent out some kind of EMP. I doubt there's power for miles."

"Eruption?" Kyle says. "The volcano erupted?"

"Huh," Linder says. "I thought you'd be smarter."

"Fuck you."

"And more polite," Linder sighs. "Grab on and I'll pull you up."

"I'm not coming up there," Kyle says, trying one last time to be brave in the face of certain death.

Then a cry rings out and Kyle's blood goes cold.

Linder gives the cable a shake.

"I don't know what that is, but it doesn't sound good, kid," Linder says. "Been hearing them since the eruption. Grab the cable so I can pull you up. I don't think you want to be stuck in a hole when whatever that is gets here."

Kyle thinks about it for a split second, but a second and a third cry makes his mind up for him and he grabs onto the cable. His feet slip and slide as he tries to walk up the side of the pit and in the end, he lets Linder pull him up and out.

"Thanks," Kyle says, instantly wishing he can take the word back as he gets to the top and rolls away from the edge of pit.

"Ah, there's the Morgan politeness," Linder says.

"My last name is Holden," Kyle says instantly.

"Please," Linder laughs. "If you're going to have any last name other than Morgan, it should be Linder, not that Holden alias."

"Who the hell are you?" Kyle asks. "And don't say you're my father. I don't believe that for a second."

"If I can't say that, then I can't answer your question," Linder says. "How about you just call me Tobias then?"

"How about you not call me little shit?" Kyle sneers as he gets up and puts some space between himself and Linder.

"Yes, sorry about that," Linder says. "My temper can get away from me sometimes. But I'm fine now and I promise not to call you names again, okay?"

"No, not okay," Kyle says. "What you're going to do is get the hell away from me. I'm going this way and you're going that way, got it? I'm going to find my dog while you fuck off and die."

"And the politeness is gone," Linder sighs. "That's your mother right there. As much as I disliked your grandmother, she at least had humility and the good Lord on her side."

Kyle glares at the man, but Linder just shrugs.

"Suit yourself, kid," Linder says. "You want to wander alone through the forest, you go for it."

A high wailing echoes through the trees and the ground starts to shake.

"I'm thinking we should stick together, though," Linder says. "Things aren't quite right."

Kyle looks at the world around him and is frozen with indecision. Huge trees are uprooted and lie at angles against each other while the ground is pocked with pits and crevices. A huge wall of stone is a few yards away, pushed straight up out of the earth by the eruption. Kyle wonders what the land must look like closer to the volcano if it's this messed up here.

The ground keeps shaking and Kyle realizes there's a rhythm to the tremors.

"Are those...?" he whispers.

"Footsteps," Linder grins. "Something wicked this way comes."

Kyle isn't sure what's scarier: that something is big enough to shake the ground as it walks or that Linder is grinning like the cat with a canary over the situation.

***

Dr. Probst jolts awake, a scream forming on her lips, but it doesn't have a chance to escape as a hand clamps down around her mouth.

"Don't make a sound," Coletti whispers into her ear. "We aren't alone."

Dr. Probst reaches up and slowly takes Coletti's hand away as she looks around them. She wants to ask were they are, but Coletti holds a finger to his lips and then points up with his other hand. She cocks her head, puzzled. Then that scream Coletti had averted previously finally makes its escape as everything shudders around her from the loudest roar she's ever heard.

Coletti glares, but doesn't try to shut her up since the doctor quickly figures out her folly and clamps her own hands over her mouth this time. The roar sounds like a foghorn filled with glass and is so powerful that the fillings in her back molars begin to vibrate. As does the earth she's seated upon.

Dr. Probst looks about and realizes the two of them are buried under a pile of fir boughs. Needles rain down on her head and she is covered in pitch, but those aren't her immediate worries. The most immediate worry is what is making the noise that should only exist in nightmares. Her eyes find Coletti's in the gloom and he points again towards a small opening between the boughs. Dr. Probst slowly shifts her position, terrified that even the slightest movement will bring their cover crashing down on them.

Outside their hide, the world is nothing but smoke and flame. Geysers of fire shoot high into the air, and Dr. Probst is able to see that they are maybe six or seven hundred yards from the edge of the massive hole. She turns her head and looks behind her, realizing Coletti has them covered and backed up against a huge slab of granite. Their backs are protected, which Dr. Probst realizes is a wonderful thing, considering what else is around them.

Monsters.

That is the only word she can think of as she watches giant creatures crawl around. Four-legged beasts that stand a hundred feet tall walk on thick, tree trunk legs, clawed toes sticking out from all sides of feet that are the size of cars. The monsters' heads are bulbous, with deep black eyes protruding from each side, covered by sharp, scaled ridges.

Eyes on each side. Predators have eyes that face front. At least, they do normally...

What Dr. Probst sees is far from normal.

The creatures hurry past, almost scurrying in fear, as they pour up out of the volcanic hole. Again, she is grateful for their position as it keeps them from being trampled by the things.

Then another roar and she jams her hands against her ears.

The creatures cry out, wailing with a fear she easily shares. They rush forward faster, their huge legs moving in a way that she has never witnessed with quadrupeds. There isn't a side by side rhythm, but more independent movement from their center mass. Dr. Probst's scientific curiosity almost makes her forget the horror of what she is seeing, until reality comes slamming down. Literally.

What the woman had mistaken for part of a mountain, or rock formation forced up from the ground by the eruption, is in fact the leg of an even larger nightmare. All bits of scientific reality she had been trying to cling to, fall away as the leg is lifted into the air and comes crashing down onto one of the fleeing monsters.

The ground under Dr. Probst and Coletti shakes so hard that small cracks form in the dirt and chunks of the granite wall behind them crack off. Neither has time to brace themselves against the tsunami of monster blood and guts that slams against their shelter.

Blue/black blood sprays in through the boughs, while nearly translucent bone fragments rip apart the tree limbs, exposing the two to the danger beyond.

Dr. Probst scurries back against Coletti and the man instinctively wraps his arms around the woman as they watch a ten fingered hand reach down and pick up the crushed carcass. They crane their necks, having to look almost straight up, as the broken monster corpse is lifted a thousand feet into the air towards an open mouth of unspeakable horror. The corpse is lost from sight as it is devoured, torn apart by a thousand teeth, each as large as one of the fir trees that used to fill the landscape around them, but are now lost and broken. Just like Dr. Probst's sanity.

"Hold on," Coletti whispers to her, his face pressed into the back of her head. "Keep it together."

But the doctor can't, and once again, Coletti finds he must hold his hand over her mouth as the woman begins to scream uncontrollably.

FIVE

The situation room is nearly silent as everyone watches the last satellite images of the supervolcano before all transmissions went dark.

"Tell me we have someone figuring out what those things are," President Nance says, breaking the silence and sending everyone back into hyperactive chaos. "Tell me I'm not witnessing giant demons coming up from Hell."

"No one knows what they are, sir," Joan says. "Images have been sent to every zoologist with the proper security clearance."

"Send the information to *all* the damn zoologists!" President Nance yells. "I don't care what their security clearance is! It's not like we can hide those things from the world!"

"Sir, we have F-15s in the Carolinas ready at your command," Air Force General Mark Tulane states, his eyes watching the president carefully. "I just need your authorization."

"The Carolinas?" President Nance asks. "Surely, we have jets closer than that. What about Peterson or Nellis?"

"We have lost communications with every base within a thousand square miles of ground zero," Joan states. "While we can talk to NORAD, we can't reach any other military installation within that zone. We think the eruption created a massive EMP the likes of which we've never seen. Even shielded equipment and facilities are down."

"Jesus," President Nance curses. "This is unreal."

"That's one word for it," Joan frowns.

"Sir?" General Tulane asks. "Your orders?"

President Nance looks at the rest of the Joint Chiefs. "Talk to me."

Admiral Quigley clears his throat, his eyes drawn to the replayed scene on the main monitor. "It is my opinion that we are under attack, Mr. President." There are assenting murmurs from the other chiefs. "We don't know what those things are or where they could be coming from-."

"They're coming from a goddamn hole in the fucking ground!" Army General Lawrence Azoul shouts. "Stop tiptoeing around this like it's some political issue! It's not! We have been attacked by goddamn monsters, Mr. President, and the sooner we come to grips with that, the sooner we can retaliate!"

"Monsters," President Nance says, shaking his head. "Do you know how you sound, General?"

The man stands and points at the main monitor. "I don't need to sound like anything! Look at those things! Look! A third of our country has lost all electronic capabilities. That means they are in the dark, literally, about what is going on. Are we going to wait around and establish diplomatic relations with these things? As unbelievable as they are, they're here! We need to blast them from this planet and then sort through the mess afterwards!"

All of the Joint Chiefs look from General Azoul to President Nance.

"How soon until we can establish satellite imaging again?" President Nance asks.

"Six hours, sir," Joan replies. "We had every major satellite positioned above the supervolcano. When the EMP hit it didn't just go out, but up as well, killing every satellite observing the volcano. The soonest we'll be able to get imaging again is six hours."

"My God, we're blind," President Nance says. He looks at General Tulane. "Launch the fighters. Orders are to engage at will. I want all video of those engagements relayed here immediately."

"Of course, Mr. President," General Tulane nods as he reaches for a phone in front of him. "They'll be up and over ground zero within the hour."

"Good," President Nance sighs. "Now someone get me reports from the ground. I want to know what people are seeing!"

"Sir, the power is out," Joan says. "We can't talk to anyone within that thousand mile radius."

"Then send people in that can! The EMP didn't make the place a dead zone! I want boots on the ground and communications set up ASAP!" President Nance yells as he gets to his feet, his fist pounding the table. "We may not know what we are at war with, but we are at war!"

***

"Found another one!" Lu yells as she hurries to a hand reaching out from under a fallen shed. "And there's someone over there!"

Lu grabs onto the sheet metal and shoves it aside. Underneath is a woman clutching her two small children and the family dog. All look terrified.

"Are you hurt?" Lu asks.

"Just bruised a little," the woman says. "What happened?"

"The volcano erupted," Lu says. "It knocked out power and fried all electronics."

Lu helps the woman and children away from the wreckage, dusting off the kids while the small dog cowers behind the mother, its tail between its legs.

"Where's the light coming from?" the woman asks, looking up at the dull, red glow in the sky.

"We aren't sure," Bolton says as he comes up, helping a limping man stay upright. "It could be the volcano erupting and reflecting down from the atmosphere. There's an ash cloud up there the size of the whole country is my guess. With all the minerals in that ash, it's a wonder we aren't seeing a rave light show."

"The wonder is why we aren't all choking on ash right now," Lowell says, standing off to the side next to a half-demolished house, his eyes studying the sky. He's dressed in dirt caked jeans and a heavy winter coat. "That shit comes down and it's bye bye lungs."

Everyone looks up for a second before Lu clears her throat and turns to the woman.

"We're heading west. We've been finding people along the way," Lu says. "If you have any food and water, plus warm clothing and salvageable bedding, you need to get it together and come with us."

"Why west?" the man asks as Bolton lets him go and he hobbles over to the woman and children. "I thought we were supposed to head south?"

"We're military," Bolton says, pointing at his uniform, even though it isn't his normal one. "We can get folks onto ships and get off the continent."

"Gonna be a long walk," Lowell says, pointing over his shoulder at a rag tag group of people standing near the cracked and broken street. "Especially with the refugee parade there."

"Hopefully we can find working vehicles soon," Lu says.

"What's wrong with the cars?" the man asks.

"Nothing electronic works," Bolton replies. "That means batteries and alternators. We haven't found a car that will start in miles."

"Maybe Coeur d'Alene wasn't hit," Lu says. "If we can get there, we can regroup and figure out how to get everyone to Seattle."

"What do you mean *if?*" the woman asks.

In answer to her question, one of the loud roars fills the air, bouncing around the area like a warning claxon telling them to flee.

"Mommy?" one of the kids whines.

"That's the if," Lowell laughs.

"We've stayed ahead of the things, but they are gaining on us," Bolton says. He pats the M-4 strapped to his back. "If you have weapons, you'll want to bring those as well."

The family just stands there.

"And they're gone. Checked out like the rest," Lowell laughs, turns, and walks back to the group out near the road. "We have to keep walking."

"I know you have questions," Lu says, getting in close to the parents. "But none of us have answers. We're just as lost as you are. The only thing we can do is keep moving and hope things get better."

"Right. Better," the man nods then looks up at the sky.

"Can you walk?" Bolton asks him. The man doesn't respond and Bolton snaps his fingers. "Hey! Can you walk?"

"Yeah, yeah, I think so," the man nods. "I broke my leg a few months ago, that's why I'm limping so bad. Must have hurt it again. I have crutches inside."

"Get them," Bolton says. "And anything else you will need for the trip. Essentials only. Don't bring pictures or mementos. They'll just weigh you down. You can come back for those later."

"Okay, yeah, fine," the man says and limps off to the half-demolished house with his family.

Lu waits until they are inside before turning to Bolton. "Come back later? No one is going to be able to come back here for a long time."

"It got them moving," Bolton says. "It's a trick I learned in Afghanistan when evacing civilians from combat zones. Tell them what they want to hear now, deal with what they need to hear later."

"So, lie to them," Lu frowns.

"Yeah," Bolton says. "If it gets their asses into gear. This isn't grey area time, Lu. This is life or death. Most non-combatants make the wrong choice without realizing it. It's my job to make the right choice for them."

"Non-combatants?" Lu asks. "This isn't a war, Connor."

More roars and several high, keening wails make the group by the road jump and cry out.

"You may be wrong on that," Bolton says. "I hope you're right, but those sounds aren't exactly friendly."

"We don't know what those sounds are," Lu says.

"I think it's safe to assume at this point that my bear theory isn't holding up," Bolton says. He looks towards the road. "How about you get people calmed down while I hurry up our new additions?"

Lu sighs heavily and nods. "Okay, but be nice and don't push them too hard."

"I'm always nice," Bolton smiles. "You know me."

***

"Your leg hurting?" Kyle smirks as Linder hobbles behind him.

"I could ask you the same," Linder says. "You've got a hitch in your step as well."

"I'm fine," Kyle replies.

"Same here," Linder says.

"Good."

"Good."

They keep walking, dodging crevices and cracked earth, working their way over or around fallen trees, fording small streams that look like they just came into existence. All while continually looking over their shoulder for the source of the wails, shrieks, roars, and giant footsteps.

"If you hurt my dog, I'm going to kill you," Kyle says.

"I don't enjoy hurting animals, you know," Linder replies. "I want you to know that."

"Whatever," Kyle replies. "Most sane people don't have to point that out."

"Your implication isn't lost on me," Linder laughs. "But I can tell you I am more than sane."

"So, what? You're super sane?" Kyle snorts. "Great. Everything is fucking peachy keen then."

"Watch your language," Linder says. "You disrespect your grandmother by saying that word."

Kyle stops and whirls on the man. "You mean the grandmother you killed? Fuck. You."

"Couldn't be avoided," Linder shrugs. "That woman wasn't the person you thought she was. She has more blood on her hands than you can imagine."

"Seeing you shoot her has helped me imagine a lot," Kyle snaps. "So, again, fuck you."

More wails, more screeches, more footsteps shaking everything.

"We should keep moving," Linder says. "Walking will cool our heads."

"Whatever," Kyle says as he turns and hikes away from the man. "If this hadn't all gone to crazy end of the world shit, I'd fucking kill you with my bare hands."

"I'm sorry to hear that," Linder replies. "I figure times like these bring families closer together."

"You're not my family!" Kyle roars.

A roar answers him. And it's close.

"See what your anger has done?" Linder hisses, hurrying faster, his hands shoving Kyle in the back. "Go!"

"Don't fucking touch me," Kyle hisses back and Linder pulls his hands away.

"Just go," Linder says, trying to keep from exploding. The little shit is making it very difficult for him, though.

Very difficult.

***

"We're going to have to move," Coletti says. "We're going to get trampled at some point."

"How?" Dr. Probst asks. "We come out of hiding and we'll get eaten."

The woman is exhausted from her screaming, and subsequent crying fit, but has enough energy to start assessing the situation the two find themselves in.

"You've seen what it's like out there," she whispers. "The big ones eat the smaller ones. That means the smaller ones will probably eat us as soon as we push these branches aside."

"I think the smaller ones are too busy getting away from the bigger ones," Coletti says, ignoring the absurdity of that statement. "They don't have time to stop and snack on us."

Dr. Probst shudders at the comment.

Coletti starts emptying his pockets and pats Dr. Probst to do the same. After some seconds of glowering, the doctor finally follows suit and pulls everything from the high-altitude jumpsuit she wears. There isn't much.

"We each have a water bottle and water purification tablets, so that's good," Coletti says, looking at the inventory on the ground before them. "Only four MREs, though, and five energy bars, so food is scarce."

"How were we going to eat before?" Dr. Probst asks.

"We were going to set up a base camp and then have supplies air dropped as needed," Coletti says, looking at the surreal sky and landscape about them. "Don't think that's happening anytime soon." He studies the sky then turns to Dr. Probst. "Why haven't we suffocated from the ash yet?"

"The eruption must have been so powerful that the ash is in the upper reaches of the atmosphere," she replies. "It's so far up it's out of the local air currents and now going global. Europe will be getting a nice surprise soon."

"But it will come down, right?" Coletti asks.

"Yes, it will," Dr. Probst replies, "but no way to know when."

"Yeah, the usual rules no longer apply," Coletti laughs quietly.

"Physics is physics," Dr. Probst says. "As a scientist, I have learned that the hard way too many times."

"Never assume," Coletti counters. "As a SEAL, I learned *that* the hard way once. Won't happen again."

"Then be prepared for an ash fall like the world has never seen," Dr. Probst responds. "And pray we have found shelter by then."

"I didn't think scientists prayed," Coletti grins.

"What's the saying? Foxholes make believers out of everyone?" She waves her hand around. "I think our temporary shelter counts as a foxhole, don't you?"

"I've been in worse," Coletti replies. He sighs and looks at the meager supplies.

The water bottles and water tablets, MREs and energy bars, two survival knives, a few feet of heavy duty cord, four pop flares, and two Mylar blankets, folded tightly into small, silver squares. Plus Coletti's .45 and three extra magazines, as well as the helmets they wore on their insane descent.

"Won't get us far, but better than nothing," Coletti says as he divides the supplies up between them, then gets up, crouching low so his back just barely touches the fir boughs. "Ready?"

"What? Now?" Dr. Probst asks. "Shouldn't we wait for morning so there's more light?"

"How much light do you think will get through that ash?" Coletti asks. "The glow from above is light enough to keep us from falling into a ravine or off a cliff. We need to move while we still have energy. We get far enough away and we might be able to find that shelter you prayed for."

"I haven't prayed yet," Dr. Probst responds. "I just suggested we pray."

"Well, I have been since the second we hit ground," Coletti says as he slowly and carefully begins to move the fir boughs out of their way. "You should take your own advice and start right away. Another thing I've learned as a SEAL is you take help where you can get it, no matter the source."

There's a wide enough gap in the boughs for them to get out and Coletti holds his hand back for Dr. Probst to take. She does, stands up, and the two of them quietly step out into a terrifying new world.

***

"Command, this is Porthos," the fighter pilot calls over the com. "We are approaching the target area. Guns are hot and missiles ready. Please confirm standing order to fire as needed."

"Standing order is confirmed, Porthos," a voice responds. "Godspeed."

"You hear that, boys?" Porthos says. "We can light up these Godzillas as soon as we have contact."

"You have got to be shitting me," someone replies. "This is a joke, right?"

"No joke, Short Stop," Porthos replies. "You've all seen the footage. Crazy shit came up out of that hole and we get to send it back! I want all wings to report now!"

"Short Stop is a go."

"Walker is a go."

"Eggs is a go."

"Downsize is a go."

"Tickles is a go." He sighs. "Can I get a fucking new call sign after this?"

"Like what, Monster Fucker?" Eggs laughs.

"Shut it," Porthos orders.

"Rocket is a go."

"Trophy is a go."

"Alright, gentlemen," Porthos says, "we have some ash to deal with. Drop hard and fast, then eyes on your targets. We're looking at creatures close to a thousand feet tall. The ash cloud is at 40,000 feet and rising. Estimates say it's got to be at least a thousand feet thick in of itself. That's a lot of time flying blind. Watch yourselves coming out the other side."

The F-15s break from formation and dive, their sleek bodies piercing the black ash that rolls below them.

Porthos watches his readings as the world around the jet fighter goes dark.

"You got anything, Athos?" Porthos asks his WSO seated behind him.

"Radar is for shit," Athos replies, his eyes studying the three screens in front of him, his hands working the dual joysticks rapidly. "Can't get a lock on anything. The ash is denser than we thought."

"And thicker," Porthos says. "We're already two thousand feet in, not just one thousand."

"Whoa, what was that?" Athos asks. "You see that?"

"No, what was it?"

"I don't know," Athos says. "I picked up something in the ash."

"Probably one of the other fighters," Porthos replies. "Everyone better stay on course or we'll have some nasty collisions."

"That's not what I'm worried about," Athos says. "If this ash doesn't thin out, we're going to slam right into a fucking mountain."

"Well, we're about to find out what's up soon enough," Porthos says. "Here we go!"

The fighters break from the ash cloud and not a single man is able to keep from gasping, praying, cursing, or flat out screaming.

"Jesus Christ!" Porthos cries. "Light 'em up, Athos!"

Porthos pulls the trigger on his forward guns while Athos targets the monsters with the air to ground missiles. The WSO watches as the missiles shoot out away from the fighter, headed for their target a few thousand feet below them.

"This isn't fucking real," Eggs says over the com.

"Keep it under control, Pilot!" Porthos orders. "Stay focused and send those things back to Hell!"

Missiles rain down as bullets fill the air in a blanket of hot lead, all headed towards the impossible monsters that lumber, shuffle, stomp around at the edge of the massive hole in the earth.

"Five seconds to impact," Athos says. "Three, two, one!"

The missiles hit their targets and fire erupts everywhere. Huge explosions climb into the sky as the fighters all pull up, aiming their noses back towards the ash.

"Direct hits!" Athos shouts.

"Hear that, gentlemen?" Porthos laughs. "Looks like we know how to shoot."

Something streaks by the side of the fighter, causing Porthos to jerk the stick.

"Whoa there!" Athos shouts. "You okay, man?"

"Did you see that?" Porthos asks. "What the fuck was that? It was huge!"

"Hey, guys?" Short Stop calls. "I don't think we're-"

His voice is cut off and there's a brief squeal of static.

"Short Stop? Come in, Short Stop!" Porthos shouts.

Nothing.

Off to the right, an explosion just below the ash cloud catches the pilot's attention.

"Athos, I need to know what the fuck is going on!" Porthos shouts.

"We have bogeys!" Walker yells.

Then the com is filled with pilots shouting as their WSOs try to lock onto the new threats.

"Athos!"

"I'm trying, goddammit!" Athos shouts. "I can't get a lock! The things are massive and keep dropping in and out of the ash!"

"Are you fucking telling me we have flying Godzillas up here with us?" Porthos asks.

"I don't fucking know!" Athos yells.

A shape appears in front of their fighter and Porthos barely shoves the stick in time to send them shooting underneath the thing. He rolls the fighter to the left and dives as Athos shouts directions at him from behind.

"Left! Right! Jesus, the thing is faster than we are!" Athos yells. "Do that voodoo you do, man! We can't outrun it!"

Porthos jams the stick as far forward as it will go, sending the fighter into a power dive that he isn't sure he can pull them out of. His eyes lock onto the monsters below and he realizes that there are more than just the big ones they attacked. Dozens and dozens of smaller things crawl from the chasm, scurrying away as soon as they are free.

But he can't think of those things right now. He has more pressing issues.

"Counter measures!" Porthos yells.

"You think flares are going to scare this fuck off?" Athos shouts.

Porthos whips the stick to the right then pulls up hard and the fighter races past the flying beast pursuing them. There's a roar of frustration that the pilot can actually hear over the sound of the jet engines. His gut clenches and he jams the stick forward, sending the fighter into a dive once more.

A huge wing whips past the fighter, and all of a sudden, alarms start to blare as lights flash along the dashboard.

"Shit!" Porthos yells. "The thing clipped us!"

The man struggles to get control of the fighter as it begins to spin wildly through the air. It plummets towards the ground, and the hundreds of monsters below. Porthos jams his feet into the bottom of the cockpit for leverage as he tries to pull the jet out of the fall.

His muscles strain and he's pretty sure he tears something in his left elbow as he grips the stick with every ounce of strength left in his body. He can hear Athos yelling in his ear, but he shuts the man out, putting all of his focus onto getting them out of the dive. His throat goes raw from screaming as the stick slowly starts to respond. He risks letting go with one hand and pushes the throttle forward, using the thrust from the engines to try to cut the spin.

It works. In a second the jet is no longer spinning and Porthos has control once more. He aims the fighter back towards the ash cloud, ready to get the fuck out of this nightmare.

Instead he runs directly into one.

The thing before them spreads its enormous wings and six massive claws reach for the jet.

"OH, FUCK!" Porthos screams as the two combatants collide.

***

Dr. Probst huddles against Coletti as they hide under a rocky overhang, their eyes glued to the aerial battle above.

"They're coming out of the ash," Dr. Probst says. "How can they breathe? The ash alone should kill them, not to mention the altitude."

"You're trying to apply that reality thing again, Doc," Coletti says. "You should stop doing that."

There's a huge explosion and one of the fighters and flying monsters come crashing towards the ground, now both just a fused ball of flame. Dr. Probst gasps as the ball of flame slams into one of the big monsters, sending it collapsing to the earth. Everything shakes from the impact and Coletti and Dr. Probst hold each other tighter as rocks bounce off their heads from the overhang.

They both stare as the big monster shakes off the fire and debris and pushes back up to its feet.

"That explains why those missiles didn't take the things out," Coletti says. "This isn't looking good."

"They'll just have to use bigger missiles," Dr. Probst says.

"How?" Coletti asks. "You think those flying things are going to let an F-35 through that ash? The only option left is to send in the bombers."

"My God," Dr. Probst says. "You think they will?"

"They might," Coletti says. "Which means we need to be far away from here when they do."

There's a second explosion and a third and two more fighters plummet towards the ground in flames. Neither actually makes contact with the earth, as they are lost in the chasm instead.

Coletti tugs at Dr. Probst's arm. "Come on. It's not going to get any better."

***

"Does anyone have any good news for me?" President Nance asks, his tie askew and face red with anger, yet white with fear, creating a splotchy, maniacal look. "Tell me we killed something!"

"Only confirmed kill is the flying creature that Pilot Hormell collided with," General Tulane says. "Otherwise, we can't say for sure if any of those things died."

"You're telling me that eight F-15 Strike Eagles couldn't kill one of those giant monsters?" President Nance snaps. "Those things took direct hits from goddamn sidewinder missiles!"

"Sir, calm down," Joan says, taking the full wrath of his anger on herself as the man whips about to face her. "We don't know what we are dealing with. Conventional weapons may not work on these creatures."

"Then get me unconventional weapons!" President Nance roars. "Nuke the goddamn things!"

"Sir, we cannot use nuclear weapons," Secretary of Defense Jeremy Borland says from down the table. Quiet for most of the crisis, the man has let the Joint Chiefs handle things, but the mention of nukes means Borland's time to step forward is now. "The thermals will take the radiation right into the upper atmosphere and spread it with the ash. We nuke those things and we could possibly win, but the Earth will be contaminated with radiation in a matter of months. We already have an ash winter to deal with, sir, we can't have a nuclear winter also."

"That's assuming nukes even work on these beasts," General Azoul adds.

"True," Borland agrees. "But the way that flying monster went down I'd say nukes would work. We just can't use that option."

"Then what other options do we have? What about MOABs?" President Nance asks.

"Mother Of All Bombs?" Joan asks. "How would we get them there? You saw what those things can do to F-15s. A bulky bomber isn't going to be able to out fly those monsters."

"They won't have to," General Tulane says. "We could drop them from above the ash. My guys will make sure they hit their targets."

"Your guys will make sure they hit *near* the targets," Admiral Quigley counters. "We won't know what the results are. They could just bounce off and make the bastards mad. Until we have visuals, we can't make a single informed decision. We need eyes on the area and now."

"Satellites are still not in place," Joan says. "We have a couple more hours until we can get them over ground zero."

"Then what?" General Tulane asks. "We stare at black ash? Even if we can get thermal imaging, we won't be able to know exactly what we're looking at."

"Especially if the things aren't warm blooded," General Azoul says. "They could just show up as rocks on the thermal. I know where General Tulane is going with this and I agree. We need eyes on the ground."

"It'll take a day to get troops in there," Joan responds. "Every vehicle within a thousand miles is nonoperational due to the EMP."

"We may have folks on the ground that are a lot closer," Borland says, leaning forward. "All we need is one or two to be spotters for us. We get them the equipment and they'll make sure the bombs hit home. And tell us if they work."

"Do I have to mention the EMP again?" Joan snaps. "We can't talk to anyone close enough to help! All electronics are out!"

"That's not quite true," Borland says. "If Coletti or any of his people survived, then we can get hold of them. Or at least point them in the right direction."

"How?" President Nance asks.

"CLDs," Borland says. "All Special Operations operators have them, from Delta Force to the SEALs. Coordinate Locating Devices. They are small and can only give operators longitude and latitude, but they are shielded from even the strongest EMPs. We start airdropping containers into the area with all the gear the men need and those containers can give off a signal that the CLDs will pick up. If Coletti's people, or any other operators, are close by then they'll know to get to the containers."

"Is this true?" President Nance asks the Joint Chiefs.

"Yes, sir," General Azoul nods. "The trick is whether or not we have any men in the area."

"Do it," President Nance orders. "Get those men the gear they need to so we can finally get some intel on the area. We have no idea how much time we have before these things start to spread."

"Yes, sir," Borland says. "I'll start making the calls."

"But let me say this," President Nance announces, standing before them all. "If we do not hear from any operators within twelve hours of the drop, we send in the bombers. We blanket the entire region."

SIX

"Where are you leading us?" Linder asks, his face dripping sweat, mouth tight with pain. "This isn't west, is it?"

"No, it's south," Kyle says. "We aren't going west, not yet."

"We aren't?" Linder asks, his voice instantly making the hair on the back of Kyle's neck stand up.

The teenager stops and turns to look at Linder.

"Do you have a problem with going south?" Kyle asks.

"West would be better," Linder says. "There are military ships waiting to take people off the continent."

"Yeah, I know," Kyle says. "That's why we're going south. My mom is south and without her, I won't be getting on one of those ships."

"You mean we," Linder states. "*We* won't be getting on one of those ships. Where you go, I go. We're a father and son team now."

Kyle is about to argue for the millionth time that the man isn't his father, but he doesn't have the energy and just turns around and stalks away.

"Hey!" Linder shouts. "Don't you turn your back on me!"

Linder hobbles after him quickly and grabs Kyle's arm. The young man rips his arm from the older man's grip and glares.

"Don't touch me," Kyle snarls. "I'll fucking kick your ass if you touch me again."

"You think you can take me?" Linder laughs. "Kid, I'm a trained federal agent of the United States of America. I've taken down murderers twice your size."

"Good for you," Kyle says and turns away again.

"I said not to turn your back on me!" Linder yells and slams his fist into the back of Kyle's head.

The teenager falls to one knee, then kicks out, nailing Linder right in the wound on his leg. The man crumples to the ground and Kyle jumps on him, grabbing him by the collar as he cocks a fist back, ready to slam it into Linder's face.

But Linder quickly counters with a knee to Kyle's groin, sending the kid falling to the side in a gasping, grunting heap. Linder shoves away from Kyle and then gets to his feet. He looks around and finds a medium sized log, picks it up and starts to move closer.

"You don't listen," Linder snarls. "Just like that cunt mother of yours. Think you know what's best, but you don't. I'm the only one that knows what's best. I'm the only one that can show you the true path of God to follow. Not that whore. Not that fucking cunt whore. Not her."

Linder smacks the log against his palm and raises it over his head, his eyes nothing but madness.

"Time you learned what's best for you, boy," Linder says. "I am the Lord's instrument; I am His lesson."

"How about you just put that stick down?" a voice says from behind Linder, followed by the distinct sounds of several rifle bolts being pulled back and then locked into position. "I'd suggest you do it slowly, unless you want to find out what lesson a bullet teaches your back."

Linder doesn't lower the log at all, just slowly turns to face the voice. He quickly sees the voice has friends. A good ten or so friends, all with hunting rifles, semi-automatic (probably converted to fully automatic) assault rifles, sub-machine guns, and various pistols.

"There a problem here, folks?" Linder asks, the log still raised above his head.

The man in the front of the group, a Winchester 94 30/30 to his shoulder, cocks his head and frowns.

"Well, mister, you seem about to brain that kid there," the man says. "And I'm not so sure that's a good idea. I could be wrong since I don't know the full story and maybe your beef with the kid is legit. But for now, how's about you lower the log and we get to the bottom of this."

"I think you should just move along," Linder says. "That's what I think you should do. This is federal business."

There's a few snorts and chuckles from the group.

"Oh, it's *federal* business, is it?" the man laughs. "Well, that changes everything." He cocks the lever of the 94 and takes two steps forward. "Now, I just want you to get on your knees."

"Oh, you're those types," Linder smirks, log still raised.

"If you mean that we're true patriots of this here United States, then yes, we are those types," the man says. "And any true patriot knows that the real enemy of this country is the federal government. Get. On. Your. Knees."

Linder sighs, then lets the log fall from his hands. He laces his fingers behind his head and lowers himself to his knees.

"Tell me more about this true patriotism," Linder smiles up at the man. "I've been thinking about making a change for a while now. Your outfit sure looks like a sound organization."

The response he gets is a rifle butt to the face and then darkness.

***

"Do I need to say it?" Lowell asks as he turns and looks over his shoulder at the straggling group of survivors. "Do I?"

"We aren't leaving people to die out here," Lu snaps.

"Not saying we should," Lowell shrugs. "Just saying maybe we need to divide this group up and let the ones with a real chance at living move a little faster."

"That's the same as leaving people behind," Lu says.

"No, actually, it's not," Lowell replies. "Leaving people behind would mean we *leave people behind*. Like not come back for them. But splitting up, and letting the healthy hurry on ahead, means we can find help faster and come back for those that can't hurry. No one gets left behind, just like no one gets held back."

"You're such a self-serving asshole," Lu says. "I should have left you in the bus." She shakes her head and looks at Bolton. "Can you believe this crap?"

"Yeah," Bolton replies.

"Uh...what?" Lu asks, her eyes wide. "What did you say?"

"I agree with him," Bolton says. "It hurts to say it, but I do. Staying in one group means we put everyone at risk. Splitting up and letting the most able bodied travel faster is a good idea."

"I thought you SpecOps guys never leave a man behind," Lu glares.

"We also never hold anyone back," Bolton says. "I would never have asked any of those men back there to die for me just so I can have my hand held."

"Good, because they can't do shit now except bloat and rot," Lowell smirks.

"I agree with you and you talk shit about my dead friends?" Bolton growls. "What the fuck is wrong with you?"

"If I knew that, I wouldn't have been on that bus," Lowell replies. "My life is a mystery, even to myself."

"No one is going on ahead," Lu says. "We stay together and we stay on the interstate."

"Not much of an interstate anymore," Lowell says as he looks about at the broken asphalt and abandoned cars. "But I guess it leads somewhere."

"Next exit will be in just a few miles," Lu says. "We'll look for more survivors and rest up somewhere for a few hours. Maybe we'll find some food for everyone."

"Or maybe we'll find a couple of burning buildings like at the last exit," Lowell says. "If some of us run up ahead and check, we'll know for sure."

"No way I could do your job, Lu," Bolton chuckles. "I'd have put a bullet between his eyes miles ago."

"What's the call, Marshal?" Lowell asks. "We stagger and stumble along, a train of losers just waiting to die? Or do you let a couple of us scout ahead and see if the next exit is even worth it?"

Lu looks at Bolton and the man shrugs.

"I hate the asshole, but he has a point," Bolton says.

"I should have kept you shackled," Lu says to Lowell.

"But you didn't," Lowell replies. "How many of us do you want to go?"

"I'll go with," Bolton says. "Keep an eye on him for you."

"Take two more," Lu says. "You double time it there and back."

"That's the plan," Lowell says and turns around, walking backwards as he scopes out the group of survivors. "You, and you."

Lowell points to a shorter man who looks like he's in good shape. Grey eyes that dart about quickly, the man points at his chest. "Me?"

"You. Come on," Lowell says. "You too."

The other man is a mountain with legs, but has a simple look to him, like he's not exactly sure what's going on. The man shakes his head.

"Don't wanna," he says in a slow, even voice.

"We're just gonna check out the next exit," Lowell says. "Give us a chance to move a little faster."

The mountain man furrows his brow. "Why?"

Lu snorts a laugh.

"We're going to need shelter soon," Lowell says. "There might be a place up there that can hold all of us, but we need to know soon."

"Why?" the man asks again.

"Juts pick another," Bolton says. "If we're going to do this, then we need to do this."

A far off screech and then howl makes everyone look about quickly and grab onto the person next to them as if that will ward off whatever is out there.

"You hear that?" Lowell asks. "Do you know what that is?"

"No," the man says, shaking his head.

"I don't either," Lowell says. "But it makes sense to be inside somewhere safe instead of finding out, right?"

"Yeah," the man says. "I guess."

"Cool. Then let's go," Lowell says, turns and starts jogging down the broken interstate.

"What the fuck?" Bolton calls. "You gotta learn teamwork."

"No, I don't," Lowell replies.

The two other men catch up quickly and all four jog as fast as they can while also keeping their footing on the uneven terrain.

It takes them less than ten minutes before they come to the next exit. The off ramp is completely destroyed and they have to climb down through massive chunks of asphalt and concrete to get to the road below.

"This doesn't look promising," Bolton says as the four men get to the lower road and walk towards a the short rows of gas stations and fast food outlets that line the road.

The buildings are dark and a couple of them have collapsed, their cracked plastic signs standing like gravestones above them. Lowell walks towards the largest building left standing, a newer truck stop that's part gas station, part convenience store, part restaurant. A couple of overturned semis lay on their sides in the shattered parking lot, but no signs of the drivers, or anyone else.

"That'll be big enough," Lowell says. He looks back at Bolton. "Want to pull your pop gun there and have a look?"

"You think I need my carbine?" Bolton laughs. "Why? This isn't the zombie apocalypse."

Lowell shrugs. "May be locals in there feeling territorial."

"Your faith in your fellow man is admirable," Bolton laughs. "You do realize all of this went to hell only a few hours ago, right? The world hasn't had time to go Thunderdome yet."

"You'd be surprised how fast things go to shit," Lowell says and the look in his eyes makes Bolton shut up and just nod.

"Fine," Bolton says and unslings his M-4 from his back. "Let's go."

"Keep an eye on things out here," Lowell says to the other two. "Give a shout if you see anything."

"Okay, sure," the short man says.

Bolton puts his carbine to his shoulder and steps cautiously towards the front entrance. One of the double doors hangs by a hinge while the other is still in the frame, its glass scattered across the ground. All of the windows are either completely shattered or severely cracked. Lowell comes up behind Bolton and cranes his neck, trying to get a better look inside.

"Dark as shit," Lowell says.

"Lack of power will do that," Bolton replies. He takes a couple steps forward so the barrel of the M-4 is just over the threshold of the entrance. "Hello!"

"Dude, don't you think quiet is better?" Lowell asks.

"If anyone is in here then they heard us already," Bolton says. "We've been crunching glass for the last two feet and chatting away." He moves a few more steps forward. "Hello!"

There's no reply and Lowell looks back over his shoulder at the other men waiting in the parking lot. The short man gives him a nervous nod while the mountain man just looks up into the glowing ash sky.

"Coming?" Bolton asks.

"Yeah, let's do this," Lowell says.

"Right," Bolton smirks, amused by Lowell's slipping courage. "Let's do this."

Bolton hurries inside, sweeping the carbine back and forth as he works his way past the front counter and towards dim lettering painted above a hallway.

"Need to shit?" Bolton smiles. "The crapper is right there."

"Why is this so funny to you?" Lowell asks.

"Because I've been in areas of the world that look like the apocalypse has hit them," Bolton says. "And Wherever, Montana doesn't compare. You're all of a sudden too worked up about all of this shit."

"I thought you were taught to approach all situations like they could be your last," Lowell says. "The way the day has gone, I'd say this is a situation like that."

Bolton shakes his head as he checks the next aisle and the next, only finding food and drinks and other assorted sundries spilled out onto the floor, fallen from the collapsed shelving. A soft tinkle in the far corner gets his attention and he whirls around, the M-4 more firmly pressed to his shoulder, his face completely changed.

"Hello?" Bolton calls out. "We aren't here to hurt you, just checking the place out. We have some injured and sick folks that need somewhere to bed down for the night. That's all."

Bolton's eyes study the darkness, looking for the tell tale signs of a person or persons. Even in the dark, a person can stand out. His eyes have been trained to see the difference between what is still and what is almost still. No matter how much a person thinks they aren't moving, the human body is incapable of total stillness.

There.

"I see you," Bolton says. "Not here to hurt you, like I said. We only need a place to stay."

A shadow pulls away from the far corner, then another and another.

Kids.

Two girls and a boy, all about thirteen or so.

"You the army?" one of the girls asks.

"Not quite," Bolton says. "Where are your parents?"

The girl shakes her head and the other one makes a soft squeak.

"You guys sisters and brother?" Bolton asks.

There's a thump and a loud crunching sound from outside.

"Bolton," Lowell says. "That doesn't sound good."

Several more thumps shake the building and the kids all hurry back to their hiding spot in the corner, crouching low as they wrap their arms about each other.

"It's back," the girl cries.

The thumps get louder and louder. Lowell and Bolton turn to see the two men outside come sprinting towards them. Then suddenly there's only one sprinting as the shorter man is yanked up into the air by something long and bright blue.

"Ohgodohgodohgodohgod!" the mountain of a man whines as he hurries towards the door.

Bolton and Lowell rush up to meet him, but just as he's about to get to the entrance, he too is yanked up into the air by the long, bright blue something. Lowell tries to stop, but his feet skid on broken glass and he tumbles out of the building and into the parking lot. His hands are scraped and cut, and he presses them to his chest as he rolls over and looks back at Bolton.

Then he looks up and sees a nightmare standing over the building.

"Grab the kids and get out," Lowell whispers.

Bolton sees the terror on the man's face and doesn't waste time asking questions.

"Come on!" Bolton shouts towards the kids. "We need to leave!"

The kids don't move, just stay in their protective huddle.

"Bolton," Lowell hisses. "Now."

The soldier slings his carbine and hurries over to the kids, grabbing at them, but one of the girls, the talker, swats his hands away.

"It's safer in here," she says. "If you stay quiet."

"Bolton!" Lowell yells. "We need to go now!"

Bolton looks behind him and almost craps himself as he watches Lowell roll quickly to the side just as the bright blue something slams down against the pavement, right where he'd been.

"That's its tongue," the girl says. "That's how it gets you."

"Holy fuck," Bolton whispers.

"Bolton!" Lowell yells as he scrambles to his feet and starts running away from the truck stop. "COME ON!"

The thumps shake everything and Bolton realizes they are massive footsteps as a shadow moves over the parking lot and gigantic feet and legs come into view. He walks towards the entrance, feeling the irrational need to get a better look, which is nothing new with his job.

Outside, Lowell is running one way then another, zigzagging and dodging as the blue tongue slams down in the spots he'd been just seconds before. Bolton is actually impressed by Lowell's ability to juke, but impressive or not, the thing will eventually catch him.

"Hey!" Bolton cries as he runs out into the parking lot, turns, and sprints towards the long rows of diesel pumps off to the side. "HEY! Over here!"

The monster stops and turns its bulk, it's black orb-like eyes finding Bolton.

"Holy fuck," Bolton swallows.

The thing is well over 75 feet tall, with four multi-jointed legs. Its body is segmented like an insect's, but with many more regions than just the standard three. The huge legs seem to work independently of the others and it's a bit dizzying as Bolton watches the monster turn its bulk around to face him.

He wants to throw up as he looks up at the abomination and sees a mouth that nearly splits the creature's narrow head in half. Teeth of all sizes poke haphazardly from the monster's maw, and

Bolton can see bits and pieces of the two men hanging from between them. An arm here, a leg there, jeans and a flannel shirt flapping in the wind.

Then the tongue comes at him and he barely has time to think before it slams down an inch from his body. The smell coming off the tongue is like nothing Bolton has ever experienced. He's seen death pits, warehouses filled with corpses, entire villages set afire, their inhabitants left like charcoal briquettes. He can recall each and every smell from those experiences and they pale in comparison to the rotted, sulfuric carrion stench of the monster's tongue.

The blue thing whips back and Bolton notices the pavement bubbling slightly where it came in contact with the tongue. The smell, the bubbling pavement, and then Lowell screaming at him to run are what pull him back from the brink of madness.

No time to worry about the impossibility of the monster that towers over him; time only to fight.

Bolton opens fire, aiming up at the creature's head, aiming for the mouth of many teeth. Bullets ping and whine as they bounce off of the teeth, and the surrounding lips, seeming to do absolutely no damage.

"Shit," Bolton says as he dives, rolls and comes up on one knee, barely dodging another tongue strike.

He continues to fire, but the bullets don't penetrate the monster's tough hide, they just ricochet everywhere, causing Bolton to quickly rethink his strategy. The tongue comes at him once more and he leaps out of the way, his back slamming into one of the diesel pumps. He ducks down as the tongue whips past, ripping the pump in half. Fuel spills everywhere as the hose is torn free and the diesel left in it from the last use leaks out onto the pavement.

Bolton barely has time to get up and run as the tongue whips back at him. Part of it catches him in the shoulder, sending him spinning to the ground in a painful lump. He cries out in pain as his coat starts to smolder and he barely gets it off before the material at that spot is nothing but a smoking mess, smelling of sulfur and bile.

"Fuck me," Bolton says as he scrambles backwards on his hands and feet, his eyes locked onto the monster that towers over him. He waits for the next strike, but the creature stops, its head turning back to the pumps.

The tongue flies down and cracks open another pump, this time staying there, the tip flicking back and forth like an angry cat's tail. Bolton can see the diesel glistening on the blue end and he wonders what the hell the monster could want with that fuel.

Then the tongue is sucked back into the creature's mouth and it seems to stand stock still for a few seconds before rushing forward so fast that Bolton is almost unsure if the thing actually moved or teleported to the pumps. It digs at the pavement, ripping the pumps from their moorings, as it tries to claw its way to the fuel lines below.

"Come on," Lowell hisses, having moved back to the building. He looks out at Bolton from the corner and waves. "Get your ass up."

Bolton doesn't have to be told twice as he scrambles to his feet and crouch runs to Lowell.

"I don't think this is the exit we want to stop at," Lowell says. "Do you?"

"Let's get the kids and go," Bolton says, his eyes drawn to the monster as it cracks open more and more pavement, quickly working its way over to the spot where the massive diesel tanks are buried.

"The kids? Fuck them," Lowell says. "They made their choice, they can stay. We need to go."

"I'm not leaving," Bolton says. "They're only kids!"

There's an ululating roar as the monster's tongue breaks through the steel tanks and into the diesel reserves. It lowers the front half of its body to the ground and begins to drink up the fuel, its tongue changing shape so it is broader and able to scoop the diesel into its mouth like a dog.

"Not something you see everyday," Lowell says.

"Hold on," Bolton says and rushes back into the building.

He looks over at the kids that haven't moved, but doesn't bother with them. Instead, he jumps and slides across the front counter and begins searching next to the racks and racks of cigarettes.

"Here we go," he smiles as he grabs a bottle of lighter fluid.

He yanks a pack of lighters from next to the register then slides back over the counter and starts searching the aisles. It takes him a couple of seconds that he knows he can't afford, but he finally finds the small housewares section. He grabs up a dishtowel, rips it into strips, and starts to soak a strip with lighter fluid. Then he snags an unbroken bottle of soda, pops the top, dumps the contents, and fills it with the remainder of the lighter fluid.

"Want to see something cool?' Bolton smiles as he stuffs the fluid soaked strip into the bottle and rips open the pack of lighters. Most of them fall to the ground, but Bolton is able to catch one and he shakes it at the kids. "Come on. After this, you won't be able to stay here anyway."

The kids slowly get up and follow Bolton out of the store. Lowell is standing outside, his mouth open as he watches the monster continue to drink up the diesel. Then he sees Bolton, and what the man is holding, and a huge smile spreads across his face.

"Now we're talking," Lowell says.

"That fucker is full of diesel," Bolton says. "I think it's about to give him an upset tummy."

"Lame," the boy behind them says.

"Not a fan of the one liners? Oh, well," Lowell shrugs and looks at Bolton. "You just gonna chuck it at the thing?"

"I figure that's the best thing to do," Bolton says. "Once I throw this, we'll want to start running. Fast."

"Yeah, I guessed that," Lowell says. He looks at the kids. "Hope you guys aren't going to start playing possum again, because anything even close to this place is about to become extra crispy."

Lowell reaches out and grabs the first girl's arm and pulls at her as he backs away from Bolton.

"Nice knowing ya, dude," Lowell says, then yanks hard on the girl's arm, tugging the kids along with him.

Bolton takes a deep breath, gagging a little on the fumes of the lighter fluid and diesel that fill the air, and then sprints forward as he places the lighter against the rag. Once he's about twenty yards from the monster, he flicks the lighter and the flame ignites the rag.

Without hesitation, Bolton cocks his arm back and tosses the impromptu Molotov cocktail right at the thing's head. The bottle shatters and flaming lighter fluid joins the diesel, instantly setting the monster, the ground, and the tanks below on fire. Bolton turns and runs as fast as he possibly can, knowing that the boom is about to be big.

He isn't disappointed when the there's a huge WHUMP and suddenly his breath is sucked from his lungs and it feels like he's being picked up by a giant hand made of air and thrown across the road. He hits the side of a wrecked minivan and crashes to the ground, his ears ringing and eyes filling with spots.

"Hey!" Lowell shouts, his face suddenly pressed close to Bolton's "You okay?"

Bolton shakes his head and looks about. The world is full of fire as fuel tank after fuel tank erupts, ripping the truck stop apart from below. He reaches up and Lowell helps him to his feet as they watch fifty foot flames lick the sky. Thick, black smoke is everywhere, making it impossible to see anything other than fire.

Then the explosions stop and Bolton looks over and smiles at the three kids as they once more huddle close to each other.

"Not bad, eh?" Bolton nods. "Come on, let's get you guys back with our-"

His voice is cut off as an angry screech nearly shatters everyone's eardrums. Bolton looks back towards the truck stop and gulps as he watches the smoke part, revealing a fire covered monster.

"No fucking way," Lowell says. "That didn't kill it?"

The monster screeches once more, then belches, sending flames shooting right towards them all. Lowell dives one way while Bolton dives on top of the kids, covering them from the heat. He can feel his hair burn and he pats at himself as he rolls off the kids and yanks them to their feet.

"Go! Gogogo!" Bolton screams at them as he shoves them towards the woods that stand back behind a windowless Burger King. "RUN!"

The kids don't hesitate and sprint towards the trees as Bolton unslings his carbine, grateful it hadn't fallen off when he was thrown across the street. He takes a knee and fires at the monster, aiming for the pitch black eyes, hoping to blind the thing. But it does nothing except let the beast zero in on his location.

The tongue whips out and Bolton instinctively throws his carbine out in front of him to block the attack. The M-4 is pulled from his grasp and Bolton falls back on his ass, stunned as he watches the monster suck the carbine inside its mouth and swallow.

"Bolton!" Lowell yells from the woods, the kids nowhere to be seen. "Dude!"

Bolton scrambles to his feet and hurries over to the cover of the trees, not even close to kidding himself that the overgrown sticks can stop the creature if it decides to pursue.

"I think there's another one," Lowell exclaims as he points off down the road towards a far off shape.

"We have to get back and warn the others," Bolton says.

"Fuck that!" Lowell snaps. "We need to hide! There's no way we can stay out in the open with those things!"

"What the fuck are they?" Bolton asks, not expecting an answer.

"Who fucking cares?" Lowell says. "They're big and they don't fucking die!"

Just as the words leave his mouth the monster rushes towards them then stumbles and stops. Its mouth opens all the way and it leans forward as it hacks and spews glowing green bile from its throat.

"Jesus fuck," Lowell says.

The monster stumbles again and this time, its front legs go out from under it as it pukes up more bile. The liquid splatters to the ground, but doesn't stay liquid for long. Right before Bolton and Lowell's eyes, the bile turns from green to grey and hardens on the pavement, looking like a weird mix of foam and plastic.

Then the monster collapses to the ground and lets out a high keening wail, forcing Bolton and Lowell to cover their ears. But even with the creature only a few yards away, the two men don't run; they are transfixed by what's happening in front of them.

"Holy shit," Bolton says as the monster's sides burst open and more of the grey gunk comes spilling out, slowly spreading across the ground until it thickens completely and stops.

"What the hell did that?" Bolton asks.

"I don't know," Lowell says.

The ground shakes and several howls and screeches cause the men to look down the road as more than one shape starts to appear from the thick smoke, headed right towards them.

"I think its friends know it's down," Bolton says. "We better go."

"No shit," Lowell says as he turns and runs deeper into the woods, not hesitating at all to see if Bolton is behind him or not.

***

"Approaching the drop site," the pilot states, his eyes watching the readings on the screens and gauges in front of him due to the complete lack of visibility in the ash cloud. "Deploy on my mark."

He flips up two red toggles, and then pulls down a lever. A siren sounds in the cockpit, but he ignores it as the rear hatch of the specialized plane opens far behind him. His hand hovers over a second set of toggles.

"In three, two, one," the pilot says and then flips six toggles, hesitating a second between each.

Behind him in the cargo bay, six massive crates fall from the plane, one after the other. They tumble through the air, followed quickly by eighteen more crates as three other planes deploy their payload. The planes, their jobs completed, pull up and accelerate out of the ash cloud, leaving the crates to fall towards the ground.

The planes are nearly free of the ash when the first creature attacks. It comes at a plane from above and wraps its massive wings about the machine, sending them both plummeting to the ground. The monster waits until they are out of the ash before it lets go, but not before its claws rip the engines right off the wings, sending the plane spinning out of control and down to the earth.

Pilots start shouting as they are set upon, but it makes no difference. In seconds, there isn't an aircraft left flying and the monsters return to hide in the ash far above the Earth.

Tumbling end over end, but ignored by the creatures, the crates fall thousands of feet before huge parachutes are released, set to deploy by automatic timers and altitude sensors. A third of the crates get tangled in their parachute lines and continue to rocket towards the surface of the earth, while the rest level out and float their way to their intended coordinates.

Or try to. The air currents are brutal as the crates leave the ash cloud and are sent this way and that. Some of the parachutes become so coated with the thick, volcanic ash that they start to lose their effectiveness, sending the crates falling much faster than intended, while others are buffeted about by the thermals and then sent flying across the sky.

The result is a random descent of crates across nearly a thousand square mile area.

One crate, its parachute intact and in working order, drifts along at a steady rate until it slams into the tops of several fir trees. The parachute lines are torn from their clips and the crate falls quickly, slamming into the ground of a mostly uprooted forest. As soon as it settles on the ground, small hatches on every side snap open and spring loaded antennas pop up, each transmitting a signal that only specific receivers can pick up.

***

"Twelve of the eighteen crates are transmitting," a tech announces as a map fills the main monitor in the situation room.

"They have a good spread," General Azoul says, studying the red dots on the maps indicating the location of each crate. "If we have any men in the area, and their CLDs are in working order, then they should be able to zero in on the coordinates."

"Those are a lot of assumptions there," President Nance says. "The timer starts now. If we hear nothing in twelve hours, I'm sending in the bombers. Are we understood?"

"Twelve hours is not much time," General Azoul says. "You have to give our men a chance to get to the crates."

"That twelve hours gives those beasts time to spread out across our country!" President Nance shouts. "You saw the video feeds from the jet fighters! How much ground can things that size cover? They'll move faster than your men will, that's for sure. Twelve hours and we say goodbye to that region of the United States. This isn't up for debate, people. Twelve hours."

"Yes, sir."

"Of course, Mr. President."

"It's your call to make, Mr. President," General Azoul says. "But I have faith in our men on the ground. If they are alive, they'll find a crate."

"You had better pray that is true, General," President Nance frowns as he studies the map and the many red dots that flash the locations of the crates.

SEVEN

Linder awakes to the light of a flickering candle on an upturned bucket a few feet from him. The candle is only a couple of inches tall, but even that small amount of illumination sends daggers of pain through his head.

"Looky here," a man says. "The Fed has decided to open his beady little eyes."

"Are you the one that assaulted me?" Linder asks as he braves the light of the candle and looks about the space he's in; all he sees is darkness.

"That would be me," the man says, seated a few feet in front of the chair Linder is tied to. "Gil Courtney is my name, Agent Linder. You can call me Gil."

"You know who I am?" Linder asks. He can tell by the way their voices echo that they are inside a very large space.

"Found your badge, Mr. F-B-I," Gil drawls. "It looks real enough, which brings me to the question of why you were about to brain a teenage boy? The kid is good sized, so self-defense I can understand, but that's not what we walked up on, was it?"

"Where is he?" Linder asks. The taste of blood is heavy on his tongue and he turns and spits, sending the bloody phlegm splatting to the ground, which he recognizes as concrete. But not any concrete- concrete that isn't cracked and broken.

"The boy? He's safe," Gil says. "A real all around tough guy, that one. We save his ass from you and he still puts up a fight. Kid won't even give us his name."

"It's Kyle," Linder says. "You can call him Kyle."

Gil smiles at Linder and nods. "This isn't no hostage situation, Agent Linder."

"Just Linder," Linder says.

"Well, Linder, I know my protocols too," Gil says. "Make sure your captors know your name. It humanizes you and makes it harder for them to kill you. Am I right?"

"Something like that," Linder says. "Where is he? Where's my son?"

"Ah, now it's interesting you bring that up," Gil says as he stands and walks closer to Linder, dragging his chair with him.

The scraping noise digs into Linder's head and he involuntarily winces, which causes Gil to smile wider. The man stops almost exactly three feet from Linder, flips the chair about, then takes a seat, his arms folded over the back.

"The one question that kid will answer is whether or not you're his daddy," Gil says. "And he's pretty damn insistent that you are not."

"He's mistaken," Linder says. "That boy is of my flesh and blood."

Gil watches Linder for a couple seconds before he shakes his head. "You are all kinds of contradictions, Agent Linder. You sound worried about the kid, but were ready to kill him only a couple hours ago."

"A couple of hours?" Linder asks. "How long have I been down here?"

"A couple of hours," Gil smirks. "It's implied. Where was I? Right, your contradictions. So, worried about the kid, want to kill the kid. You're a Fed, but act more like a criminal. You sound all official, but then that tone changes and you start to sound like a preacher man I knew back outside Missoula, God rest his soul."

"How'd he die?" Linder asks.

"That's a strange thing to ask," Gil replies. "But, to be truthful, I don't completely know he's dead. I'm just assuming on account of the hole."

"The hole?" Linder asks. "What hole?"

"You don't know?" Gil laughs. "Man, there's a hole the size of Rhode Island out there! Nearly swallowed Missoula right up! Probably would have been more merciful if it had, considering."

"Considering what?" Linder asks. "Stop talking in redneck riddles!"

Gil frowns deeply and stands up. He cocks his head, licks his lips, then turns and walks away, lost in the thick darkness beyond the candle's light.

"Hey!" Linder shouts. "HEY! Where are you going? Where's my son? Take me to my son right now!"

"We'll see," Gil's voice calls out. "I'm gonna let you sit there and think about how you talk to people. Sometimes a little alone time is good for the soul."

"Get your ass back here!" Linder yells. "You backwoods fuck! You think you can hold me? Do you? I get free and I'll gut you! Slit you wide open from nuts to neck!"

A door opens far off and faint light spills into the space for a split second before the door slams shut behind Gil.

"Hey! HEY! I'M GOING TO KILL YOU, YOU DAMN REDNECK PIECE OF SHIT!"

Linder strains at the wire that binds his hands together and to the metal chair he's seated in. The metal cuts into his skin, adding that pain to the agony already pumping through his head. The man focuses on the pain, drinking it in like a secret elixir, and starts to twist his wrists slowly back and forth, over and over, until he has a perfect feel of the tension and strength of the wire that holds him.

***

"He say anything?" Gil asks as he walks into a large room outfitted with old worn couches as well as rows of shelving laden with canned goods and various supplies.

Kyle is seated at a table made of thick wood, his hands handcuffed to a solid metal ring at the edge of the table. His eyes watch as Gil moves to the table and takes a seat across from him.

"He hasn't said a damn thing," a thin, wiry man says from one of the couches, an old paperback in his hands. The man, Moss Owens, sets the book down on a stained coffee table in front of him, stands and stretches then looks over at man sleeping on a second couch. "Fin. Hey, Fin! Get your ass up!"

Moss walks over and gives the couch a hard kick.

"What?" Fin asks. "I was sleeping."

"I know," Moss says. "Your time up top. Go find Lorelei and Brian. You all can relieve Jim, Scoot and Tomboy."

"It's damn cold up there," Fin says as he sits up and swings his legs over the edge of the couch. "And we're already out of whiskey."

"I'll add that to the list of provisions we'll need to scout for," Moss says. "Now get."

"Fine, whatever," Fin says as he stands, hitches his camouflage cargo pants up around his hips, and stomps out of the room.

Moss waits for the door to click shut before he turns to Gil. "That should give us a few minutes. What you learn from the Fed?"

"Not much," Gil says, eyeing Kyle. "Except that he says he is the kid's daddy. I'm inclined to believe him."

"He's not my father," Kyle snarls.

"Yeah, you keep saying that," Gil says. "But I'm not so sure."

"That's it?" Moss asks. "That's all you got out of the guy?"

"These two don't know shit about what's going on," Gil laughs. "The guy didn't even know about the hole."

"How the hell can you not know about the hole?" Moss laughs with Gil. "It's a giant fucking hole in the middle of the country."

"What hole?" Kyle asks.

"See?" Gil says, pointing at the teenager. "That's what I'm talking about."

Moss looks at Kyle then at Gil.

"I say we bring them with us," Moss says. "Take a trip down the mountain and get some needed supplies."

"Booze ain't needed," Gil says.

"It is if we're going to be cooped up in the bunker forever."

"Those things are out there," Gil says. "One nearly got us on our way back here."

"But it didn't," Moss replies. "You afraid of those things, Gil?"

"Hell yes, I'm afraid of those things!" Gil snaps.

"Don't be," Moss says. "They can't get in here, and they're too big to catch us on the horses."

"The things are fast," Gil counters.

"That they are," Moss nods. "But they move funny and can't handle the ridges like we can. Damn monsters must be from the plains."

This makes both men cackle and Kyle looks from one to the other, puzzled by the behavior, and the situation he's found himself in. At first, he was sure that Gil was the guy in charge, but after listening to the interactions between the men, he isn't so sure. Everyone seems to go to Gil first, but when Moss speaks, they also listen. Kyle doesn't know who he's supposed to focus on.

And one thing his grandma taught him was always figure out who is in charge; saves a lot of time and hassle that way.

"What was that thing?" Kyle asks. "That went by us?"

"Don't know," Moss shrugs. "But there's more and they are ugly as sin."

"And those are the small ones," Gil says.

Once Linder had been knocked out, the people with Gil and Moss had picked Kyle up and dragged him through the woods to a small clearing where several horses were waiting. They draped the unconscious Linder over a pack mule and then shoved Kyle up into a saddle of an extra horse. Kyle stayed silent as his hands were cuffed and the reigns shoved into his palms. Luckily, he'd been riding horses most of his life or he would have fallen once the group got moving.

Maybe an hour of hard riding had gone by when they heard the screeches and howls coming through the woods. Trees that still stood snapped in half as something big moved past them quickly. Kyle barely got a glimpse of it before it was lost from sight, but what he saw, he didn't like.

"Kid needs an education," Moss says. "So does the Fed. We take them with us and head to Missoula. Might find some survivors along the way."

"We don't need more people here," Gil snaps. "They'll just waste our resources."

"Oh, come now, Gil," Moss says. "The more the merrier." He gives Gil a wink. "And we could use more ladies than just Lorelei, Janey, and Tiff."

"Can't argue there," Gil says. "May have to repopulate Earth someday, won't we? It's God's will."

"I'd say so," Moss nods. "I'd certainly say so."

"Oh, great," Kyle says. "You two should get along with Linder just fine. Crazy God nuts."

***

It takes two hours to get down the mountain on the horses, and another full hour before they are in sight of the outskirts of what used to be Missoula, Montana. It would have been a much faster trip if it wasn't for the fact they had to constantly change routes each time they heard the loud howls of the unknown creatures.

By the time they reach a ridge, just above their destination, the horses, as well as the group, are exhausted and it's all Kyle can do to keep his eyes open. At least until he catches sight of what lies just beyond Missoula.

Instead of the hills and mountains that should be visible, there is only a vast chasm for as far as Kyle can see. And standing at the edge of the chasm are monsters that make him wish he was a little boy again and could just crawl into his mother's lap to make it all go away.

"And he laid hold on the dragon, that old serpent, which is the Devil, and Satan, and bound him a thousand years," Linder says.

"Hoohoo. Someone knows their Revelations," Gil smiles. "Good thing, 'cause I think the end of the world is at hand."

"What are they?" Kyle whispers as he sees the beasts that stand close to a thousand feet tall. "They look like Godzilla."

"Boy, you don't know your monster movies if you think that's what Godzilla looks like," Gil says, pointing towards the creatures. "Godzilla is thick, with huge haunches and short arms. Kinda like a T-Rex that don't work out no more."

"But with a smaller head," Moss says.

"Yeah, with a smaller head," Gil says. "In proportion to its body, that is. Godzilla is way bigger than a T-Rex. But the proportions are different. But these things?" He moves his hand, indicating the distinctive differences as he starts to describe the beasts. "That head there? Too flat and wide to be like Godzilla. And look at all those horns! Must be like ten horns on top of that head. Godzilla has scales and ridges, but no horns."

"Mouth is all wrong too," Moss says. "Godzilla has a mouth like you and me, all up front. Them things have a mouth that near wraps all the way around the back of their heads."

"Too many teeth too," Gil adds. "All sticking out and shit. And the arms are too thin and long. Plus, the ugly things have two sets of lower legs. Godzilla has only two legs."

"Like it should be," Moss says. "What the hell do these things need four legs for? Especially when they are just sitting there."

"You guys are fucking crazy," Kyle says. "I'm not kidding. You're flat out bug fucking nuts."

"Why? Because we know our monsters?" Moss asks. "The world didn't used to be ruled by the internet. When I was a kid your age, I had to watch whatever movies came on TV. I didn't get to dial up anything I wanted on Netflix."

"We watched a lot of Godzilla movies late at night, didn't we, Moss?" Gil laughs. "And Frankenstein and Dracula and that wolfguy."

"If it was on, then we watched it," Moss nodded.

"Are you two brothers?" Linder asks. He keeps wiggling his wrists in the wires that now have him secured to the pommel of the saddle. He knows eventually he'll figure out their secret. And when he does, he plans on truly teaching the men around him what he knows of Revelations.

"We ain't brothers," Moss says. "Just grew up together."

"The smaller ones are gone," Gil says. "Must have cleared out. Tired of getting picked on by those big guys."

This gets Linder's attention and he looks over at Gil. "Picked on? How do you mean?"

"The big ones don't like the little ones," Gil replies. "We watched from up on that other ridge back over there for like an hour."

"Using binoculars," Moss says.

"I figured," Linder nods. "What did you see?"

"The big ones seem annoyed by the little ones. Constantly stepping on them and eating their asses," Gil explains. "Squish then chomp. Those little ones finally got cleared away from here, looks like." He turns in his saddle and his eyes scan the hills and the mountain ridges above them. "Kinda makes me wonder where they all went."

"Makes me wonder why the big ones aren't leaving too," Linder says.

"That's what you're wondering?" Moss laughs. "We show you a huge hole in the ground, with giant monsters all about it, and you wonder why the monsters aren't taking a stroll through our fair state? And your kid thinks we're the crazy ones."

"Where they came from or why they are here are questions that are almost philosophical in nature," Linder says. "Might as well ask why man is on this earth."

"Because God put us here," Gil says.

"I'm not disagreeing there," Linder nods. "But, the question that really needs to be asked is now that the things are here, what do they plan on doing? That's the reason I wondered why they are staying by the hole and not spreading out across the land."

"Huh," Gil nods. "Never thought of it that way."

Kyle rubs at his face over and over, hoping his brain will kick in and make sense of everything. Here he is, riding a horse, with a bunch of what he thinks must be survivalist militia types, not to mention there's a man on the horse next to his that keeps saying he's his father, while all around them the world is broken and dead and giant fucking monsters stand guard over a hole that's so big he can't see to the other side.

"Am I the only one about to freak out?" Kyle blurts out. "What the fuck are we doing here? We should be up in that bunker staying safe and as far away from this shit as possible!"

He looks around, and other than Linder, only sees blank stares.

"We need booze," Moss says. "And maybe ladies." He looks over his shoulder and nods to the only woman in the group that rode down. "No offense, Tiff."

"Ain't no thing," Tiff replies. "Go ahead and look for more ladies, 'cause ain't none of you getting in my pants."

The whole group bursts out laughing and Kyle can't help but hunch his shoulders in some instinctive reflex to shield himself from the insanity that surrounds him. He glances over at Linder, but for once, the man isn't looking at him, instead he's staring at the giant monsters that stand miles away.

"Come on," Gil says. "Moss needs booze. Let's go find him some."

He clicks his mouth and gives his horse a quick kick to the haunches, overriding the animal's natural, and understandable, fear of what is before them all.

***

"What is that?" Dr. Probst asks as she and Coletti crest a large hill and look down at the ravaged city below. "Where do you think we are?"

"Missoula," Coletti replies. "Hard to tell by looking at it the way the landscape has changed so much. But this is where we're supposed to go and the map says Missoula."

"You're sure about this?" Dr. Probst asks. "Why do you think that little black disc isn't sending us on a wild goose chase?"

Coletti looks at the thick, round piece of metal in his hand. Even though it's only the size of a large pocket watch, it's surprisingly heavy, the weight part of the heavy duty shielding that keeps the disc from being fried by an EMP. In the middle of the CLD is a small glass circle and Coletti puts the disc to his eye, double checking the coordinates that flash within.

Slipping the disc back into his pocket, he crouches down and opens a pouch on his pants leg and takes out a plastic coated map and a small compass with a magnifying glass attached.

"This is where we were," Coletti says, pointing to the spot several miles north. "This is where we are." His finger traces a route down to a new point on the map. "The coordinates on the CLD are on the edge of that city down there. Something is waiting for us and we need to find it right away."

"What do you think it is?" Dr. Probst asks. "Food? Water? Weapons?"

"You're probably right on the last part," Coletti replies. "There could be food and water, but I doubt that's the priority at the moment."

"Why the hell not?" Dr. Probst asks, her voice rising an octave. "Why wouldn't someone send food or water to us? We'll die without it!"

"Doctor, calm down," Coletti says. "Getting pissed isn't going to change reality."

Dr. Probst laughs and turns to look towards the chasm. And what stands by it.

"Don't talk to me about reality, Lieutenant," she sneers. "That ship sailed a long time ago."

Coletti places the map and compass back into his pants and stands up.

"I'm not saying there isn't food and water waiting for us," Coletti says. "I'm just saying that there are bigger priorities than just keeping us alive. Odds are there's some type of com system that got dropped down there." He pats his pocket where the CLD sits. "I saw twelve sets of coordinates before the CLD locked onto these as the closest. That means the brass is fishing for eyes on the ground. They are hoping someone is alive to tell them what's going on."

"Because of all of that," Dr. Probst says, pointing up at the ash that is the sky. "The satellites can't see through there, can they? Even the military ones. Our government is blind and has no idea what we're dealing with."

"That could be," Coletti says. "Which is why they need us more than ever. We have to get down there and find whatever it is they dropped for us. If it is a com system then that may be better than food or water."

"We have been hiking all night long," Dr. Probst says. "There's nothing better than food and water right now."

"How about a ride home?" Coletti grins. "That would be way better."

Dr. Probst's eyes go wide and she stares at the lieutenant.

"You think that? You think they'll come get us?" she asks, her voice a hopeful squeak.

"They aren't going to find two people with better intel on the situation," Coletti shrugs. "They'd be crazy not to come get us."

The thought of being rescued brings new hope to Dr. Probst. She shoves the fatigue from her mind and straightens her back, eyes fixed on the ruined city below.

"Then what are we waiting for?" she asks. "Let's get our asses down there."

"My thoughts exactly," Coletti says, giving her a reassuring smile.

He turns and heads off down the hill, the reassuring smile instantly dropping from his face.

***

"Where are all the people?" Kyle asks as he is helped down from his horse.

One of the group, a man Kyle thinks is named Scoot, leads the horse over to the others that are tethered to a porch railing as they all stand in the front yard of one of Missoula's many abandoned homes. The horses snuffle through the ash on the ground, trying to find some grass they can munch on, but come up empty, their nostrils flaring and feet stamping in frustration.

Kyle knows just how they feel.

"Missoula was evacuated weeks ago," Gil says. "Most everywhere was."

"Only people left here are the crazies," Moss says. "And they ain't all bad."

"They ain't all good neither," Gil says.

"True," Moss nods. He glances around at the quiet, ash covered neighborhood and then claps his hands together. "Let's find some booze."

"What? Here?" Kyle asks.

"Where'd you think we'd look? The liquor stores?" Gil laughs. "Those got looted a long time ago. Best place to find booze now is in people's homes. Most folk didn't have time to pack up the vodka and bourbon when the National Guard came through and goose stepped everyone out of town. They were too busy trying to convince the Jackboots to let them keep their precious Fluffy and Rover."

"Government had no right taking people's pets away from them," Moss sighs. "No right at all."

Linder snorts then tries to stifle a laugh as Gil and Moss turn on him.

"Something to say, Agent Linder?" Moss asks.

"Nope," Linder says, shaking his head, a smile barely contained.

"Spill it, Fed," Gil grumbles. "What government propaganda do you have for us?"

"None," Linder says. "Just strikes me as funny that of all the offenses and mistakes this government has perpetrated during this crisis, the one you focus on is how pets had to be left behind or put down."

"You ever had a dog or cat, Fed?" Gil asks.

"Not since I was a kid," Linder says.

"Well, then maybe you don't understand the bond between a pet and their owner," Gil says. "There's a loyalty there that can't be bought. Killing that loyalty just shows the evil lengths the government will go to in order to crush our spirit. They gassed Fluffy and shot Rover to show us that we are the pets now and Washington DC is our master."

"Ain't my master!" Scoot calls out.

"Mine neither!" Tiff says.

The rest voice their agreement, but Linder just shakes his head.

"They killed every animal except for livestock, because pets take up resources and space that we can't afford right now," Linder says. "There's no room or food for cats, dogs, birds, gerbils, lizards, or even goldfish. Do you think they have a 'pets only' cruise ship waiting down in Galveston or New Orleans? They don't. And you aren't even considering the waste disposal issue. Pets were a noose around people's necks; an anchor weighing them down and keeping them from getting priorities straight."

"Yeah, you'd say that," Kyle snaps. "You killed my dog."

All eyes fall on Linder.

"I didn't kill your dog," Linder replies. "I shot it. As far as I know, it could still be running around out there somewhere."

"That true?" Moss asks, looking at Kyle. "He shot your dog?"

"Yeah."

"Fucking Fed," Gil says and spits in Linder's face. "We should shoot you."

"Then shoot me," Linder says. "Go ahead. Do it."

"We might," Gil says. "But then again, we might not."

"Could find a use for you," Moss says. "Maybe use you as a bargaining chip when the government marches through here looking for our bunker."

"You actually think the government is going to send ground troops anywhere near here?" Linder laughs. "What they're going to do is drop a nuke on this place and kill those Leviathans and Behemoths!"

Gil and Moss stare at him for second then both shrug.

"I say we tie him up with the horses and leave him," Moss says.

"Good idea," Gil replies. "I sure don't want to hear his bullshit anymore. Scoot, you stay here with the Fed. Keep an eye on him."

"Do I have to?" Scoot asks.

"Yeah, you have to," Gil says. "And gag the asshole while you're at it. Don't let him try to get in your head. Federal agents are trained to make you believe stuff you don't wanna."

"You going to leave me here too?" Kyle asks.

"He really shoot your dog?" Moss asks.

"I already said he did," Kyle snaps. "Not something I want to keep thinking about."

Moss and Gil share a look.

"What do you think?" Moss asks.

"Kid hasn't shown any love for this guy since we found them," Gil replies. "We have to trust him at some point. Or just go ahead and kill him."

"What?" Kyle shouts.

"Hush," Moss hisses. "Sounds carry, kid. We may not seem like we're worried about the big monsters, but they're just right over there."

Moss points to a random spot over the houses that surround them. Everyone turns and looks, their eyes wide with caution and fear as if they can see the monsters as clearly as they did from up on the ridge.

"And we don't want to rile up the crazies," Gil says. "Maybe one or two hiding around here."

"No, wouldn't want to stir up the crazies," Linder says. He watches as the cuffs are taken off of Kyle's wrists and someone hands the teenager a backpack for any supplies he may find. "Be careful, son."

"I'm not your son," Kyle snaps. Linder just smiles at the boy. "I'm not!"

"See?" Gil says, pointing at Scoot. "They try to get in your head."

Scoot nods and takes a step away from Linder.

"You're with me, kid," Moss says to Kyle. "Tiff's with Gil. Morgie and Paul. Jim and Tomboy."

They all split up and take off in different directions. Kyle glares at Linder then hurries to catch up with Moss as the man strides away, his eye on a two story, brick colonial diagonal from them.

Linder looks over at Scoot. "Have any water?"

"None for you," Scoot says and takes another couple of steps away from the man, not wanting to get close enough to gag the man, let alone give him water.

***

"When was Missoula evacuated?" Dr. Probst asks quietly as she struggles to keep up with Coletti. "I didn't expect it to be such a ghost town."

"Pretty much all of Montana, Wyoming, and the Dakotas were cleared out weeks ago when the first major tremors started," Coletti replies, his eyes on the CLD. When the red lettered coordinates turn green, then he knows he's within 400 yards of the beacon. "Everything I heard was that it wasn't an easy task getting people around here to leave. Kinda independent population in the west."

"I wouldn't know," Dr. Probst says. "I'm from Maryland."

"And I'm from Ohio," Coletti says. "Which was once considered the west a century and a half ago. Not so much anymore."

"I don't think I could live in a place like this," Dr. Probst says. "So remote. Out in the middle of the wilderness."

"Trust me, Doctor," Coletti laughs. "Missoula is not remote. I've been deployed to areas that haven't seen electricity yet, even in the 21st century. That's remote."

Coletti stops and holds up a hand, his eyes staring at the CLD.

"What?" Dr. Probst asks. "Are we close?"

"Yes," Coletti says as he hurries a few yards forward. Dr. Probst starts to follow, but he shakes his head. "Stay there. I'm trying to zero in on the direction."

Dr. Probst stands still as she watches Coletti run from one point to another; his eyes looking at the black disc then up at his surroundings, down at the black disc then back up to his surroundings.

"I think it's this way," Coletti says, pointing towards what looks like was once an affluent area of Missoula. "Now you can follow me."

The two make their way through the empty streets; the direct path blocked by high fences and locked iron gates. Coletti swears under his breath every time a street takes them away from the signal, but then sighs with relief when it turns and doubles back, taking them closer once again. All around them the houses get bigger and bigger until they are surrounded by mini-mansions with front yards alone bigger than the house Dr. Probst grew up in. Of course, most of the mini-mansions are demolished and stand as piles of rubble, but they are expensive looking piles of rubble.

Dr. Probst is almost glad to see the symbols of American excess looking so shabby, until she catches sight of a hand sticking out from underneath a collapsed stone chimney. Then she remembers that no matter what people were before the supervolcano, they are now just refugees and survivors. At least the lucky ones are.

Coletti stops and follows Dr. Probst's gaze.

"Don't dwell on it," Coletti says. "Better to just keep moving and shove it from your thoughts."

"How?" Dr. Probst says. "How do you compartmentalize the horror and violence?"

"You just do," Coletti shrugs. "Or go crazy. And you might as well kill yourself once you get there."

Dr. Probst nods and they keep walking.

"Highlands Country Club?" Dr. Probst asks. "What you're looking for is on a golf course?"

"Could be," Coletti shrugs. "We're almost there."

The green light in the CLD is flashing faster and faster as Coletti and Dr. Probst walk through the broken iron gates of the country club entrance. They go a few more yards and the light starts to flash so fast it almost looks like it isn't flashing at all. Coletti looks about the landscape, his eyes studying the golf course for signs of anything that would resemble a military drop.

"It should be right here," Coletti says as he cuts across the ruined golf course.

The grass is brown and the greens are no longer smooth, but ripped apart by the seismic nightmare of the eruption. Yet, in the middle of it all, a deep water hazard is still intact and that is where Coletti finds himself as the flashing green light becomes solid, telling him he's reached his destination.

"In there?" Dr. Probst asks.

"In there," Coletti nods. He squats down and peers into the murky, muddy water. "Somewhere."

"Do you know exactly what you're looking for?" Dr. Probst asks as she opens a water bottle, leans over and fills it, and then drops two purification tablets inside. She caps and shakes the bottle for a second, then opens it and gives a sniff.

"Gonna taste like crap," Coletti says. "But it won't kill you."

Dr. Probst takes a sip and almost gags at the sulfuric taste. Coletti smiles.

"Told you," he says as he unlaces his boots, slips them off, then unzips his jumpsuit and slips it off. He takes off his shirt and begins to remove his pants.

Dr. Probst blushes and looks away, her eyes focusing on the horizon to the east.

"Why didn't the big ones leave the chasm?" she asks aloud. "The smaller ones did, but the big ones stayed. What are they waiting for?"

"Not sure I want to know," Coletti says as he wades into the water. "But from what we saw, I think those smaller ones are plenty happy to be away from the bigger ones."

"Why invade a place, but turn on your own kind?" Dr. Probst asks.

Coletti is about to dive into the water, but stops and looks at the doctor.

"What do you mean by invade?" Coletti asks.

"Well, isn't that what's happening?" Dr. Probst replies. "I mean what else would you call it? There are giant monsters coming up out of a hole in the earth; some are moving out into the land while others remain back by the point of entry. An advance guard and then a defensive force. Oh, and an air force to control the skies. That's textbook, isn't it?"

"Yeah, I guess it is. Interesting," Coletti says. "I never saw it like that. I was thinking more of just a mad attack by unthinking monsters. You're framing it as an intentional invasion by a foreign force."

"Doesn't get more foreign than thousand foot nightmares coming out of a supervolcano," Dr. Probst says. "And they haven't exactly asked us to take them to our leaders, so I'm guessing the goal is to conquer and destroy us, not start diplomatic relations."

"Keep thinking like that," Coletti says. "I'll be right back."

He takes a deep breath then dives down into the water, lost from sight in seconds. Dr. Probst sits by the edge of the water, her knees up against her chest as she takes another disgusting sip from the bottle.

***

Linder watches as Scoot paces back and forth along the broken sidewalk. The man's eyes are looking at everything around the area, except what he should be looking at.

"You sure I can't have a sip of that water?" Linder asks, moving his body at an angle so Scoot doesn't see the warm blood trickling down his wrists. "I'm really thirsty, buddy. Just one sip and I promise not to bug you anymore."

"Shut up, Fed," Scoot snaps. "I'm not going to talk to you and let you get inside my head."

"Do you think FBI agents have super powers or something?" Linder laughs. "I'm just a regular guy like you. I used to get up in the morning, put my clothes on, and go to work. Sure, I got to have a badge, but doesn't make me any different than you. I had bills, I watched football, and I liked to go to the movies. Regular guy with a regular life."

"That's what all the Germans said after World War II," Scoot replies.

"Wow, really?" Linder laughs. "I used to work bank robberies and missing persons, buddy. I wasn't in charge of gassing people. This is the USA, not Nazi occupied Europe. Huge difference, buddy."

"Stop calling me buddy," Scoot says.

"Fine...Scoot, is it?" Linder asks. "Come on, Scoot. All I need is one sip. My throat is killing me. Just one."

Scoot looks over at the man secured to the porch railing and sighs. "I ain't even supposed to be talking to you, man. Gil said I should gag you."

"Give me one drink and then you can gag me. Deal?" Linder smiles. "This air is bad, Scoot. My throat feels like sandpaper."

"At least the ash isn't falling anymore," Scoot says as he looks up at the dark sky. "Gonna suck when it does start again, though, ain't it?"

"Yeah, Scoot, it is," Linder nods. "That's why a drink of water now would go a long way. That ash up there could start falling any second. When it does, I'd rather have a wet whistle than a dry tongue."

Scoot frowns at Linder. "You talk weird sometimes, you know that? You don't sound like a fed."

"Really? What do I sound like?"

"I don't know," Scoot says. "Like this preacher guy my parents took me to when I was little. He was all nice and friendly, then he'd start talking and I'd get scared. But I got to have pop and cookies afterwards."

"I'd settle for just water," Linder laughs. "Although soda and cookies would be pretty great right now, huh?" His shoulders slump and he coughs a little. "Come on, Scoot, just one little drink. Please. I can't do anything to you when I'm tied up."

Scoot watches Linder for a second, nods his head and walks over, his water bottle held out like a crucifix warding off a vampire.

"You're gonna need to pour it into my mouth," Linder says, turning his body some more so his back is almost all the way to Scoot. He looks over his shoulder and opens his mouth.

Scoot moves slowly closer until the bottle is near enough to angle and pour a small bit of water into Linder's open mouth.

"Thanks," Linder says, smacking his lips once Scoot stops pouring. "That was more than I could have hoped for. You sure are stupid."

Scoot looks puzzled. "I'm what?"

Linder spins about, his hands free, wrists bloody, metal wire gripped in both fists. He rushes forward and jams the wire into Scoot's eyes, then sweeps the man's legs. Before Scoot even has a chance to cry out, Linder drops down with all his weight, his knee crushing Scoot's throat. A couple of bloody bubbles gurgle from between Scoot's lips and Linder grinds down with his knee some more until he hears the cracking of Scoot's vertebrae.

Scoot's eyes gloss over and Linder gets to his feet, a look of pure contempt on his face.

"How's that for your pop and cookies, you fuck?" Linder snarls, then spits on the man's face. He looks about, scanning the area for anyone else, kneels down and takes the .38 pistol from Scoot's hip. "Thanks."

Linder turns and hurries off, heading in the direction he last saw Kyle go with Moss.

EIGHT

"Most of these folks aren't going to make it," Lu says, looking back at the struggling band of survivors as they work their way through the dense woods and broken ground. "I still think we should stick to the interstate."

"You think that because you didn't see what we saw," Bolton says. "Trust me. We can't afford to be out in the open."

"We have got to be getting close to Coeur d'Alene," Lowell says. "These people can rest when we get there."

"If they make it," Lu scowls. "You really saw a monster? Like some alien thing?"

"No idea what it was," Bolton says, "but it was huge. Like three stories tall. Thick legs, mouth full of teeth."

"And that tongue," Lowell says, shivering. "Won't get that image out of my head for a long fucking time."

"It drank diesel fuel?" Lu asks. "Then tried to eat you?"

"It tried," Lowell laughs nervously. "But all it got was soldier boy's rifle."

"Carbine," Bolton says.

"You know what I mean," Lowell replies.

"There's a difference."

"Boys? Knock it off," Lu sighs.

"Rifle or carbine, I think it gave it indigestion," Lowell says.

"My bet is on the diesel," Bolton suggests. "You don't drink a gas station's worth of diesel and not walk away with, well, gas."

"Good one," Lowell smirks.

Lu looks from one man to the other and shakes her head. "No way. Are you two bonding? Connor, this man is a cop killer! Not to mention two judges! The only reason he's not behind bars is because a goddamn fucking volcano erupted!"

"And you need me to help keep the meek alive," Lowell smiles.

"Don't do that," Lu snaps.

"What?"

"Smile. You look like Hannibal Lector," Lu says. "But not as sane."

"Ouch," Bolton says. "Listen, Lu, I know who this guy is, trust me."

"You do?" Lowell says.

"Yeah," Bolton says. "I know your type. Seen it on a hundred battlefields. You don't live for the blood or the killing. You live for the chaos. That's your fix. Pure chaos." Bolton spreads his arms. "And now you have all the chaos you want. I'm betting this is the calmest you've ever felt in your life. Kinda like coming home after a long, tiring vacation."

Lowell looks at Bolton and nods. "You ain't as dumb as you look, GI Joe."

"Gee, thanks," Bolton says.

"No bonding," Lu says, wagging a finger at the two men. "I have no problem putting a bullet in Lowell's head if I have to. I need you to be the same way, Connor."

"I can put a bullet anywhere without hesitation," Bolton says. "That isn't a problem."

"Chaos buzz kill, dude," Lowell says to Bolton. "And here I thought we'd shared a moment."

A loud wailing echoes through the woods and the party stops dead in their tracks.

"That one was close," Bolton whispers.

"I think we just need to get up over that ridge there and we'll be looking down at Coeur d'Alene," Lu says. "We're almost there."

"Then what?" Lowell asks. "We haven't found a single working car along the way. That means the EMP hit this far too. What makes you think getting to Coeur d'Alene is going to be better than out here in the woods? It's just a city and cities have a lot of gas stations. According to Sergeant Slaughter, those things like gas stations, right? Aren't we just walking towards a monster buffet?"

"We get up over that ridge and then we'll see what is happening," Lu says. Another wail rings out and the party starts moving quickly, "unless you want to stay here and just wait for whatever that is?"

"Not really," Lowell says. "But I also don't want to walk into a city where those things could be waiting for us."

"What if Coeur d'Alene doesn't work out?" Bolton asks.

"Then we head north," Lu says.

"Uh, pretty sure Seattle is west," Lowell counters.

"If Lu says north then we go north," Bolton replies.

"You are so pussy whipped," Lowell grumbles. "Nut up, dude."

"Not even going to dignify that with a response," Bolton says and walks off.

"Well, you are!" Lowell calls after him. Lu just glares. "What? I'm right. If you didn't have a pussy, he wouldn't even consider doing what you want. Simple nature."

Lu shakes her head and stalks after Bolton.

"You two just don't want to face the truth!" Lowell calls after them. "The sexual tension is thicker than that ash up there!"

A couple of the others in the group hike past him, not making eye contact.

"What? Like you can't see it? Whatever!"

***

"Wait here," Moss says as he hands Kyle his pack. "I think I can squeeze through that."

Kyle looks at the collapsed mansion and frowns. "Why? You need to get drunk that bad? That place could come down on your head any second."

"Just wait here," Moss says. "And don't think of running off. I know this town way better than you do. You won't get away."

"Get away to where?" Kyle asks. "I'm standing in a city only a couple miles from a hole in the planet where giant monsters are hanging out. Where exactly am I going to go? Right now that bunker of yours sounds like the best place in the world to be."

"And that bunker is out of booze," Moss grins just as he slides between two hunks of concrete and is lost from sight.

Kyle turns away from the destroyed mansion and looks off towards the east and where the hole should be. He knows the monsters can't see him from there, since he can't see them from here, but he still has a weird feeling like he's being watched. He checks the area, studying each of the other collapsed mansions that line the once posh street. It strikes him as funny that of all the damage he's seen to the city, the most is in the rich part of town. Guess they don't build these houses quite as sturdy as the one story ranch houses back towards the center of town.

He hears Moss curse and swear, but there's no screams or calls for help, so Kyle keeps looking around, his mind wondering what life must have been like for the people that had lived in the mansions. He has spent all his life living in a log cabin tucked away in the woods, keeping a low profile and staying out of other people's business. The neighborhood around him strikes him as the complete opposite of that.

A sound catches his attention and he cranes his neck, trying to see past two mansions that sit on the edge of what he thinks is a golf course. He's never seen one in person, so he's not 100% sure. It could just be a big backyard for all he knows.

"What you staring at?" Moss asks, making Kyle jump.

"Thought I heard something," Kyle says, then sees the two bottles of brown liquid in Moss's hands. "You found some. Good for you."

"Okay, okay, this is getting tiring," Moss says, holding up the bottles. "Do you really think we're looking for booze because we want to party?"

"Yeah," Kyle says. "Why else would you be looking for it? You said you wanted booze and ladies."

"Have you seen any ladies?" Moss asks.

"No," Kyle says. "I haven't seen anyone."

"That's because there isn't anyone here," Moss says. "Me and Gil was just fucking with you. We thought it would be funny to make you think we were just some drunk guys ready to party and fuck our way through the end of the world, and you bought it."

"I bought it? What the fuck, man?" Kyle snaps. "Why would you do that?"

"Because we were bored," Moss shrugs. "You have any idea how long we were in that bunker?"

"I don't know," Kyle says. "A week? A couple of days?"

"Since July, man," Moss says. "As soon as the first earthquakes started. Gil and I had found that place a ways back. Spent years fixing it up and adding supplies. We were in there for two weeks during Y2K."

"During what?" Kyle asks.

"Never mind," Moss smiles. "Before your time, kid. Doesn't matter anyway. We went in there and some of our friends started showing up over the next couple of weeks as everything got shittier and shittier. We have enough supplies to last us for about two years." He shakes the bottles of liquor. "Except for booze. Which can be used as a cleanser, an antiseptic, a solvent, and a pain killer."

"You want the alcohol for its uses, not because it gets you drunk?" Kyle nods. "Why didn't you just say that?"

"Like I said, we've been bored," Moss shrugs. "Seemed like fun to play the post-apocalyptic nutjob role."

"Gil doesn't seem like he's playing," Kyle states.

"Nah, Gil's okay," Moss says. "Hates the government, but he's not totally whacked out. Luke's the one to be careful of."

"Luke?" Kyle asks.

Moss watches him for a second then nods. "Yeah, you haven't met him. His mom was like Carrie's mom, you know, from that Stephen King movie? Used to lock him up in closets and shit. I think the end of the world has brought some of that out in him." Moss sighs. "But you probably know that with how your dad is."

"He's not my dad," Kyle snarls.

"You sure, kid?" Moss asks. "Because there is a kind of resemblance."

"No, there isn't," Kyle snarls again. "So shut the fuck up about it." He's about to say more, but the wind carries the sound of splashing to them and they both turn to look towards the golf course.

"That what you heard before?" Moss asks.

"Yeah, I think so," Kyle says.

"Weird time for someone to go for a swim," Moss says. He hands Kyle the liquor, then reaches inside his jacket and pulls out a 9mm pistol. "Come on. Let's go have a look."

"Really?" Kyle says. "Maybe it's those crazies you were taking about? Unless that was part of the joke."

"I wish," Moss says. "That's the one part of the end of the world that's held true. There are always crazies."

***

Morgie, a man that would stand about six and a half feet tall if he didn't slouch his shoulders and back so much, stops just as he's about to try the doorknob to the front door of yet another apartment. He's sick of checking the shitty little one bedroom boxes, sure there isn't any booze hiding in a single one of them, and is about to turn around and tell Paul those very words, when someone taps him on one of his hunched shoulders.

"What, Paul?" he asks, then starts to shout as he sees Linder's smiling face instead of his friend.

The shout never makes it past the gash across his throat as Linder steps back from the spray of blood, wiping the knife he holds on his pants.

"I'm not Paul," Linder says, then points the knife at the railing of the second floor walkway that opens onto the parking lot below. "Paul's down there. Here, have a look."

Morgie's hands are jammed against his neck, desperate to stop the flow of blood, so he doesn't even try to fight as Linder grabs him by the elbow and yanks him over to the railing.

"See? There's Paul," Linder says, pointing down at a body, head nearly sliced off, as it lies in a pool of blood that slowly flows down into the cracks in the pavement. "You should go see how he is."

Linder gives Morgie a shove and the big man topples over the railing. His hands come away from his neck as he flails just before slamming into the ground. The man's skull cracks open on impact and his brains spill out, adding to the gore of Paul's blood.

"Dammit," Linder swears. "I meant to ask him if he knew where Kyle was." Linder shrugs and looks towards the stairs. "Oh, well, I'll find someone else."

***

Coletti's head breaks the surface of the water and he frowns at Dr. Probst.

"I can see it," he says, "but there's no way we'll get it out of here."

"Can you open it under water?" she asks.

"I can," Coletti replies. "But who knows what's in there."

He takes a deep breath and dives once more, his hands cutting through the water as he swims towards the dark shape of the airdropped crate. It takes Coletti a bit to locate the sensor on the crate that will pop it open, and he's forced to swim back to the surface for another breath of air.

"Well?" Dr. Probst asks.

"Just getting a breath," Coletti says. He breathes in and out, quickly stretching his lungs so he can get as much air as possible before his next dive. Dr. Probst keeps looking over her shoulder towards a stand of leafless trees. "What?"

"Nothing," Dr. Probst says. "Thought I saw something move."

Coletti searches the area, turning his body around as he treads water. "If it's one of those things then you get the hell out of here fast, got it?"

Dr. Probst frowns at him. "If it's one of those things, we'd be able to see it clearly. Not like those monsters can duck behind a juniper bush or something and hide."

"Just be careful is what I'm saying," Coletti replies. "And don't wait around for me. Anything comes at you while I'm underwater, you run like hell. I'll find you later."

"If that something doesn't get you," Dr. Probst says.

"Here's hoping," Coletti says, takes a deep breath, and dives once more.

He swims as fast as he can down to the crate, pulls the CLD from his pocket and places it into a small depression in the crate's metal. He starts to worry about the air he's burning as he waits for something to happen. There are several loud clicks and the crate starts to split open from the other side. He smiles and heads back to the surface for one last breath before he searches through the crate.

He's a little surprised by what he finds when he surfaces.

"Hey, there," Moss says, holding onto Dr. Probst's arm, his 9mm pointed at her head. "Kinda weird time for a swim, don't ya think?"

"You okay?" Coletti asks Dr. Probst. She nods, but doesn't say anything, her eyes wide with fear as she looks at the barrel of the pistol. "What do you guys want?"

Coletti sizes up Moss, noting his lanky body type, the way he holds his pistol, where his feet are placed, the distance between him and Dr. Probst. Civilian. And an amateur one. Coletti's eyes move to Kyle and he's surprised at the kid's age. He's also surprised that the boy doesn't have a weapon, but holds himself like he knows how to fight. Or at least has had some training. Kid's probably too young to have ever gotten into a real fight.

"If you're going to rob us then just do it and go," Coletti says. "All of our stuff is right there. Take it and leave us alone, okay?"

"How about you come out of that water?" Moss says. "Take a seat on the grass and tell me what the hell it is you're doing."

"I needed a bath," Coletti says. "Just take the stuff and go. We don't want any trouble."

"I don't want any trouble neither, pal," Moss says.

Coletti catches the fact that Moss keeps saying "me" and "I," not "us" and "we." That tells him quickly that the man sees himself as separate from the teenager. Or they just met and haven't gotten used to each other yet. Whatever their relationship, Coletti figures he can use it to his advantage.

"This what you do?" Coletti asks Kyle. "Point guns at unarmed women? This guy your dad?"

129

"I don't have a dad," Kyle snaps and Coletti realizes he's hit a hot button.

"That so? Your dad bail on you?" Coletti asks. "He leave you alone in all this crap? Who's this guy to you then? He your uncle? Nah, I don't think so. He take you captive, is that it? Hold you hostage like he's doing to my friend now?"

"We're old friends," Moss says. "Now shut up and get out of the water."

"Old friends?" Coletti asks, swimming closer to the shore. "Really? What's the kid's name?"

"Kyle," Moss smirks. "So shut up."

"What's his last name?" Coletti smiles, getting closer to the shore with every word.

Moss doesn't answer. He looks over at Kyle then back at Coletti. "Shut up."

"Yeah, you two are best buddies," Coletti laughs as he reaches the shore and pulls himself out of the water. He grabs onto the dead grass, but a clump comes away in his hand and he slips back, falling on his ass.

"Jesus, you retarded or something?" Moss asks.

"That is not a nice word to use," Dr. Probst says.

"Gee, I'm sorry," Moss replies. He jabs the pistol at her head and she cringes, a small cry escaping her lips.

"Calm down," Coletti says. "I'm getting out. Just be cool with that gun, okay?"

Coletti gets to the shore again and this time, he gets all the way out of the water before slipping and falling into the dead grass at Moss's feet.

"Son of a bitch," Coletti mutters. "This just sucks."

Moss looks down at the man and shakes his head, and then points with the pistol at the pile of clothes. "Now, why don't you go over there and empty those pockets. Show me what you're holding."

Yep, total amateur.

As soon as Moss points his pistol away from Dr. Probst's head, Coletti reaches out and grabs the man's ankles, pulling his feet out from under him. Before Moss's ass hits the ground, Coletti is up and leaping onto the man, his fist hitting Moss square in the jaw.

The 9mm goes flying and Coletti gets three more hits in before Moss starts crying out for him to stop. He tries to bring his arms up to block Coletti, but his pathetic attempts to defend himself are just swatted away and more blows slam into his face.

"Hey!" Kyle yells, the 9mm in his hand as he stands a few feet away from everyone. "Stop it!"

Coletti lets one more punch connect before he rolls off of Moss and gets to his feet, his eyes locked onto Kyle.

"You aren't going to shoot me," Coletti says.

Kyle pulls back the slide and grips the pistol, his finger close to the trigger and his other hand cupped underneath. Coletti recognizes that the boy knows how to shoot, but is banking on the kid not knowing how to kill.

"Put it down, son," Coletti says, taking a step towards Kyle.

The gunshot is loud in the dead city and Dr. Probst screams as the bullet kicks up a chunk of dirt at Coletti's feet.

"Tell us who you are," Kyle says. He looks Coletti over. "What are you? Navy SEALs? You have a trident tattoo."

"Very good, kid," Coletti says. "I am Navy." He points at the water trap. "And there's something in that water I need to get. You are keeping me from that duty."

"What is it?" Kyle asks.

"I don't know yet," Coletti says. "It was airdropped. Probably under the president's orders."

"The president? Why would he airdrop something to you?" Kyle asks.

"Kid, I've told you what I know," Coletti answers. "I won't know the whys or whats until I go down there and check it out. So either shoot me and end this or put that damn gun away and let me do my job."

Kyle and Coletti lock eyes and stare at each other.

"Fine," Kyle says, easing the hammer home on the pistol. "Go get whatever it is. We'll wait here."

"I don't know how I feel about that," Coletti says as he looks over at the bloody Moss.

"We won't hurt your friend," Kyle says. "And it's Morgan, by the way."

"What?" Coletti asks, confused.

"My last name," Kyle says, putting the 9mm in the waistband of his pants. "My last name is Morgan."

"Good to know," Coletti smiles then nods at the pistol. "Gonna shoot your dick off if you keep that there, Kyle Morgan."

"Yeah, well, not like I'll ever get to do anything with it," Kyle snorts. "The end of the world is here and like Moss said to me, there's no ladies left."

Coletti shakes his head and chuckles. "You're a strange kid, Kyle. But you seem like a good one too. Keep Dr. Probst safe and make sure your old friend there doesn't try anything."

"You're a doctor?" Moss asks, looking up at Dr. Probst. "Can you look at something on my leg? It's like a mole or something."

"You're going to leave me here with them?" Dr. Probst growls.

Coletti looks over at Moss as the man, still lying on the ground, starts to unbuckle his pants. He looks at Kyle who just stands there like every other bored teenager in the world.

"Yeah, I think you're good," Coletti says as he wades back out into the water. "Back in a second."

A huge cry from above makes them all look up towards the ash cloud. Shapes move in and out of the ash, barely visible in the gloom.

"I'll try to be fast," Coletti says as he stretches out his arms and dives under the water.

***

The sound of the gunshot makes Linder hesitate as he straddles the fallen form of Tomboy, his hand cocked back for another hit. The hesitation gives Tomboy the split second he needs to lash out and rake his nails across Linder's cheek.

"You godless fuck," Linder says and lets the cocked arm come down with all his strength. He winces as one of Tomboy's teeth cracks and cuts his knuckle. "Shit!"

Linder brings his arm back and then down, back and then down, over and over until Tomboy's face is nothing but bloody pulp. Linder stops, his chest heaving from the exertion, and gets up off the dead man. He leans down and wipes his bloody knuckles on Tomboy's coat then stands straight and takes a deep breath.

"Now, who is shooting?" Linder asks as he leaves the corpse in the middle of the street.

Up against the curb to his left lies Jim's broken body, his head split open from a little romper stomper action. Linder had always wanted to put someone's open mouth against the edge of a curb and then stomp on the back of that unfortunate someone's head. One loud, bloody crunch and it was all over.

Several screeches make Linder glance up at the sky and he glares at the shapes of the monsters that flit in and out of the ash, as if the monsters are an inconvenient annoyance.

"What are you?" he asks as he walks down the middle of the street. "Demons from above? Fallen angels ready to wage war on humanity?" He cups his blood covered hands to his mouth and shouts. "Then come get me! Come on, demons! I'm standing right here!"

He stops and holds his arms out, then thumps his chest over and over.

"I'm! Standing! Right! Here!"

***

"You hear that?" Moss asks, buckling his pants back up after Dr. Probst insisted for the tenth time that she was a geologist, not a medical doctor. "Somebody yelling?"

"I don't hear any yelling," Kyle says, sitting on the dead grass next to Dr. Probst as they both stare up at the ash and the increasing numbers of monsters flying about the cloud. "I just hear those things."

Moss follows their gaze and says, "I sure hope they don't take a shit on us like pigeons do."

Kyle and Dr. Probst look over at Moss and stare.

"What?" Moss asks. "Monsters probably have to shit too. I doubt they fly down and dig a hole. I'll bet they let their droppings just fly where they, uh, well, *fly.*"

"I didn't need to hear that," Dr. Probst says. "Those things are bad enough without having to worry about being defecated on by one of them."

"That means shit on," Kyle says to Moss.

"I know what it fucking means," Moss scowls. "Don't be a dick, kid."

Coletti bursts from the water and tosses two large packs up onto the grass.

"There's more," he says and points at the packs. "Go through those and inventory what's in there. Double check them against each other to see if they are duplicates or if each pack is specialized."

Moss starts to reach for a pack and Coletti snaps his fingers.

"Not you," he says. "Dr. Probst. I trust her to not miss anything."

"I can check one," Kyle says.

Coletti looks at Dr. Probst and she nods.

"Fine," Coletti says as he turns back, ready for another dive. "Make it fast. I'll get the last two and then we need to get away from here." He looks up at the sky. "This spot is too open."

"Exactly!" Moss exclaims. "Those things could shit on us at any moment!"

"Sure. Whatever," Coletti shrugs then dives once more.

Kyle gets up and grabs the two packs, surprised by their weight.

"I think they sent everything but the kitchen sink," he says as he sets the packs down by Dr. Probst. "How do you want to do this?"

"We open them up, take everything out carefully, then start calling the items off, comparing what we find," Dr. Probst says.

"Okay," Kyle nods as he undoes the top straps of his pack.

A high pitched screech causes him to look up quickly and he sees one of the monsters shoot from the cloud, its wings pulled in tight to its body. The thing dives a few hundred feet then its wings come out and it swoops back towards the ash cloud.

"We should hurry," Dr. Probst says.

"No shit," Kyle nods.

***

"Dear God...," Lu whispers as the group of survivors crest the ridge and look down on Lake Coeur d'Alene and the city of the same name that lies below them.

Smoke rises from the city and every person can see that what's left isn't the sanctuary they were hoping for. People turn to each other and the looks of exhaustion are replaced with looks of disappointment and desperation.

"What now, boss?" Lowell asks. "Doesn't exactly look like they have a vacancy."

"It's better than being out in the open," Bolton says. "We can't be caught standing here when that ash cloud finally decides to come down."

"Why hasn't it?" Lowell asks.

"We don't know," Lu snaps.

"I know we don't know," Lowell replies. "It was a rhetorical question."

"Are we going down there or not?" a man asks and the same question ripples through the group.

Lu looks at Bolton and he shrugs.

"You're in charge, Marshal," Bolton says. "I'm just along for the ride."

"Thanks," Lu smirks, then turns to address the people around her. "You can see what we're looking at down there. It's not pretty. We could go down and help out and maybe find somewhere safe to stay or we could go down there and find nothing but chaos and murder."

"Way to sell it," Lowell mutters.

Lu glares at him and continues. "Or we keep going and look for someplace else. We might make it to Spokane."

"No way can we get to Spokane!" someone yells. "Not with those things all around us!"

There are murmurs of agreement and Lu holds out her hands.

"I know, I know," Lu says. "But we don't have a lot of options."

"There was a farm a ways back," someone says. "We could just stay there. I bet they have food stored somewhere."

"Those things are back there, you idiot! Didn't you hear me?"

"Don't call me an idiot, asshole! It was just a suggestion!"

"Who you calling an asshole, cocksucker? I'll fucking kill you!"

"Jesus," Lu snarls as she wades into the crowd and grabs the two men about to come to blows. Her fingers pinch deep into the backs of their necks and the men, both much taller than Lu, come to heel quickly.

"Knock it off!" she roars. "We do not have time for this! I'm going down there! You all can come with me or not, I don't care! End of discussion!"

She lets the men go and smacks them both upside the head before turning and stomping away from the crowd.

"You coming?" she barks at Bolton as she pushes past him.

Lowell chuckles and then holds up his hands as Lu turns her anger on him.

"Whoa, Marshal. That look is considered a deadly weapon," Lowell smirks. "Better put it away before someone gets killed."

"Fuck off," Lu says and starts down the trail carved into the hillside below the ridge.

"That could have gone better," Lowell says as he looks at the angry and stunned faces of the group.

"I don't think so," Bolton says. "I know Lu pretty well and that's about as good as it could have gone. I'm surprised she hasn't smacked someone before now."

***

"A fleece jacket, clothes, some rations, water, purification tablets, a multi-tool, binoculars, compass, a gas mask, and this," Kyle says as he hands over a small, black sat phone. "I'm guessing it's for you. I can't get it to turn on."

"No weapons?" Coletti asks.

"No," Dr. Probst says, "but there's a phone in each pack."

"That's good," Coletti says. "We'll need backups since we have no way to charge these. Once one dies, I'll switch to a new one. You sure there're no weapons?"

"None," Kyle says. "Not even a survival knife."

"Then these were random, blind drops," Coletti says. "Even though the crates can't be opened unless someone has a CLD, they made sure there weren't weapons in case one broke open and happened to be found by a civilian."

"Is that good or bad?" Dr. Probst asks. "I'm guessing by the look on your face it isn't good."

"It means the brass is flying blind," Coletti says. "They have no idea who is on the ground and that means a rescue team isn't coming anytime soon."

"How can they not know who's down here?" Moss asks. "It's the government. Don't they have spy satellites? They have like drones and shit that can see a mouse fart at ten miles up."

"The EMP must have hit a huge area," Coletti says, pointing at the sky. "Could have been big enough to take out satellites. And do you see any drones flying around? All I see is a huge amount of ash blocking out the sun."

"Is it morning yet?" Dr. Probst asks. "I don't even know what time it is anymore."

"It's time to make a call," Kyle says. He nods at the sat phone in Coletti's hand. "Get on that thing and find out what's happening."

"Good idea," Coletti says. He takes a few steps away and sees the looks of surprise. "This call is considered classified. Sorry."

"Not classified from me!" Dr. Probst snaps.

Coletti nods and then walks off, followed closely by Dr. Probst. And Kyle and Moss.

Coletti ignores the eavesdroppers and presses the CLD against the sat phone. The solid black face lights up and the phone instantly starts to dial. Coletti takes a couple of deep breaths as he waits for an answer on the other end.

***

"One hour, sir," Joan says, her face drawn and tired. "One hour before we launch the bombers."

"Sir!" a tech shouts. "Mr. President! We have an incoming call from one of the sat phones!"

President Nance stands up, his eyes locked onto the main monitor. "Where is it coming from?"

"Missoula, Mr. President."

"Jesus H crackers and toast," Admiral Quigley says. "Someone's right next to ground zero."

"Put it through now," President Nance says. "Hello? Hello, who am I speaking with? This is President Charles Nance speaking, identify yourself."

"Mr. President? This is Lieutenant Jason Coletti, sir. I'm here with Dr. Probst. We made it in, but it's not good, sir."

"Holy shit," Admiral Quigley laughs. "Leave it to Team Six to get a man inside."

"Lieutenant? What can you tell us about the situation? We need details, son."

***

Coletti looks up at the sky and the creatures flying about the ash. He then turns his attention to the direction the hole is in.

"Sir, I don't exactly have good news," Coletti says. "Whatever these things are, there are a lot of them."

"Tell us what you know."

"Dr. Probst and I landed close to ground zero and was only maybe a half mile from the edge of the chasm, sir. What we saw was like out of a nightmare. There are so many of these monsters, sir. And they aren't all the same."

"We know that, son," President Nance replies. "We know of the smaller ones, the big ones, and the flying ones. Any others?"

Coletti laughs at the use of the word "smaller."

"Those are the three types we know of, sir," Coletti replies. "And we aren't sure they are all working together."

"Lieutenant? This is Admiral Quigley. What do you mean they aren't working together?" Several voices start shouting as once. "Shut up!" The voices quiet down. "Keep talking,

Lieutenant. Why would you think these monsters would be, or wouldn't be, working together?"

"The doctor and I watched as the smaller ones kept getting squashed and then eaten by the bigger ones, Admiral," Coletti explains. "The smaller ones were trying to get as far away from that hole as possible, as fast as possible. They did not like being near the big ones."

"How many?" a different voice asks.

"Total, sir?" Coletti asks. "Or how many of each type?"

"Each type."

"I can't say how many of the flying ones there are," Coletti replies, his eyes drawn back to the monsters above. "But there are a lot and they are getting more active."

"Son, this is General Tulane," General Tulane snaps. "I saw them take down some of my best pilots. That's pretty damn active right there!"

"Yeah, we saw that too," Coletti says. "The missiles didn't even faze the big ones. The explosions just rolled off their backs."

"And how many of those are there?" General Tulane asks.

"No way to say, sir," Coletti replies. "I couldn't see the entire hole, just the part I was closest to." He looks at Dr. Probst. "But the big ones were standing by the edge, spaced out every quarter mile or so." Dr. Probst nods to him in agreement.

Moss sits back on the ground, his arms wrapped about one of the wet packs. His face looks pale and he glances at Kyle, but the boy is too busy listening intently to Coletti to notice.

Coletti waits as several voices start talking at once again. "Sirs? Hello? Admiral Quigley? General Tulane? Mr. President? What do you need me to do?"

"Get somewhere safe, son," President Nance replies. The other voices quiet down immediately. "Any place that will shield you from the blasts."

"I'm sorry, sir, but did you say blasts?" Coletti asks.

Dr. Probst and Kyle both take a step back at the words while Moss looks like he's going to faint.

"Son, those things have left me no choice," President Nance says. "I'm ordering the area be blanketed with MOABs. The bombers will be launched within the minute. I am truly sorry, but we cannot risk these things, as you said earlier, working together. Godspeed, son."

"Wait!" Coletti shouts into the sat phone. "Mr. President! We watched those missiles hit the monsters! They didn't even scratch them, sir! Their skin is like slick looking leather and must be impervious to fire, Mr. President! All you'll do when you drop the MOABs is kill any survivors in the area!"

Coletti waits, but there's no response.

"Sir? Mr. President? Son of a bitch!"

He nearly hurls the phone into the water trap, but restrains himself and carefully places it in his pocket instead.

"That did not sound promising," Dr. Probst says. "What's a MOAB, by the way?"

"Massive Ordinance Air Blast," Kyle replies.

"That's right," Coletti nods. "Most people call it the Mother Of All Bombs." He looks at Dr. Probst and sighs. "It's the most powerful conventional bomb in our arsenal."

"The things set the air on fire," Moss says. "We are so dead."

"It doesn't set the air on fire," Coletti says. "But, yeah, we're dead."

NINE

The streets of Coeur d'Alene, Idaho are strewn with rubble and debris. Barely a building is intact, with most of them collapsed in on themselves. Smoke drifts everywhere as fires burn, spreading to whatever buildings still have combustible materials left in them.

Lu stares at the horror of it all, her lips pressed together in a tight line.

"There's nothing here for us, Lu," Bolton says at her elbow. "Look around. This place is done. We need to just keep moving."

"The buses from Champion were supposed to meet here," Lu says, her voice even and calm.

The even and calmness worries Bolton.

"Buses? You saw what happened to our buses, right?" Lowell snorts. "Whatever buses you're looking for, I doubt they made it."

Lu whips around on the man and decks him with one punch. The even and calm is gone. Lowell, sitting on his ass in a puddle of mucky water, wipes his mouth then looks at the blood on the back of his hand.

"I'm just stating reality," Lowell says as he gets to his feet.

Lu sends him back to the ground.

"What the fuck, Marshal?" Lowell yells. "I know you don't like me, but stop fucking hitting me!"

"Kyle and Terrie were on those buses, right?" Bolton asks.

"They were following in the Bronco," Lu replies. "They had to leave sooner. It's complicated."

Kyle and Terrie?" Lowell asks.

"Her son and mom," Bolton says.

"Jesus," Lowell says. "Why didn't you just say so? I'd have shut the fuck up without you breaking my fucking jaw."

Lu looks down at Lowell, and then extends her hand. He eyes it warily, but finally grabs it and lets her pull him up. Then she punches him again and he's back where he started.

"Mother fucker!" he snarls and gets to his feet, his eyes red with anger, his fists clenched.

"Hold it!" Bolton shouts and stands between the two. "Not the time for this!"

"You," Lowell snarls at Lu. "You think you're in charge? Rule of law is shit now."

"Really? Because I'm declaring marshal law!" Lu says, lunging for him. "And when I say marshal, I mean it like-"

"Yeah, I get it!" Lowell spits. "Stupid fucking pun!"

"Jesus, you two," Bolton says. "Just fuck already."

This stops Lu and Lowell instantly in their tracks.

"No way, man."

"Are you fucking kidding me?"

"There. You two done now?" Bolton asks. "I figured that would shut you up."

"Not cool, dude," Lowell says, shivering with disgust.

Lu looks behind them at the group of survivors that have walked for hours and hours, miles and miles, following her, thinking she has a plan. Now they just stare at her as she loses her shit on a prisoner that has no business being in the position he is in.

"Let's see what we can find," Lu says. "Look for anything useful."

"We can cross the whole city off the list of useful," Lowell says, looking around at the destruction. "What the hell could cause this so fast?"

"Looks like artillery," Bolton says. "Except I'm not seeing blast marks like we should."

Lu turns to the group behind them. "Find supplies," she orders. "Anything we may need like food, water, warm clothing, face masks, anything. Keep moving and looking and we'll meet on the other side of the city." She takes a deep breath, her eyes truly seeing the desperation and hopelessness for the first time. "Then we start walking to Spokane."

"What about Terrie and Kyle?" Bolton asks.

"If they are here, they are here," Lu replies, taking a deep breath. "If they aren't, then they aren't."

"Now she's seeing reason," Lowell says and quickly steps out of her reach.

"Shut the fuck up," Lu says and stomps off.

The emotions inside her wage war. One side insists she is abandoning her family by not doing everything needed to find them. The other side keeps showing her the faces of the dozens of men, women, and children that have been traveling with her all this way. If she ditches them for her own personal needs, she's no better than Lowell.

Back and forth her mind goes, keeping her so wrapped up in her thoughts that she almost doesn't notice what sticks out from the second story of the building next to her when she rounds the street corner. If it wasn't for the brake fluid that drips down in a constant stream, Lu would have walked right past it.

"What the fuck?" she says as she wipes a drop of brake fluid from her cheek. She looks up and does a double take. "Hey, Connor?"

"Yeah?" Bolton replies as he jogs up next to her. "What…?"

"How the hell do you think that got up there?" she asks. "Some explosion?"

"No, the car would be more damaged," Bolton says. "And look at how the building is? If I didn't know better, I'd say it was dropped."

"Dropped?" Lu asks. "How the hell could that happen?"

"I said if I didn't know any better," Bolton replies. "Which I do. It would take a construction crane to get it high enough to drop like that. I don't see any cranes around here."

"Bizarre," she nods. She studies the car for a minute then looks up at the rest of the building. Movement above catches her eye and she glances at the ash cloud. "Oh, shit."

Swirling in and out of the cloud are dozens and dozens of the flying monsters. They swoop and dive, roll and rise, a multitude of slick, leathery wings and sharp talons.

"Holy crap," Bolton says. "Look at them all. What are they doing?"

***

"What are we doing?" Dr. Probst asks as they run from the golf course. "Where are we going?"

Coletti looks over at the geologist then at Moss. "Where can we find the best cover?"

"I don't know," Moss says. "Haven't had to hide here before. We always just salvage and then head back to the bunker."

"The bunker? Where is that?" Coletti asks.

"An hour ride northwest," Moss says. "But that's too far, right? They're sending in the bombers now, aren't they?"

"Yeah, that's too far," Coletti says. "We need somewhere closer. Where are the municipal buildings? Usually those have underground storm shelters."

"Center of town," Moss says. "This way."

He takes off running and is almost out the front gate when he stops in his tracks.

"Dude, what's wrong?" Kyle asks as he catches up to the man.

Moss turns around and they see the large knife sticking from his belly.

"There you are," Linder smiles as he steps away from one of the large stone columns by the gate. "I was worried."

"Fuck...," Kyle whispers.

Linder pulls the .38 from the waistband of the small of his back and aims it at Coletti and Dr. Probst.

"Introduce me to your friends, Kyle," Linder says. "I always want to know who my son is hanging out with."

"I don't know who you are, but we don't have time for this," Coletti says.

"I've been hunting for this boy for almost his entire life," Linder says. "We'll make time."

"Great. Just fucking great," Dr. Probst says. "I'm going to die on a fucking golf course."

***

"Command, this is Halo Alpha," the pilot calls out. "Approaching the target. Cannot confirm visuals due to the ash cloud, but targeting is locked. Ready to deploy payload on your orders."

"Deploy when ready," a voice replies. "Presidential order Tango One One Nine Delta is a go. Good luck."

The pilot looks down at the ash cloud only a thousand feet below his B-52 bomber then glances at the altimeter before him. 62,000 feet. That's a few thousand feet higher than the massive plane's service ceiling threshold of 55,000 feet. But the squadron was told to get above the cloud and stay above the cloud at all costs.

"Truman Squadron," the pilot calls over the com. "Commence bombing run. Empty your payloads on my mark. Three, two, one."

The eighteen B-52 bombers flying in formation around Halo Alpha all dip lower, getting as close to the cloud as possible before their bomb bay doors open. Massive, bright orange missiles are lowered from the planes, six per bomber, their size and weight causing increased drag, forcing the pilots to compensate instantly.

It's that hesitation by some of the pilots that makes them miss what comes up at them from the cloud.

"Sir!" a gunner shouts over the Halo Alpha com. "Bogeys! Coming up fast!"

"Drop ordinance now!" the pilot shouts. "NOW!"

A winged beast rushes straight at the bomber, its six legs outstretched, talon claws reaching, reaching, grabbing.

"What the hell?" the pilot shouts. "It's on us!"

The monster grips the six orange missiles in its talon and rips them free from their harnesses, then dives back towards the cloud. The violence of the attack sends the bomber spinning out of control and it soon involuntarily follows the creature into the thick ash.

"DROP EVERYTHING NOW!" the pilot screams. "DO NOT LET THE ENEMY TAKE YOUR PAYLOAD!"

He can hear several voices shouting into the com, most announcing they have successfully dropped their payload and are now trying evasive maneuvers to get away from the attacking beasts. Many other voices are shouting and calling out that they've been grabbed and are falling out of control through the ash.

The pilot fights the controls, desperate to get the bomber steady and level so he can get his crew out of this nightmare. But the plane is too heavy, the ash cloud too thick, and the situation too unreal for even his trained mind to grasp.

The bomber shoots out from the ash cloud and the pilot gasps, and then cries out as he gets a whirling look at what lies below. The chasm is massive, easily 200 miles across. But that isn't what makes him cry out. It's what's in the chasm.

He sees fire and darkness, but also something else. Something moving.

"Mother of God," he whispers. "What is that?"

Then a flying monster whips past him, the MOABs clutched in its claws. If the pilot wasn't stunned before, he is now when he watches the monster spread its wings wide and slow its descent.

Then it lets the bombs go, sending them falling directly into the chasm at what lies within.

***

"Tell your dad to put the gun down," Coletti says to Kyle.

"He's not my fucking dad!" Kyle shouts. "He's some crazy fucker I've had to hide from my whole life!"

"You never had to hide from me," Linder says. "No child should hide from their father."

"Oh, for fuck's sake," Kyle says and throws his hands up in the air.

"Mister, whoever you are, you need to understand something," Coletti says, hooking a thumb over his shoulder. "The President of the United States just ordered that the entire area be carpet bombed with MOABs. Do you know what a MOAB does?"

"Yes, I do," Linder says. "They have a blast radius of what, 200 meters? Maybe 300 meters? They incinerate anything and everything in that radius. Not to mention a shock wave that can bring down buildings." Linder shrugs and glances quickly around. "I don't think we have to worry about that. Looks like Missoula came pre-leveled."

He laughs at his own weak joke. Coletti shakes his head.

"There is something seriously wrong with you," Coletti says.

"What gave it away?" Dr. Probst mutters under her breath.

"Listen, in minutes there will be MOABs raining down on this area," Coletti says. "We have to get somewhere deep underground. We have to find shelter or we're going to be nothing but ash like that cloud up there."

Linder glances past Coletti for a split second in the direction of the hole. He looks back at Coletti and sneers. But the sneer falls away quickly and his eyes are forced to look over Coletti's shoulder once again.

"I don't believe *that* is what President Nance had in mind," Linder laughs. "Do you?"

Coletti eyes Linder for a minute, but can see the man's attention is focused squarely on the sky behind him. He debates whether to use Linder's distraction and take the crazy fuck down, but the multitude of wails and shrieks ends the debate. Coletti turns, as do Dr. Probst and Kyle, and they all stare.

"Holy fuck," Kyle says.

"No fucking shit, kid," Coletti responds.

The sky is filled with flying creatures, all swooping and zooming through the air under the ash cloud. They are everywhere. Coletti watches as two dip their wings and rocket towards a set of orange missiles. They grab them up in their claws, and then roll to the side, turning back towards the massive hole. Once over the chasm, they let the missiles fall, sending them directly into the maw of the massive hole.

Over and over, the monsters maneuver through the sky, collecting the falling bombs, and depositing them right where they want them. In a matter of minutes, there are no longer missiles in the air, just flying monsters, all circling, circling, circling the hole.

"Go," Coletti says. "Run! Now!"

"No one is running!" Linder shouts, cocking the hammer back. "We are staying right here!"

"No, you ain't," Moss coughs as he pulls the knife from his body and jams it into Linder's calf.

The man falls to the ground screaming and the gun goes off. Coletti grunts and falls to a knee, his hand going to his pocket.

"Here!" he shouts and tosses Dr. Probst the CLD. "Take that and run! You have a sat phone. Call this in once you find shelter. The President needs to know what's happening."

Dr. Probst catches the CLD easily, but just stares at it. Another gunshot, this one hitting the ground right next to Coletti, wakes her from her daze and she shakes her head and glares at Linder. Then she turns and runs full out past the country club entrance.

Kyle watches her for a second, but then takes off after her.

"Kyle! KYLE!" Linder yells as he tries to stand, but his leg crumples under him, the knife bobbing in the meat of his calf. "COME BACK!"

"You crazy fuck," Coletti says as he gets up and stumbles over to Linder.

The man whips the gun up at him, but Coletti kicks it out of his hands and then stomps on Linder's arm. With his other arm, Linder yanks the knife free of his leg and swipes at Coletti, but the lieutenant is able to jump back out of the way. This frees up Linder's other arm and he pulls himself forward, his hand inches from the fallen .38.

Coletti lunges and brings a fist down into Linder's face, but he gets a slash across his cheek for the trouble. Blood pours from the wound as Coletti rolls backwards, out of Linder's reach, and presses his hand to his face. A flap of skin about six inches long squirms under Coletti's fingers and he realizes he can kiss his good looks goodbye. This thought seems to amuse his fatigued mind and he starts laughing.

"What's so funny?" Linder snarls as he struggles to get up, but his leg just won't hold him. "Shut up! Stop laughing!"

"There's always you," Coletti says. "Some guy like you that has to gum things up."

Coletti is able to get to his feet, but the world swims around him and he looks down to see a lot of very dark blood staining his uniform. He keeps laughing, but it takes on a jagged tone.

"I knew a guy in Afghanistan that had one day before his tour was up," Coletti says, limping towards the .38, racing Linder for the gun. It's a slow race, as both wounded men bleed like stuck pigs. "This guy, he had a friend in the local village. Just some merchant that he liked to have tea with."

Coletti gets to Linder's hand before he gets to the pistol and presses his boot down on the man's fingers. Linder cries out, and then tries to slash him with the knife again, but Coletti is ready for the attack. He blocks the knife with his other foot, letting the blade slice a huge hunk of the heavy duty rubber sole, and drops fast, sending his knee right into Linder's face. The crunch of bone echoes loud, even with the horrendous noises the beasts above make.

"My friend was having tea one afternoon," Coletti says, sending a fist into Linder's face as he grabs the man's knife hand and twists the wrist quickly, snapping the bone. "They were busy talking about kids and family and normal stuff two husbands and fathers would talk about. All while sipping this awful black stuff that tastes more like cough syrup than tea."

Coletti lands another punch and another and Linder spits a broken tooth up at him.

"I got to go have tea with the two of them since it was my bud's last day," Coletti continues. "He wanted to introduce me to his friend and hoped I'd take his place during tea time when I could."

"I'm going to kill you," Linder spits.

Coletti responds with two more punches, making Linder's eyes start to roll back in his head. "Shut up. I'm telling a story."

Coletti coughs hard and a spray of blood shoots from between his lips.

"Got...ya," Linder says, quietly, his voice nothing but a semi-conscious rasp.

"Hardly," Coletti says as he elbows Linder in the face then boxes his ears. "Be quiet and listen."

Coletti tries to take a deep breath, but his chest hitches and he lets loose with a long, wet cough. More blood sprays from his mouth and he's forced to fall back on his ass. Which gives him the angle and leverage to kick Linder in the face, adding to the bloody mess.

"Where was I? Right. Afghanistan," Coletti says, his breath coming in ragged starts and stops. "So I'm sitting there in this man's house, which is really a hut made of mud and stone and old wood, but the place was clean. Like really clean. Made my apartment in the states look like a frat house dive." He kicks Linder again and then again. "Anyway, we're having tea and the man's brother-in-law comes walking in. He sees us and his face just turns to rage."

Coletti pauses as a harsh coughing fit overtakes him. It's a couple of minutes before he gets it under control.

"This guy's brother-in-law is pissed and starts yelling at the man in Arabic," Coletti says. "My pal and I stand up, ready to just leave and diffuse the situation, but the brother-in-law pulls out this handgun from his robes. I don't even get a chance to see what kind it is before he puts a bullet in our host's head then turns and fires into my pal."

Coletti looks at Linder and reaches towards him, slapping the man on the cheek weakly.

"Hey? You awake?" Coletti says. Linder's eyes flutter open. "Good. You need to listen to this. So, our host is dead and my pal is lying on the floor bleeding out when the brother-in-law turns the gun on me. He pulls the trigger and it clicks empty. I jump the guy and take him down. I want nothing more than to snap his neck right there, but I know the situation is going to look bad. If an American comes walking out of a local's house, leaving two dead locals behind, then the village is going to think I did it all. Had to keep the mother fucker alive."

Coletti taps his head.

"That was the training taking over," Coletti continues. "Thinking smart in a bad situation. I radio it in and soon the whole village is locked down. The local tribal leaders are called and I've got the head shed up my ass. It takes days to get the story straight. Finally the brother-in-law confesses. He tells the whole thing just how it happened. And you know what?"

Linder just stares blankly.

"Hey? Pay attention. You know what the brother-in-law said? You know why he killed his own wife's brother? Because he said it was the right thing to do. That was it. The right thing to do."

Coletti jabs a finger into Linder's cheek.

"You're just like that guy. You justify your actions, thinking the world owes you because you were wronged somehow and only you can set things right."

Coletti slaps Linder on the forehead.

"How's that working out for you now, asshole?" Coletti laughs, and then begins to choke as his lungs fill with blood.

He falls to his side, his body shuddering with the wet, heavy coughs. He tries to breathe, but there's no room for air in his chest. He looks over and sees Linder smiling.

"Fuck...you," Coletti says just before life leaves him.

"No...fuck...you," Linder gasps. He struggles to get free of Coletti and winces and cries as every movement tears at his wounds. "Kyle..."

***

"This way!" Kyle yells, pulling at Dr. Probst. "The horses are one street over!"

"Horses? What fucking horses? You have horses?" Dr. Probst shouts. "I don't know how to ride a horse!"

"You'll learn!" Kyle yells.

They turn the corner and see the house where the horses are tethered to the porch. They also see Scoot's body in the broken and dead lawn.

"Dear God," Dr. Probst says, her hand going to her mouth as they approach the body. "Did your dad do that?"

"Jesus fucking Christ!" Kyle tells. "He's not my dad! Not! My! Dad!"

"Okay, calm down, kid," Dr. Probst says.

"And everyone needs to stop calling me kid," Kyle mumbles. "I'm not a kid."

"Who the fuck is this, kid?" Gil asks as he hurries from the other side of the house, his pack heavy with goods, Tiff right behind him. "Where's Moss?"

"Dead," Kyle says. "Linder killed him."

"Your dad killed Moss?" Gil shouts. "How the hell did that happen?" He looks at Dr. Probst. "Did you have something to do with this? Did you set that Linder guy free?"

Gil raises his rifle, but Kyle steps in front of him.

"She's part of the government," Kyle says. "Moss and I found her and some soldier on the golf course. They had these."

Kyle pats his pack and points at the one on Dr. Probst's back. Then he looks behind him at the flying mass of monsters circling where the hole is.

"We need to get out of here," Kyle says. "There are a hundred bombs about to go off."

"Bombs? What bombs?" Gil asks, the rifle still pointed at Kyle. "Is that what those things were dropping? How'd they get bombs?"

"B-52s," Dr. Probst says. "The president ordered the area destroyed. When the bombs go off, this place will be vaporized."

Gil looks at Dr. Probst, then Kyle, then the flying monsters. He thinks for a second then lowers the rifle.

"Come on," he says. "Get on the horses."

"I can't ride," Dr. Probst says.

"You'll learn," Gil says.

"That's what the kid said, but it's not that easy," Dr. Probst protests as Kyle takes her pack and straps it to the back of one of the horse's saddles.

"It is if you want to live," Kyle says. "Give me your foot."

Dr. Probst eyes him, nods and sticks her foot in Kyle's laced hands. The teenager boosts her up into the saddle, helps her get situated, then takes the reins and wraps them around her hands.

"Don't let go, got it?" Kyle says.

"Yeah, okay," Dr. Probst says, obviously terrified. "Not letting go."

Gil looks down at Scoot then at Kyle.

"You seen the others?" he asks.

"No," Kyle says. "But if they were between here and the golf course, then Linder probably got them."

"Shit," Gil says as he gets up into his saddle. "We can't wait around to find out if that's true."

Kyle turns his horse towards the street and looks over at Dr. Probst. "What did that Coletti guy give you?"

"It's classified," Dr. Probst says.

"Goddamn government," Gil says. "We should just leave you here."

"No, she knows what's going on," Kyle says, looking over at Dr. Probst. "More than we do, at least."

The earth starts to shake and the horses whinny with fear. Kyle walks his over next to Dr. Probst and grabs onto her reins, steadying the doctor's mount as they all look to the east.

"What is that?" Gil asks, his eyes nearly squinted shut as he tries to see through the hazy air. "You see that?"

They do and it takes everyone's willpower not to freak out.

"Ride," Kyle says in a low voice then clears his throat and shouts, "Ride!"

Gil and Tiff take off first and Kyle lets go of Dr. Probst's reins then reaches back and smacks the horse on the haunch, sending it galloping after the other two. He kicks back hard and his horse takes off.

Kyle risks one last glance over his shoulder, not believing what he's seeing.

"The big ones are on the move!" he shouts. "Go!"

***

"Why haven't the bombs detonated yet?" President Nance asks, his eyes meeting only puzzled stares. "They should have detonated on impact."

"Reports from the bombers say they were attacked," General Tulane reports. "Half the squadron was knocked out of the sky. The other half was able to drop their payloads, but…"

"But what, General?" President Nance snaps.

"A couple of the pilots report that they saw the flying monsters snatch the missiles out of the air," General Tulane says. "They caught them and took them down into the hole."

"They did what?" President Nance asks. "Why the hell would they do that?"

"Sir?" a tech says. "A satellite was able to catch the transmission from one of the missiles' cameras. Should I put it up on the monitor?"

"Yes," President Nance snaps.

The image on the main monitor is replaced by a grainy, low resolution of nothing but darkness. Then suddenly the darkness parts and the whole situation room watches as the missile races down towards the chasm.

"What is that?" President Nance asks as they all stare at the image. "What am I looking at?"

"It's too dark to tell, Mr. President," the tech says. "This is the best image I could get."

"Is there something in there?" President Nance asks, looking at the Joint Chiefs, his cabinet members, and all the advisors seated around him. "Someone tell me I'm not seeing what I'm seeing!"

Everyone stays quiet because no one can tell him that.

***

The horses race through the destroyed streets of Missoula, finally getting to the edge of the city and the open land beyond. Gil leads the way as the earth around them all trembles, the force of massive footfalls shaking the trees left standing. Kyle constantly has to keep helping Dr. Probst keep her horse on track, but at least she hasn't fallen out of the saddle.

They ride and ride, putting as much distance between them and what's behind them as they can. Kyle's guts clench with every shudder. Then the roars begin.

The horses scream, actually scream, at the deafening sound, and their panic makes them sprint even faster. Dr. Probst's horse no longer tries to stray from the rest. Instead it rides closer as the horses move tighter together, their instinct for herd protection from what's coming after them now driving them forward.

The roars grow louder and louder, and the massive footfalls stronger and stronger. Kyle looks back and can actually see the top halves of the giant monsters. They are nothing short of pure nightmare.

Kyle's breath comes in quick gasps and he realizes he's going to hyperventilate from panic if he doesn't get his shit together.

"No time for weakness, Kyle," his grandma's voice echoes in his head. "You be a man now and do what has to be done. I didn't raise you to fall apart when things get tough. Suck it up, boy and trust in the Lord to deliver you!"

Kyle's not so sure about trusting in the Lord, but he's always trusted his grandma. And even though it's just his imagination creating her voice, it works and he digs deep for the courage he needs to keep going.

***

"Gotta keep going," Linder says as he pulls himself, hand over hand, along the cracked pavement of the road in front of the country club. "Can't stop. So close."

The tremors increase, making his body bounce and flop on the ground like a kid lying flat on a trampoline. A fingernail snaps free as he tries to keep going, but the increased frequency of the quakes makes it nearly impossible for him to continue. After only a few yards more, his body gives out and he's forced to roll over on his back.

What he sees makes his bladder let loose, but he doesn't even notice.

Towering high into the sky, and coming at him fast, are six massive monsters. So big that the ash cloud far above can only be seen as glimpses between the monsters' giant bodies and heads. Linder starts to shake his head back and forth as he watches the giant beasts come at him.

"Yea, though I walk through the valley of the shadow of death," Linder says, then chuckles. "Though I *crawl* through the valley of the shadow of death, I will fear no evil, for thou art with me, thy rod and thy staff, they comfort me."

He holds his hands up and extends both middle fingers.

"But as for the cowardly, the faithless, the detestable, as for murderers, the sexually immoral, sorcerers, idolaters, and all liars, their portion will be in the lake that burns with fire and sulfur, which is the second death."

He spits to the side.

"No second death for me," Linder growls as the monsters get closer and closer. His whole body is shaking so hard he actually comes up off the ground as the footfalls get nearer. "For I am the righteous! I am the chosen amongst the sinners! But he that doeth truth cometh to the light, that his deeds may be made manifest, that they are wrought in God."

The monsters are almost on top of him and the earth cracks and splits just feet from his body. He looks up and all he can see is Hell. A foot so big it defies comprehension is lifted high above him and he laughs.

"Fuck you, abomination!"

Then the foot comes down and Linder becomes one with the earth, his body obliterated along with the pavement and everything around it for blocks.

TEN

"Find cover!" Bolton shouts at the group of survivors as the flying monsters start to dive down towards the city. "Get out of the open! Go!"

"We need to do the same thing!" Lowell yells as he grabs Bolton's arm. "They've all panicked! We can't save them!"

"We can try!" Bolton yells as he pulls his arm free and runs towards where Lu is helping a young girl stand up. "We aren't abandoning them!"

"Stupid asshole," Lowell mutters as he looks around. He sees the three kids from the gas station huddled together by a demolished Starbucks and starts to go to them.

He stops in the middle of the street as a pickup truck falls from the sky and crushes all three, their bodies flattened like berries under a boot.

"Oh, fuck," he says and stumbles backwards, his eyes drawn to the monster that flies by.

The thing shrieks and climbs into the sky, joining the other things that constantly swoop down and attack, intent on wiping the city clean of all humanity.

"No," Lowell says. "Not going out like this."

He kicks it into gear and looks over at a large stone building that still stands. The windows and doors are shattered and broken, but the walls look sturdy and the place isn't ravaged by fire.

"There!" Lowell yells, smacking Bolton on the shoulder as he runs by. "Get everyone in there!"

Lowell dodges holes in the road and the husks of burned out cars as he sprints towards the building. He gets to the stone steps and turns, his hands cupping his mouth.

"Come on! This way!" he yells. He's about to say more, but the words won't come out.

Anson Lowell has seen horrors in his life that would force most people to just eat a gun or swallow a handful of pills, but he's always pushed on. He has never let anything take him down, no matter how violent or brutal. He's watched murder and rape, seen cruelty in all of its many forms. Experienced it first hand.

But nothing in his life has prepared him for what he sees as he stands at the base of the stone steps, his eyes glued to the city around him.

The monsters swoop down from above, snatching up screaming survivors in their claws. They take them high into the air then let go, sending the people falling hundreds of feet before they explode onto the pavement, onto abandoned cars, onto piles of rubble.

Over and over, Lowell watches as the things hunt down those people that haven't found cover and scoop them up, talons piercing bodies, holding them tight in their vile grips. Up in the air they go, then down come the terrified victims. Again and again.

The air is buffeted around Lowell as giant wings flap towards him. The shriek from above rips him from his nightmare trance and he scrambles up the steps, diving into the open doorway just seconds before claws snap closed on the spot he just vacated.

He keeps scrambling until he's sure he's far enough inside that the thing can't get at him. The monster hits the pavement and lunges for the doorway, but it's too big to get through and just shrieks and shrieks at Lowell before turning and flying off.

"Holy shit," Lowell says and looks down at his crotch to make sure he hasn't pissed himself. He hasn't and says thanks for small favors.

"Lowell!" Lu shouts as she appears at the doorway. "Lowell!"

"In here!" he cries. "Come on!"

An older woman covered in blood has her arm around Lu's shoulders and the two stumble inside. They get to Lowell, and Lu eases the woman to the floor.

"You okay?" she asks, following the woman down and collapsing next to Lowell.

"Yeah," Lowell says. "No piss."

Lu looks at him and raises an eyebrow then shakes her head. "Whatever. Where's Bolton?"

"Still out there," Lowell says.

"Shit," Lu says and starts to get up, but Lowell grabs her arm.

"No, you stay with her," he says. "I'll get him."

He forces himself to get up and stumbling runs to the entrance. Looking out at the chaos, Lowell almost loses the small amount of courage he was able to dig up.

There's no sight of anyone left alive. All that's left are corpses.

And the monsters that have landed to feed on the corpses.

He slowly crouches low and slinks down the stone steps, his eyes searching everywhere for a sign of Bolton, but the man is nowhere to be seen, not even as one of the bloody snacks the monsters are busy crunching on.

Despite every instinct in his body, he hisses, "Bolton."

He gets to the bottom of the steps and freezes, waiting for one of the things to notice him and decide that hors d'oeuvres are best when alive and squirming. But none pay him any attention. They are too busy gulping down torsos in one bite.

"What the fuck?" Bolton whispers as he grabs Lowell and yanks him down behind a pile of broken bricks just feet from the steps. "What are you doing?"

One of the monsters stops mid-gulp and swings its bulbous mess of a head towards where the two men hide. It swallows and keeps staring, but after a few seconds, it decides there's nothing of interest and looks about for another corpse to eat. It finds a particularly nicely mangled body and goes to grab it, but a second beast shrieks and snaps at it, hungry for the same corpse. The two creatures start to circle and howl at each other, neither willing to give up the tasty treat, their huge bodies destroying more of the city, sending bricks and stone crashing about.

"Now," Lowell mouths and tugs at Bolton's sleeve, nodding his head back towards the steps. "Move."

The two men stay low and hurry out from their hiding place. They rush to the steps and start to climb when they both notice that the sounds of crunching and munching, shrieking and bickering, have stopped.

Both freeze and look over their shoulders.

"Oh, fuck," Lowell says as they see nothing but black eyes pointed in their direction.

"Come on!" Bolton yells and yanks Lowell up the steps and into the building as a dozen winged monsters rush at them.

The whole building shudders as the beasts collide with the stone walls. Dust falls from the already cracked ceiling and plaster chunks crash down on the floor. Lowell and Bolton run towards Lu and both men yank her to her feet as they hurry past. Lu doesn't fight them and Lowell looks back to see the older woman lying there still, her eyes glazed and lifeless.

"We need to get deeper into the building!" Bolton shouts. "Try to find the basement!"

All three skid around a corner and stop, their stomachs rising into their throats.

"Ah, shit," Lowell says.

From the front, the building looked secure, but that was just a facade. Once around the corner, they see an entire wall and side of the building has collapsed out into a parking lot beyond. And in that parking lot, standing on the fallen stones and debris are another dozen monsters, all frozen mid chomp, their eyes locked onto Lowell, Lu, and Bolton.

"Stairs," Bolton says, seeing a door to their side. "Now!"

The monsters shriek, their mouths full of meat and bone, and lurch forward at the building.

***

Foam flicks from the horses' mouths as they push their muscled bodies to the extreme. Total fear drives them on and the riders can only grip the reins, hoping they aren't thrown from the saddles.

Dr. Probst, eyes wide open, screams at the top of her lungs as her horse takes her past Gil and Tiff and to the front of the stampeding group. But even screaming at full volume, her voice is lost in the discordance that fills the air.

The thousand foot monsters continue their lumbering, multi-legged march across the landscape, shaking trees loose from their roots, sending boulders falling from ridges, causing already unstable ground to split wider, creating fissures in the earth the horses barely maneuver around.

The world darkens even more and Kyle looks back over his shoulder to see the sky blocked from view by the pursuing behemoths. The things keep coming, their roars tearing at his eardrums, sending spikes of pain deep into his brain. He almost wishes he could lose control and just scream his head off like the doctor.

Gil turns his head towards Kyle and shouts something, but Kyle can't hear what he's saying. Taking a risk, Gil lets go of the reins with one hand and points towards a bend in the road up ahead. Kyle doesn't understand and shakes his head to indicate so. Gil frowns and points harder then makes a zigzag motion with his hand.

Kyle squints into the gloom and then sees what the man is trying to show him. A trail. Just before the road curves, there is a barely visible trail. It must have been the one the group originally came down off the mountain by. That means the bunker isn't too far away.

Even with the size of the creatures bearing down on them, Kyle clings to the hope that the bunker will still hold up and be the sanctuary they need. He nods enthusiastically and then realizes their problem.

The doctor. Her horse is ahead of the others and he has no idea how to get it pointed in the right direction.

He kicks his heels and spurs his horse faster, which is a feat unto itself considering the speed the animal is already going. His horse protests, but a luckily timed roar from half the monsters gets it moving and it gallops up to Dr. Probst and her horse.

"You have to turn him!" Kyle yells.

"WHAT?" Dr. Probst screams.

"YOU HAVE TO TURN HIM!" Kyle repeats, pointing up at the curve and the trail that has become more visible as they get closer. "WE HAVE TO GO UP THERE!"

Dr. Probst looks ahead then down at the reins in her hands. "Are you fucking nuts?"

"You don't have a choice!" Kyle yells. "The bunker is up there!"

"The fucker is where?" Dr. Probst shouts.

"No, the BUNKER! THE BUNKER is up there!"

"OH!" She shakes her head. "I can't steer this thing!"

"Just hold on tight with both hands!" Kyle says. "Then yank to the right when I say so! You have to yank hard! Got it? Yank hard!"

Kyle isn't sure if the doctor understands him or not, since she just keeps looking from where the trail is, and down to the reins in her hands, over and over.

"PAY ATTENTION!" Kyle shouts and a wave of sadness hits him as he realizes he sounds just like his grandma.

Dr. Probst finally stops her Rain Man act and nods at Kyle.

The curve gets closer and Kyle lowers his head as he leans his body down over his horse. He starts to count off in head, trying to figure out the timing of when he's going to yell at the doctor. The trees fly past him and he takes a deep breath.

"NOW!" he shouts and pulls hard on his horse's reins. The animal protests with a loud whinny, but is going so fast it can't stop or pull up. It changes its direction slightly and heads right for the trail.

Kyle looks over and is pleasantly surprised to see the doctor's horse is right behind his, same with Gil and Tiff's, as the ground switches from broken asphalt to cracked and loose earth. The horses slow slightly as the trail starts to climb and the land goes from level to a steady slope. But the animals' speed only decreases a small amount as they drive themselves madly forward up the trail and along the mountain.

More foam flicks from Kyle's horse's mouth and the animal's eyes are almost rolling in its head. He knows the horse doesn't have long before it pushes its body to collapse. Yet as much as he'd like to stop so the animal doesn't drop dead under him, he knows he has to keep it going as far as possible. Stopping means the monsters will catch up and Kyle doesn't want to think about what will happen then.

The trail twists into a switchback and Kyle is almost certain his horse is going to just jump off the side of the mountain, but it slows enough to follow the marked path and keep climbing.

Still heading up, but facing a new direction, gives Kyle a view he's not sure he wants to see. There before him are the monsters. Four legs each, they stomp through the forest, crushing everything in their way. Trees snap like toothpicks, boulders crack and turn to dust under their weight. The few birds left in the area cry out as they try to fly out of the way, but many are swatted to the ground by gargantuan hands, knocked out of the way like gnats.

The trail switches once more and Kyle is thankful he no longer has to stare at the abominations. Then he feels his horse stumble a bit and his heart leaps into his throat. The trail keeps going and going and Kyle's horse is struggling against the ever increasing incline. He can feel the thing under him start to shake uncontrollably and he knows it's not just fear making the animal quake. He leans forward and yells words of encouragement into the horse's ear, while patting the animal's neck over and over, but he has no idea if it makes a difference.

They make it to one more switch in the trail before the horse lets out a harsh cry and grunt. The poor thing's front legs collapse underneath it and in a split second, Kyle finds himself flying through the air as he's thrown over the horse's head. He slams into the trail and rolls a few feet before grabbing onto a small pine. He swallows hard as he realizes he is inches from rolling right off the trail and taking a nice hundred foot plunge down the mountain to the lower switchback.

"You okay?" Gil asks as all the horses pull up, the trail blocked by Kyle's suffering horse.

"Yeah, I'm fine," Kyle says as he gets to his feet. "But we can't stay here."

"No shit, kid," Gil says. "Climb on the doctor lady's horse and let's keep moving."

But in answer to that, Dr. Probst's horse snorts, coughs, and then sits down hard. Its eyes roll up in its head and it falls to the side, dead before it fully hits the ground. Dr. Probst is able to jump free and keep from being crushed, but it's Kyle that really saves her as he lunges forward and grabs her by the pack.

She stands at the edge of the trail, her arms out and eyes looking down at the drop as Kyle slowly pulls her back.

"You alright?" Kyle asks.

"No," she states bluntly. "I'd be fucking crazy if I was."

More roars get them focused again and Kyle pulls at the doctor as Gil and Tiff get down from their horses. They grab what gear they can, and start jogging up the trail, their exhausted bodies being pushed almost as hard as the poor horses they leave behind.

"How much further?" Dr. Probst asks.

"A couple miles," Gil replies.

"Oh, God," Dr. Probst says. "We'll never make it. They'll get us before then."

As they keep climbing, they take another switchback and are once again facing the giant monsters, but this time, they are close to shoulder level on the things.

"I can't understand them," Dr. Probst says, more to herself than to anyone around her. "They aren't possible."

"They look possible right now," Gil says. "Scary fucking possible."

In seconds, the beasts are parallel with the four terrified humans. Kyle focuses on the trail, but his whole body tenses, waiting for when they will be snatched from off the mountain and popped into a monster's mouth like a handful of peanuts. He laughs at the thought since the things' hands are so big, they wouldn't even come close to being considered a handful.

"What the hell could be funny right now?" Dr. Probst snaps. "This is no time to laugh."

"It's always time to laugh," Gil says. "Let the kid laugh. Could be his last."

Kyle stops laughing.

***

Lu huddles between Lowell and Bolton as they sit in the dank, dark basement of what they figure out is one of the city hall annexes. Above them, they hear the sounds of stones crashing down as the monsters rip at the walls to get in at them.

"Persistent fucks," Lowell says.

"We can't just wait here for the building to come down around us," Bolton says. "We need to figure a way out."

"Just kick back and relax, Sergeant Slaughter," Lowell says. "We aren't going anywhere. Might as well get comfortable, because this is where we die."

"We aren't going to die here," Lu says. "I refuse to die in a municipal basement with a criminal and an ex-boyfriend. We are getting out."

"Really? And how will we do that, Marshal Optimist?" Lowell laughs. He coughs as he chokes on a breath of dust that fills the air. "Slip up through the air ducts like in the movies? You realize that nowhere in the world are there buildings with air ducts big enough for real people to crawl through, right?"

"Yeah there are," Bolton says. "Been stuck in a few."

"Stuck, exactly," Lowell says, "because they weren't big enough!"

"No, because I had to wait three days before my target showed his face," Bolton says.

"Three days in an air duct? How'd you take a piss?" Lowell laughs.

"I held it for 36 hours," Bolton replies. "Then I went in my pants. I always take adult diapers on a long hide op."

"Bullshit," Lowell says. "You did not piss in your pants."

"I did," Bolton says. "Pretty common to do. The only problem is I couldn't move around after that. The piss smell would leak out and since I was in an air duct that meant someone would come looking for the source."

It's too dark in the basement for Bolton to see Lowell's face, but if he could, he would have seen the man shaking his head in a mixture of awe and disbelief.

The crashing from above grows louder and Lowell pounds his fists on the floor.

"What we need is a fucking airstrike to come in and kill those fucks," Lowell says. "But that's not happening."

The thought of an airstrike makes Bolton realize he's forgotten something very important during all of the chaos and running for their lives.

"Son of a bitch," Bolton says as he scoots away from the other two and starts unlacing one of his boots. "I'm a fucking moron."

He gets his boot off, and then grabs the heel. He carefully works a fingernail into one of the grooves and gives it a flick. That section of the hard rubber slides a fraction of a millimeter and he keeps at it until a small compartment in the heel is revealed. Bolton laughs and holds up a small black disc with a glowing red center.

"Here's our airstrike," Bolton says. "Well, not quite, but it could be our way to talk to the outside world."

"How is that mini Magic 8-Ball going to get us out of this basement?" Lowell asks as he watches the glow disappear when Bolton lowers his head to the disc.

"It's not," Bolton says. "But it does give us a reason to try."

"I already have a reason," Lowell says. "It's called staying alive."

"We're safer down here than out there," Lu says then crawls over to Bolton. "What is that?"

"Coordinate Locating Device," Bolton replies. "The CLD tells me where I need to go when all other forms of communication have been cut off."

"Great," Lowell says. "Where do you need to go?"

"Not a clue," Bolton says. "I need a map of the area in order to figure out where the longitude and latitudes of the location are."

"You don't have that shit memorized in that super soldier brain?" Lowell laughs. "Some hero you are."

"Shut up," Lu snaps. "I'm sick of your wise cracks."

"My wise cracks?" Lowell replies. "Gee, Officer Krupke, I'm so sorry for misbehaving."

"We need to find a map," Bolton says. "This is a municipal building, right? They have to have maps around here. Anyone see what offices this place holds?"

"Nope," Lowell says. "Missed that when running from the things trying to eat us."

"What are we going to find if we can get a map and then make it to the coordinates?" Lu asks. "Is it an extraction point?"

"No," Bolton says. "It'll be something they've airdropped. Should have a sat phone at the very least. Maybe supplies, if we get lucky."

"And you know how lucky I'm feeling right now," Lowell snorts.

Lu stands up and looks towards where the old stairs lead up to the first floor. "Let's get going."

"Whoa! Shouldn't we think this through?" Lowell protests. "If you listen very carefully you'll notice that our company hasn't left."

A massive crash punctuates his words.

"I doubt they're going to leave anytime soon," Lu says. "And I'm sick of waiting around. Let's find a map, figure out where we are going, and get the fuck out of here."

"Sounds like a plan," Bolton says and makes his way to Lu.

"That sounds like more of an outline," Lowell says, getting to his feet and following the other two to the stairs. "But, hey, I always thought I'd die in prison staring at three grey walls and a set of bars. Getting eaten during the flying monster apocalypse is a much cooler way to go out."

The three make their way carefully up the dark stairs, with Bolton taking point. He wishes they had weapons of some kind, but they lost everything on the streets of Coeur d'Alene fighting the monsters. Not that the bullets did any good. They might as well have been throwing rocks.

"That way," Bolton whispers, pointing down the dark hallway as he pushes open the stairwell door. "See if you can find a directory, something to tell us what offices are here."

Bolton watches the space in the building where there should be a wall, but is nothing but open air looking out onto the hellish street beyond. The monsters have stopped attacking the building and are back to concentrating on cleaning up the streets, their giant mouths hungrily gobbling up every corpse they can find.

Bolton swallows hard as he backs up the way Lu and Lowell went, his eyes never leaving the nightmare. He can't stop himself from staring as one of the monsters tears a man's arms off with its two front legs, and then tosses the meat into its open, multi-toothed mouth. He can almost swear that the thing is smiling and happy as a dog with a bone.

Then it stops chewing and looks towards the building. Its black eyes bore right into Bolton and it instantly reminds him of a mission that almost went very wrong when he and his team found themselves in the middle of nearly fifty sharks down in the South Pacific. The monster's black eyes are just like a shark's, nothing but predatory hunger and violence.

With half an arm hanging from between its teeth, the thing turns and lumbers over to the building, its neck stretching as it gets closer and closer. Bolton doesn't move. He freezes up against the wall, his pulse rate skyrocketing.

"Connor?" Lu whispers as she starts to come back around the corner to find Bolton.

"Stop," Bolton hisses. "Stay right there."

At the sound of his voice, the creature growls low, making Bolton's balls want to crawl up into his stomach. The thing lowers its head and extends its neck as it gets to the building. Bolton watches in terror as the monster's head gets closer and closer, filling most of the hallway with a stench of sulfur and rotted meat.

Another growl, this one much louder, tests the strength of Bolton's bladder, but the soldier doesn't budge from the wall. Foot by foot, the beast pushes its head and neck into the building and Bolton can see that the thing doesn't have nostrils so much as a row of pits along its upper lip, similar to a lot of snakes he's seen. Are the monsters reptiles of some sort? Do they have the same cold-blooded characteristics? Bolton makes a mental note not to forget that observation.

The head stops only a meter from Bolton and only his years of training keep him from running screaming.

Bolton's eyes are on the creature's eyes and they stare, a stalemate of species. He studies the thing's body, how its neck is almost snake like, how the wings seem to fold into the beast's back as if they could be tucked away and hidden, how it doesn't seem to breathe, or at least Bolton can't feel a breath on him or see the monster's chest moving like it would with normal respiration.

But it has lungs enough to produce an earsplitting shriek as its head lunges towards Bolton without warning.

"Move!" Lowell yells as he pushes Bolton out of the way, a fire axe in his hands.

The monster's head comes right for him and Lowell brings the axe down with all of his strength, the blade hitting the beast right on the snout. It rocks back and howls, but for all Lowell and Bolton can see, the axe did nothing but piss it off.

"Title office!" Lowell yells, grabbing Bolton's arm and pulling him around the corner. "Maps! Lots of maps!"

"I got one of the whole region!" Lu yells as she comes rushing from an office up ahead. "As long as whatever it is, is in Idaho, Eastern Washington, or Western Montana, then we are good!"

The building shakes as the monster shoves its whole body inside and giant claws lash out, splitting the floor right where Lowell and Bolton had been standing.

"Go!" Bolton yells, waving Lu on. "Run!"

Plaster falls everywhere and the building shudders and takes a lurch to the left as the monster rips apart the hallway behind them, its body too big for the narrow space. Walls crack and collapse and Bolton can actually see the building start to sag around them, its structural integrity beyond compromised.

"There! That window!" Bolton yells as he points ahead of them towards the end of the hallway and a large double window.

He grabs the axe from Lowell, not missing a step, and cocks it over his shoulder as they race at the window. Just as they reach it, Bolton brings down the axe, shattering the surprisingly intact glass, and he lowers his shoulder and leaps through. Shards of glass tear at his clothes and he feels cut after cut along his arms and back. Lowell and Lu are yelling at the top of their lungs as they leap after. They all find themselves in a narrow alleyway between buildings.

"Oh, God," Lu says as she looks at the mouth of the alleyway. "What is that?"

"Bodies," Lowell says. "Looks like our winged overlords are stashing corpses as a snack for later."

Bolton looks behind them and sees nothing but trash cans and a three story brick wall. He hefts the axe and turns back to the wall of bodies that blocks their way out.

"Only one way through," he says as he steps up to the bodies and starts cutting.

He hacks and whacks at the corpses, sending offal and blood flying everywhere. Limbs come loose and tumble at his feet while bloated bellies burst, spilling putrid guts onto the dank concrete. Bolton tries not to gag, but his gorge won't obey and his vomit joins the puddle of yuck that stands an inch around his boots.

"My turn," Lowell says, taking the axe from Bolton, letting the man turn away from the rotten entrails and give in to the heaving that threatens to knock him to his knees.

The thought of falling into the blood and guts around him is all that keeps Bolton up on his feet.

"Clear enough," Lu says as she reaches past Lowell and starts pulling at bodies with her hands. "Up and over."

The wall behind them explodes outward and the flying monster's head whips around the alleyway, taking a second to search for them before zeroing on their location with those cold, black eyes.

"You first," Lowell says and gives Lu a shove. She doesn't argue and clambers up over the pile of corpses. "You too."

Bolton shakes his head and points at the pile, but Lowell just frowns.

"Dude, get going," Lowell says. "Don't leave the marshal all alone out on that street."

The monster darts its head forward, but its shoulders are still held back by the building. It roars at Lowell as Bolton makes his escape.

"Fuck you," Lowell says and throws the axe as hard as he can at the beast. But the blade just bounces off the monster's thick skin and ricochets right at Lowell. He dives out of the way, but realizes too late that he dove the wrong way and is now closer to the monster. The thing opens its mouth wide and comes for Lowell so fast that the man doesn't even have a second to think, he just acts.

His hand falls on something and Lowell instinctively grabs it and throws it at the attacking monster. Turns out to be a woman's lower leg and Lowell watches in amazement as the monster's jaws clamp shut the second the hunk of meat hits its wide, blue tongue.

"No yo yo tongue in you, huh?" Lowell mutters as he watches the monster chew and swallow quickly. "Oh, shit."

Lowell turns and grabs up every stray limb he can, pushes up to his feet, and starts chucking the body parts at the monster. The creature wants to get at Lowell, but it can't help itself and snatches the arms and legs, feet and hands, out of the air as they come flying at its maw.

His feet moving slowly backwards, Lowell keeps his eyes glued on the monster, making sure he keeps a steady stream of bloody bits and gory pieces headed right at the thing. He doesn't stop throwing until his ass hits what's left of the pile.

"There you are," Bolton says, grabbing Lowell's shoulder and pulling him up and over the pile and out onto the street. "Stop playing with thing and let's go!'

Lowell is about to snap at Bolton, but sees the smirk on his face and just nods. Then the pile of corpses bursts around them as the monster follows Lowell from the alleyway, its bulk tearing chunks of stone from the corners of the two buildings it squeezes out from.

"Fuck off!" Lowell yells and throws the last limb he holds.

He watches as the arm flies end over end and wants to kick himself as he sees what's gripped in the dead hand: a pistol. And it looks like a good sized one.

"Fucking Desert Eagle," Bolton says. "That may have been useful."

"Too late now," Lowell says as he and the sergeant turn to run, but stop as they realize that all the commotion has made them the number one attraction in Coeur d'Alene.

"We can't outrun them," Lu says, her hand out towards Bolton. The man takes it and she looks over at him. "This is it."

Lowell steps up and takes Lu's other hand as the flying monsters all rear up on their six legs and tower over the three humans. Lu looks down at her and Lowell's hands, grimaces and then nods. He nods back and they face their death head on, eyes open, heads tilted towards the beasts that have taken everything from them.

There's a shriek from behind them and Lowell finally closes his eyes, waiting for the chomp that will swallow him whole. Then the shriek turns into a howl which turns into a gurgle and a thick, wet cough.

Lowell opens his eyes and sees that the street of monsters has turned their attention to their fellow beast. He risks a look over his shoulder and can't help but smile as he sees what's happening.

"Bolton," Lowell says. "Check it out, dude."

Bolton tears his eyes from the monsters in front of them and looks back at the one halfway out of the alley. Grey foamy gunk leaks from the holes above the monster's lip and then from between its misshapen teeth. Bolton knows that foam, and he tugs on Lu's hand.

"Time to move out of the way," Bolton says and pulls Lu to the side with him.

Lowell, on the other side of Lu, follows, but makes sure his movements are slow and deliberate, not wanting to take away from the choking and gagging monster that has all the other beasts' attention.

They get a couple yards away when the monster let's out the loudest shriek yet and then freezes, its head and neck stretched taut. Then that head and neck explode from the rest of the body as the grey foam bursts out of the monster's neck hole, solidifying as it spurts into the air. The foam comes down onto the street and tumbles to the feet of the other monsters and Lowell is surprised to see the giant beasts actually take a step back from the gunk.

"This way," Bolton says and leads them down a street away from the monsters. "We need to get the fuck out of here and find a place where I can study the map."

"I like the getting the fuck out of here part," Lowell says. "I have no idea what help the map will be, but I don't give a shit. Lead on, Captain America."

"Knock it off with the nicknames," Lu snaps.

"Got it," Lowell nods. "No nicknames."

Behind them, all of the winged monsters howl and shriek so loud that the three escapees can almost feel the air thicken with the sounds. They don't look back as they sprint down the street, dodging the destruction around them, their goal to get as far away from Coeur d'Alene as possible before even thinking of stopping.

ELEVEN

"What is this place?" Dr. Probst asks as Gil lights a candle and leads the group down a long concrete tunnel towards a set of double doors set into a granite wall.

"We think it was some abandoned military storage facility," Gil says. "Moss and I found it a few years back and started loading it up with supplies, ready in case the Muslims invaded us again."

"Seriously?" Kyle asks. "You really thought that Muslims would invade the US?"

"What do you mean by again?" Dr. Probst says. "Please don't tell me you count 911 as an invasion."

"I ain't ruling anything out," Gil says. "But you should be thankful Moss and I did what we did. Otherwise, you'd still be out there with those things."

Dust falls around them as they still feel the ground tremor from the monsters that raced past the mountainside.

"Why'd they take off like that?" Kyle asks, turning to look at Dr. Probst.

"I don't know," Dr. Probst replies. "I missed the lecture on giant fucking monsters when I was getting my PhD."

"They have that?" Tiff asks, looking at the doctor.

"No," Dr. Probst replies, not bothering to hide her contempt.

"Don't need to be a snooty bitch," Tiff frowns.

"In we go," Gil says as he holds open one of the double doors and ushers the rest inside. "Tiff, go see who's here and let them know what happened."

Tiff picks up a candle from a basket set on a stool by the door, lights it off of Gil's, then hurries off into the darkness of the huge space before them.

"There's more to it than this," Gil says, seeing the look on Dr. Probst's face. "Right, kid? Tell her."

"Yeah, there's more than this," Kyle says. "There's a place they'll tie you up and interrogate you for hours."

"We had to be sure you weren't dangerous," Gil says. "And I'd say your pop was."

"He wasn't my pop," Kyle says, his voice exhausted.

"Whatever he was, he was dangerous as all hell," Gil says. "I'm hoping you didn't fall from the same tree."

"Whatever," Kyle says.

"Is there a restroom?" Dr. Probst asks. "I kinda need to, well, uh, use the facilities."

"You need to clean the shit outta your pants, right?" Gil smiles. "Gonna be doing some of that too." Dr. Probst gives him an embarrassed smile and he nods towards the side of the space. "Follow me."

They walk to a set of doors and Gil pushes them open, showing a small hallway with several doors along the opposite wall.

There's another stool with candles on it across from them and Gil lights one. Then he hands it to Dr. Probst.

"Fourth door down," he says, pointing to the right. "Want me to take that pack?"

"No, no, I'll take it with me," she smiles. "I think it may have a change of clothes inside. They may be wet, but they won't be...soiled."

"Right, yeah," Gil replies. "Oh, and try not to use too much toilet paper. That's the one thing Moss and I didn't get enough of. At least for all the people that ended up here." He sighs and rubs his face. "Guess there's a lot less now. God rest their souls."

"Sorry about everyone," Dr. Probst says. "I lost several colleagues when the EMP knocked our jet out of the air."

"Your government jet." Gil nods towards the door. "Hurry up, so we can get down to business."

"Down to business?" Dr. Probst asks.

"Yeah, so you can tell us what the government is doing," Gil says. He glances over at Kyle. "I may not be the Fed's biggest fan, but I wouldn't mind some of those fighter jets that my tax dollars paid for to come and blast the creatures right off the face of this here Earth, thank you very much."

Dr. Probst doesn't reply, just nods back at him and pushes the bathroom door open. She steps into the darkness and lets the door close. Then she turns and presses her ear up against and listens. She can hear Gil and Kyle talking, but their voices are very faint. She steps away from the door and studies the small bathroom. Two stalls and a sink is all there is, but Dr. Probst doesn't care. She's not here to shit, but to get some privacy so she can do what she has to.

"This better work," she says as she steps into the last stall and pulls Coletti's CLD from her pocket.

She takes off her pack and riffles through it, her hands blindly searching for the sat phone. Once she finds it, she almost clutches it to her chest like a lost child, desperate to make sure it's real and not some fantasy her mind has made to help her cope.

After a few deep breaths,s she listens hard, doesn't hear anything from outside the bathroom, presses the CLD to the sat phone, and waits.

***

"Mr. President?" a tech says. "Incoming call, sir."

"Lieutenant Coletti?" President Nance asks.

"No, sir, it's a Dr. Probst," the tech replies.

Everyone at the table frowns and all eyes turn to the president.

"Dr. Probst?" President Nance answers. "Where is Lieutenant Coletti? Why isn't he calling?"

"Coletti is dead," Dr. Probst replies. The tension in the room doubles at the words. "But that's not the problem, sir."

"That damn well is a problem," Admiral Quigley barks. "Coletti was a good man and a hero to this nation. You will do well to speak about him with more respect, Doctor!"

"I know *exactly* how much of a hero Coletti was!" Dr. Probst snaps. "The man saved my life and the lives of others. He took on a madman so we could get away."

"A madman?" President Nance asks. "What the hell is going on there?"

"Never mind," Dr. Probst sighs. "What I meant by Coletti's death not being the problem isn't because it's not tragic, because it is. It's because the missiles didn't work, Mr. President. The flying ones grabbed them and dropped them into the hole."

"We know, Doctor," President Nance replies. "We were able to retrieve camera feeds from some of those missiles."

Dr. Probst can tell that the president is holding back important information. You don't get to the level she has in her profession without learning how to read men's voices. She'd need a hundred hands and feet to count how many times she's been shut out of vital research findings by that misogynistic tone.

"Sir? What did you see?" Dr. Probst asks. "Did you witness the missiles detonate? Because we didn't see any signs that they blew, sir."

"No, Doctor, they did not detonate," President Nance replies. "But that is all I can say on the subject. Where are you now?"

"Safe," Dr. Probst says. "Or as safe as I can be. I found some other survivors and they took me back with them to their bunker."

"Bunker?" President Nance says, looking at General Azoul. "Is it a military bunker?" He flicks his finger across his throat and the tech mutes the connect. "What bunkers do we have in that area, General?"

"Outside Missoula?" General Azoul asks. "Probably quite a few. I'll have a list pulled up so we can narrow down her location."

"Good," President Nance says. He gives a thumbs up and the transmission is taken off mute. "Dr. Probst? You still there?"

"Where am I going to go? Yeah, I'm still here," she responds. "Sir, with all due respect, you need to tell me what you saw in that hole. Any information you have could give me insight into what we are dealing with."

"Dr. Probst, I highly doubt you will be able to help us with what we saw," President Nance says. "Unless you are a, what do you call it?"

"Cryptozoologist," Joan says, her eyes rolling with contempt for the word. "And we have one on the way."

There are few sneers and smirks at the table, but no one voices their misgivings. President Nance glares at them and everyone returns to their former stoic looks.

"Is there anything else you can tell us, Doctor?" President Nance asks.

"Probably nothing you can help me with, sir," she responds. "Unless you happen to be a cryptozoologist."

The president clenches his fists at the slight, but keeps his temper in check.

"That's cute, Doctor," President Nance grumbles. "If that is all then we have pressing business to get back to."

"Is anyone going to come get me?" Dr. Probst asks. "Because that would be really great if they could."

"As much as we'd like to, Doctor," President Nance says. "We cannot get anyone to you in less than a day. And even then, since you aren't exactly sure where you are, we can't afford to send troops on a wild goose chase."

"Well, you should figure out how," Dr. Probst says. "Especially since I've actually seen the hole first hand as Coletti and I parachuted over it. I have some valuable information into its geological formation and composition."

"If you have information, then you are duty bound to share it with us, Doctor," President Nance states. "This is not the time for bargaining!"

"Not the time for you, maybe," Dr. Probst says. "But it's the perfect time for me."

"Doctor, I'm warning you-"

"Oh, cram it up your ass, Mr. President," Dr. Probst snaps. "I want the fuck out of here and if you want the information I have, you are going to need to figure out how to get me out of here!"

President Nance is silent for a few seconds, before saying, "Hold on, Doctor."

He motions again for the call to be muted and the tech gives him a nod when it is.

"Tell me you have an idea where she's at, General?" President Nance says.

"I do, sir," General Azoul replies. "There's an old special munitions storage bunker that matches the coordinates her sat phone is giving off."

"We can send in a team to get her," Admiral Quigley says. "But it's still going to be..."

He looks at an aide that stands a few feet back from where he's seated.

"Twelve hours, sir," the aide says.

"Twelve hours," Admiral Quigley says. "But these are not men I want to risk losing, sir. She better be worth it."

"Yes, she better," President Nance agrees, nodding to the com tech. "Dr. Probst? The soonest we can have someone there is twelve hours."

"Jesus," Dr. Probst sighs. "Fine. Do whatever it takes. Can you find me from this sat phone?"

"We can, Doctor," President Nance says. "I hope the information you have is worth risking men's lives for you."

"I think so," Dr. Probst says. "And to show I'm not the most selfish person in the world, I'll tell you what else I know."

"What's that, Doctor?"

"That the big ones are on the move," she replies. "Six of them took off this way and trampled Missoula on a mad dash away from that hole. Could be related to whatever you think you saw or not, but those things wanted as far away from that place as possible. They could have given two craps about us little humans. They just wanted to be gone."

Everyone seated at the long table look up at the many monitors that surround them. They find the monitor that's replaying the missile video feeds on a loop and stare at the undulating mass that lies at the bottom of the huge hole.

"Yes, I believe they do want away from the hole, Doctor," President Nance replies. "Will it be a problem getting away from where you are? Can you slip out in twelve hours without the others seeing?"

"Wait...what?" Dr. Probst asks. "You're going to leave these people here?"

"Do you want to be rescued or not, Doctor?" President Nance asks. "Because I am sending a team to extract you, not everyone you are with. Is that understood?" There is silence for couple of seconds. "Dr. Probst? Are you still there?"

"Yes, Mr. President," Dr. Probst says. "And yes, I think I can get away."

"Good," President Nance replies. "In twelve hours, you'll want to slip away from the others and make sure that sat phone is with you. It's how the team will know you're the one to extract. Understood?"

"Understood, sir," Dr. Probst replies.

"Good," President Nance says. "I look forward to seeing you in person, Doctor, and hearing what you have to say."

He motions for the com to be cut completely and then settles into his chair, his eyes looking about the table.

"Where the hell is that cryptozoologist? We need someone to at least tell us what we could be looking at," President Nance says, his eyes also drawn to the monitor with the missile video feed. "I know some of you are laughing, but I don't see we have much choice in the matter."

"Damn eggheads are holding us hostage," General Tulane says. "Are we sure we can't solve this using the nuclear option? We have silos waiting for the launch orders, Mr. President."

President Nance looks over at Joan and she shakes her head. "The fallout would spread across the world. We launch nukes and every friendly country will close their borders to us, sir. We wouldn't just be burning bridges, we'd be nuking them. And we can't lose a single bridge when we have a couple hundred million American refugees we have to secure homes for."

"No nukes," President Nance says to the general. "Not yet, at least."

"Mr. President," Borland exclaims, joining the argument. "Not ever. You have to take the option off the table."

"I'm not taking any option off the table, Jeremy," President Nance says. "Not now, not ever. We do not know what we are dealing with here and if I have to launch a nuclear strike on these *things* then that is what I'll do!"

***

Dr. Probst screams as she steps out from the stall to find Gil standing right there.

"Calling your mom? Your boyfriend?" Gil growls. "Or was that the President of the United States you were talking to? Anything you want to share?"

"They're, uh, sending a team to get us," Dr. Probst says.

"Yeah, I don't think they are," Gil sneers. "I think they're sending a team to get you and leave our asses here."

He grabs the doctor by the arm and yanks her towards the bathroom door. The candle in his other hand shakes then sputters out, leaving them in darkness. She takes that opportunity to rip free of his grasp and lash out, throwing punches wildly. Several connect and Gil cries out as he's knocked aside.

Dr. Probst runs towards where she thinks the door is. Her outstretched hands smack into it and she fumbles for the handle. She manages to get the door open just as Gil slams into her back, instantly closing it again. The doctor whirls around and rakes her fingernails down his face, tearing gouges in his skin. The man screams and stumbles back. Dr. Probst doesn't waste any time, rips the door open and bursts out into the hallway.

"What the hell?" Kyle cries as she rams right into him. "Are you okay?"

Dr. Probst has a split second to decide what she's going to do.

"You have to get us out of here," Dr. Probst says. "Can you do that?"

"I don't know," Kyle says. "Maybe. I think I can figure out the way."

Gil's pained howling makes him look towards the bathroom.

"What happened?"

"You aren't with them, right? They found you and your dad?" She holds up a hand before he can protest. "I don't know the guy's name, so I'm just going to keep calling him your dad, got it?"

"Fine, whatever," Kyle says. The bathroom door starts to open and Dr. Probst turns and kicks it in as hard as she can. There's a loud cry, then a shuffle and a thud, followed by complete silence. "Jesus."

Kyle moves to the bathroom and pushes open the door slightly, shining his candle inside. He sees the unconscious form of Gil lying on the stained and dirty floor.

"Damn," Kyle says. "You knocked him out. We better gag him and tie him up before we try to escape. If he wakes up and we're anywhere close to this place, they'll find us."

Dr. Probst hesitates then nods.

"So you're with me on this?" she asks. "You didn't bond with these nutjobs, did you?"

"Moss was okay," Kyle says as he pulls her out of the bathroom and closes the door. "He said they were just messing with us and not really a militia." He looks down at the bloody faced Gil. "But I don't think he knew his friend as well as he thought he did."

"Or he was feeding you a line of bullshit so you'd trust him," Dr. Probst suggests.

Kyle stares at her in the candlelight then shakes his head. "Yeah, maybe," he says. "Guess I trust too much. My grandma always said that. She was constantly telling me I can't talk to strangers whenever I want. Because sometimes people may be strangers to us, but we may not be strangers to them."

"What does that mean?" Dr. Probst asks.

"Long story," Kyle says.

"Well, tell me part of it while we get him tied up," she says. "You can tell me the rest when we get out of here and are getting down the mountain."

"What about those things outside?" Kyle asks.

"I don't think they are what we need to worry about right now," Dr. Probst says. "Whatever they were running from is the real problem."

"What's that?" Kyle asks.

"I don't have a clue," Dr. Probst. "I doubt anyone does." She helps shift Gil's body to the side then gasps. "No…"

"What?" Kyle asks and moves the candle closer.

"This," she says, holding up a cracked and broken sat phone.

"Sat phones can be run over by a truck without breaking," Kyle says. "That shouldn't happen."

"Welcome to government work, kid," Dr. Probst says. "Where the shouldn't is always possible."

***

"Can you give me some context?" Doctor Blane Hall asks, his eyes glued to the monitor. "I mean, that's not something you see everyday. What scale am I looking at?"

"Ten miles across," Borland replies, the Secretary of Defense, as well as the rest of the cabinet and Joint Chiefs, all watching as the cryptozoologist stands in front of the bank of monitors. "That's our best guess. The chasm itself is 200 miles across."

"What are they?" Joan asks. "Can you identify them at all?"

"Are you joking?" Dr. Hall chuckles. "Can I identify a writhing mass of something that's ten miles across?"

"Can you tell us if we are looking at one creature or multiple creatures?" Admiral Quigley asks.

The video feed loops over and over and Dr. Hall watches it again and again.

"Dr. Hall?" President Nance asks, clearing his throat loudly enough to interrupt the man's thoughts. "Is it just one or multiple? If you are going to be in this room, you need to answer the questions that are posed to you."

"What? Oh, right, sorry," Dr. Hall replies. Average height, average weight bordering on pudgy, with short blond hair and deep brown eyes hidden behind thick glasses, the man looks from the monitors and over to the President of the United States. "I have no idea."

"Then why are you even here?" General Azoul snaps. "You aren't even a real doctor!"

"That's not true," Dr. Hall says. "I actually have many PhDs. I'm a zoologist, ethnobotonist, anthropologist, as well as a cryptozoologist, xenoarcheologist and senior researcher and fellow at SETI."

"Dear Lord," Admiral Azoul says. "He's a Sagan nut."

"You're looking at a nest," Dr. Hall says, his eyes locked onto General Azoul's. "Would you like to know what kind of nest I think it is?"

"That's why you are here, Dr. Hall," President Nance says, looking from the man to the general. "I am sure General Azoul would like to hear as well, wouldn't you, General?"

"I'm all ears," General Azoul replies. "Please tell us what your best guess is."

"Snakes," Dr. Hall says. "It looks like a nest of vipers to me."

"Ten miles across?" Borland asks. "That's not possible."

"If it was in the realm of the possible," Dr. Hall says, turning back to the monitors. "Then you would have called a zookeeper and not me." He stretches and yawns. "I'm going to need a macchiato, two tuna fish sandwiches on wheat, a bag of kettle chips, barbecue preferably, and an apple."

The table is silent until Joan finally stands up and walks over to the man. She studies the images for a minute then turns to Dr. Hall and smiles. "Any specific type of apple?"

"Whatever isn't mealy," Dr. Hall replies. "I can't eat mealy apples."

"Ms. Milligan? You aren't actually going to humor this crackpot are you?" General Azoul snaps, ignoring the glare from the president. "I've seen this before and he's playing us. He'll give us just enough information so we keep him safe down here. In the end, we'll get no useful intel and we'll be right back where we started."

"I'll bet you're a water boarding fan," Dr. Hall says without looking away from the monitors. "Do whatever it takes to get what you need to know, right? I'll save you the trouble, General Azoul, was it? You think I want to drag this out so I can be safe down here?"

He points at the monitor and then turns to look at the general.

"If that is what I think it is, and those things are as big as they look, then there is no safe place left on this planet," Dr. Hall says. "So before I die, I'd like a macchiato, some tuna fish sandwiches, a bag of chips and an apple."

"Not mealy," Joan says.

"Not mealy," Dr. Hall nods. "And every bit of video you have on this hole. I need all of the data right now."

***

"Were you really talking to the president?" Kyle asks as he and Dr. Probst slowly make their way from one concrete corridor to the next.

"You were listening?" Dr. Probst asks.

"As soon as you went into the bathroom, Gil started eavesdropping," Kyle answers. "I followed him and we heard everything."

"Great, just great," Dr. Probst says. "Yes, I was talking with the President of the United States."

"You said you had information about the hole," Kyle presses. "What was it?"

They keep walking and Kyle looks about the dark corridor, his eyes looking for landmarks. Instead, he just sees more old, cracked concrete. They must have really built the bunker to withstand a lot considering the way the earthquakes from the hole demolished all of Missoula and tore up the whole countryside, but the bunker is still standing fine. Kyle has to wonder if leaving with the doctor is such a great idea. At least the bunker is secure.

"If I'm not telling the POTUS what the info is then I'm sure not telling some teenage kid I just met," Dr. Probst replies.

"I'm not with these guys," Kyle says. "I was taken prisoner by them when they found me and Linder."

"Linder?" Dr. Probst asks.

"The guy you keep calling my dad," Kyle explains. "Which he isn't."

"Right, you've made that clear," Dr. Probst says. "Why'd they take you?"

"They found us fighting in the woods," Kyle answers. "Linder was beating the crap out of me and Gil and some of the others stopped him. Once they found out he was FBI, Gil went a little nuts and started spouting all this anti-government stuff. He knocked out Linder and took us back here."

"And that's it?" Dr. Probst asks. "That Linder guy wasn't looking too good. Looked like they did more than just knock him out."

"They beat him for a while," Kyle shrugs. "Thinking they'd get intel or something out of him. Gil kept saying he thought this whole volcano thing was a government conspiracy. Linder wouldn't play along so they kept beating on him."

"Why take you with them to Missoula?" Dr. Probst asks.

"I don't really know," Kyle says. "I think Gil might have wanted to leave Linder there or something."

"Why not just kill him?"

"You know what? I don't have a goddamn clue why anyone does anything," Kyle snaps. "No one has ever told me the whys, they've only told me the whats. What to do, what to say, what not to say, what place is safe, what place isn't, what the warning signs are if we're spotted, what to do when I see those warning signs. The whats. Never the whys."

"When you are spotted? What does that mean?" Dr. Probst asks.

"Never mind," Kyle says. "It doesn't matter. You have your secrets and I get to have mine."

"Fair enough," she replies. "Don't ask me for my answers and I won't ask you for yours." She stops and grabs Kyle's arm. "Do you know where we're going?"

Kyle looks around, sticks out his chest, starts to speak and then looks around and stops.

"No," he says, shaking his head. "I thought I did, but this place is a lot bigger than I thought."

"Let's try this way," Dr. Probst says. "And hope we don't run into anyone." She smacks the pack on her back and sighs. "They didn't drop any weapons for us and it doesn't look like your crazy militia friends trusted you enough to even give you a .22."

"They aren't my friends," Kyle says.

"And Linder wasn't your dad," Dr. Probst says. "I know. It was a joke. You need to lighten up, kid."

"Don't call me kid," Kyle says, then smiles as Dr. Probst is about to respond.

"Ha ha," Dr. Probst smirks. "Here's another corridor. Maybe it leads to the backdoor."

***

"Hold on, hold on," Bolton says, grabbing Lu's arm as they crest the same ridge they'd been on before when they were first looking down on Coeur d'Alene. "Let me get my bearings. I don't have a compass and I need to figure out which way is which before we take off."

"You have a map," Lowell says. "Won't that tell you where we are?"

"You were never a Boy Scout, were you?" Bolton laughs as he looks about the landscape, his eyes studying the few features he can see in the gloomy, ashen light."

"Not my gig," Lowell says.

"But your father was military. Right?" Bolton asks.

"You know what? Instead of talking about me, how about you get those bearings and figure out which way to go, Magellan."

"Knock it off, boys," Lu says. "Or I'll have to separate you two."

"Sorry, Mom," Lowell says as he plops down on the ridge, lays back, and closes his eyes. A shriek from above causes him to jump right back up. "Ok, no more bullshit, which way?"

"You aren't going to like which way we have to go," Bolton says, his eyes going from the map to the land that stretches east, and then to Lu.

"That way?" Lowell says. "You realize there are more of those things that way, right? That being the way they came from."

"Doesn't matter," Bolton says. "It's the way we need to go." He taps at the map. "We don't have a choice. I have to find whatever was airdropped. It's my job."

"Yeah, it's your job," Lowell says. "Not mine."

"Kyle is north," Lu states, her eyes fixed on Bolton. "We didn't see any sign of the Champion buses. They must not have made it to Idaho."

"I know," Bolton says. "But that's a pretty optimistic view, Lu. They could be anywhere. Right now, though, I have to get to these coordinates. I understand if you need to head north. Don't worry about me, I'll be fine."

"Oh, great!" Lu snaps. "As long as you're fine, then everything is okay!"

"Lu, like I said, this is my job," Bolton replies. "This is what I do. I have to head east and find whatever it is I'm supposed to find. I don't have a choice."

"There's always a choice," Lu sneers. "I made mine seventeen years ago and haven't regretted it once. You didn't have to make that choice. I did."

Bolton watches, completely puzzled. "Are you talking about Kyle? Having him? You didn't have to, no one would have judged you for terminating that pregnancy. Not after what Linder did to you."

"Linder? Who's Linder?" Lowell asks. "What'd he do to you?"

"You need to shut the fuck up and walk away," Lu says. "In fact, how about we call things even and you go your way and I'll go mine."

"What's this?" Lowell smiles. "The uber tough Marshal Morgan is going to let me just go free? And here I thought being in your custody meant something. Now I find out I'm no better than an unwanted dog you leave by the side of the road."

"Not even close," Lu says. "I'd never leave a poor dog by the side of the road. You? Yes. As of this moment, you are free to die alone wherever and however you want."

"Don't deflect and change the subject," Bolton says. "What the hell are you talking about, Lu? I thought you didn't have any doubts about keeping Kyle?"

"I didn't," Lu says. "I've never had doubts. That...that wasn't the choice."

"Yeah, I'm totally confused," Bolton says. He smacks the map with the back of his hand. "I have to go, Lu. Are you coming or not?"

"I have to find Kyle," Lu says. "You have to find Kyle. It can't end like this."

"Goddammit!" Bolton roars and he's answered by several shrieks from above. The three move closer to a stand of fir trees.

Bolton gets himself under control and faces Lu full on. "Talk to me. Tell me what you mean. If keeping Kyle wasn't the choice, what was?"

"Telling you the truth," Lu says. "Telling you about Kyle."

"Man, I wish I had some popcorn right now," Lowell says as he takes a seat on a rock close to one of the fir trees.

"Fuck you," Lu snaps.

"Last chance, Lu," Bolton says. "After this sentence I'm leaving. What truth are you talking about?"

"Dude, you don't know?" Lowell says. "I figured it out like two sentences ago."

Bolton ignores him and keeps staring at Lu.

"The truth is," Lu says. "Kyle isn't Linder's son, he's yours."

"Bam," Lowell says. "I knew it!"

Bolton takes a step back and shakes his head.

"No, you said you were raped by Linder," Bolton responds. "You said Kyle was his. And the guy was a psycho. A connected psycho that would stop at nothing to get to Kyle. That's why you had your mom take him. That's why they've been in hiding for all these years."

"Those are some of the reasons," Lu says. "Linder did rape me, but I was already pregnant. Kyle is yours. I was going to tell you, but after what Linder did, I just couldn't."

"Why, Lu? Why wouldn't you tell me something like that?"

"Because I didn't think you'd believe me that Kyle was yours," Lu says. "I figured you'd always think Kyle could be Linder's. And you know the man is crazy. He thought he owned me. It took all of my mother's connections to keep that man from getting to me while I was pregnant. I was able to keep my job as a marshal by saying I'd given Kyle up for adoption. If he knew you were the father, he would have killed you out of spite. He couldn't have me, he couldn't have Kyle, so he would have killed you."

"I can handle myself," Bolton laughs. "Special Forces and all that shit."

"Not with Linder," Lu says. "You have no idea how hard those first few years were. It's why Kyle thinks he and my mother are in witpro. He thinks that someone I put away a long time ago has been hunting my family as revenge."

Lu throws her hands up in the air.

"I'm a fucking US Marshal and my life is nothing but lies!"

"Why didn't you ever tell me?" Bolton asks. "All those times I met Kyle and you for camping trips and you never said a word. I thought I was being some noble guy looking out for my old girlfriend and her rape bastard. Turns out I had my son in a sleeping bag right next to me the whole time. Not cool, Lu."

"You think I don't know that?" Lu snaps. "I have lived with this for seventeen years. Now the truth comes out and I can't even tell Kyle myself. Linder is after him and my mom and I'm stuck here, no way of knowing if they are alive or dead."

"Wait? What?" Bolton asks. "Linder found them?"

"He used the chaos of the volcano to somehow track them down," Lu says. "He was following them when the convoy left Champion. I...I haven't heard anything since the gas station when you and your men joined us. I don't know what's going on." Tears well up in her eyes and she chokes back a sob. "I don't know what to do."

"Hey, hey," Bolton says and starts to wrap his arms around her.

'No!" she yells and shoves him away. "No, you don't get to swoop in and make it better! I've done this all on my own and I'll keep doing it on my own!"

"Like hell you will! He's my son!"

"But you have a job to do." Lu sneers. "You have a job to do."

Bolton takes a deep breath, his eyes studying every pained feature on Lu's face.

"You're right," Bolton says, pointing up at the sky. The ash roils with movement from the flying monsters, their shrieks muted, then loud, as they continually dive in and out of the cloud. "Come with or not, but I'd advise not staying right here."

"That's it?" Lu shouts, bringing more shrieks from above. "Come with or not?"

"You aren't giving me a choice, Lu," Bolton says. "Not then and not now."

He turns and walks away.

"You have to be kidding?" Lu yells. More shrieks and some of the monsters start to circle down away from the cloud.

"I'm thinking we use our inside voices from now on," Lowell says.

"I have a better idea," Lu says. "How about we shut the fuck up all together?"

"Then we can't talk about you two's storied past," Lowell says.

"You also won't piss me off more than I am so I tear you apart and leave you to get eaten one piece at a time," Lu says as she walks off after Bolton. "Life's a trade off."

Lowell is ready to respond, but another shriek shuts him up quickly. He hurries after the other two, constantly looking back and forth from where he's going and up at the beasts above.

"I'm only coming so I can find out how this soap opera ends, you know," Lowell says as he catches up to Lu and Bolton. "I just have to find out if Bolton has a twin brother. You do, right? But he's all disfigured and shit? Right?"

TWELVE

"This look familiar at all?" Dr. Probst asks Kyle as they stand before two very large doors.

"Nope," Kyle says. "Sorry, I probably took a wrong turn back a ways."

"More than likely we've taken several wrong turns," Dr. Probst says. "But here's hoping that the way out is on the other side of these doors."

She reaches out with both hands and gives the handles a yank, but the doors don't budge.

"Hold the candle closer," she says and Kyle steps up, placing the candle right next to the handles. "Huh. No locks."

"They're sealed," Kyle says and nods at a large keypad. "And gonna stay that way since the power's out."

"Has to be a manual way to open these," Dr. Probst says.

"It doesn't matter," Kyle replies. "If these doors are this secure then I doubt we'll find a backdoor through there."

"We can try," Dr. Probst says. "At the very least, we could hide in there if we can close and seal the doors again behind us. Give us some time to think and regroup. We have a little less than ten hours before my ride shows up."

"Shouldn't we try to find a different way out then?" Kyle says.

"I want to see what's on the other side of these doors," Dr. Probst says. "Maybe there are some weapons."

"You know how to shoot?" Kyle asks. "You don't look like you know how to shoot."

"Just help me find a panel that might have the manual release behind it," Dr. Probst says.

The two look along the walls by the doors, double checking both sides before they shake their heads and give up.

"Must be further back down the corridor," Dr. Probst says.

She turns and then freezes, her hand shooting out and gripping Kyle's elbow so hard he cries out.

"What the hell?" he snaps, then follows her gaze. "Oh."

"Oh, is right," Gil says, his rifle trained on them as three men stand behind him, equally armed. "You want to see what's in there?"

Neither Kyle nor Dr. Probst responds.

"I'll take that as a yes," Gil says. "And, you are right, Doctor, in there will be a great place for you to hang until your ride gets here. Maybe I'll wait with you and you can tell me what you wouldn't tell the kid." He steps forward, the rifle pointed square at Dr. Probst's chest. "You can tell me what you saw inside that big, old hole. You know, what your precious federal government put there."

"Oh, for Christ's sake," Dr. Probst says. "There's no point in telling you anything if you are going to just jam the information inside a brain that believes the government has had anything to do with this nightmare."

"Then there's no point in keeping you alive," Gil says. "Moss was always the softy around here, but Moss is gone now. We do things my way and my way only. Luke?"

A man steps forward, cocks a rifle, and puts it to his shoulder.

"Good bye, Doctor," Gil smiles.

"Stop!" Kyle yells and gets in front of Dr. Probst. "She told me what she saw!"

"No, she didn't," Gil says. "We've been following you in the dark almost the whole time. I would have heard."

"No, she did," Kyle insists. "And it's big. Like really big. You promise not to hurt her and I'll tell you."

"Kyle," Dr. Probst warns. "Don't."

"No, it's cool," he says. "They promise not to hurt you and I'll tell them what they want to know."

"And they show us what's behind the doors," Dr. Probst says.

"Oh, that's not a problem," Gil says. He nods towards the door. "Luke? Show them."

Luke slings his rifle, hurries ahead and kicks at the bottom of the wall next to the door. A panel in the floor slides open.

"Son of a bitch," Dr. Probst mutters.

"Now, kid, how about that info?" Gil smiles.

"Inside first," Kyle says.

Gil shrugs. "Makes no difference to me. I kinda like showing this off anyway. Luke?"

"Just about got it, Gil," Luke replies as he works at several dials and levers in the panel. Then there's a loud click followed by a series of clangs.

The doors recess slightly and then slide back into the walls until the handles prevent them from going any further. Dr. Probst and Kyle watch in fascination as a massive space is revealed, easily four times as large as the main area of the bunker when they first came in. But the most surprising part is the fact that florescent lights start to kick on as soon as the doors stop moving. Row after row of lights begins to buzz and slowly build up to strength.

"Don't know why the lights work here," Gil says. "Guess the government gets lucky sometimes."

"What is all of that?" Dr. Probst asks.

"That is the future," Gil says. "Or our future, at least. Once the outside world sorts itself out, we'll be ready for it. Nothing's gonna stop us with that in our back pocket."

Crates ten high and one hundred deep forms dozens of rows, leaving just enough space for a small forklift to maneuver between them.

"Forklift don't work," Gil says. "Probably out of propane, but we haven't bothered getting a new tank for it. Not like we need to move any of this stuff."

"What's in the crates?" Kyle asks. "Guns?"

"Only about a quarter of them are guns," Gil says. "Pistols, rifles, carbines, sub-machine guns, you name it. The rest of the crates are full of ammunition."

He smiles big and walks past Kyle and Dr. Probst and starts pointing with his rifle.

"That row right there will keep me in 30/30 rounds until the end of time," Gil says. "The government can send who they want after us, but they ain't getting in without a fight."

"I think you'd be surprised," Kyle says.

"What's gonna surprise me is if you actually have info to tell and not just a bunch of bullshit," Gil says, stepping up to Kyle and jamming him in the chest with his finger. "Spill it, kid."

Kyle looks at Dr. Probst them at Gil, then over at Luke.

"Hell," Kyle says.

Gil waits a second then, "Hell, what?"

"Hell," Kyle says. "The hole leads to Hell. Not just because of the monsters, which are really demons, but because that's what the government was looking for. They tried to find Hell and instead it found them. Now the Apocalypse is upon us."

Gil frowns deepens and he looks at the other men. Their eyes are wide with shock and disbelief. Except Luke's; his eyes believe.

"Kid, you gotta think I'm fucking stupid if I'm going to listen to that happy horse shit," Gil smiles.

"But the fearful, and unbelieving, and the abominable, and murderers, and whoremongers, and sorcerers, and idolaters, and all liars, shall have their part in the lake which burneth with fire and brimstone," Kyle says, smiling. "I'd say the fire and brimstone is pretty spot on. *Kid.*"

"Gil?" Luke says. "You don't think this is true, do you? That Hell has come to earth?"

"Shut up," Gil snaps. "Of course, it's not true. Those things out there are created by the government. Probably by the *Chinese* government and we had to babysit them since *our* government has bent over and turned us all into their bitches."

"I'm looking at a few of the fearful and unbelieving right now, aren't I?" Kyle says, taking a step forward, his chest bumping Gil's. "That what you are in this bunker? The fearful hiding from God's will? The unbelievers waiting for the righteous to come?"

"The righteous?" Gil laughs, but it sounds weak and hollow. "We're the righteous, kid."

"Oh, I don't think so," Kyle says. "I've met the righteous and they don't look a damn thing like you scraggly fucks."

***

"Humvees still secure, sir!" Sergeant Helmut "Hellmouth" Kreigel yells over the roar of the rotors coming from the two Chinook helicopters. "Ready to lift off once we're refueled!"

"Good!" Lieutenant Mallory Taylor responds. "Make sure everyone is done taking a piss and mounts up!"

"Rogue Team, listen up!" Kreigel shouts as he walks to the edge of the tarmac where four other men are busy relieving themselves on the ash covered, winter withered grass and weeds.

"Let me shake off first, Hellmouth!" Sergeant Chuck Ybarra replies. "Unless you want to do that for me!"

"Not in your wildest dreams, bitch!" Kreigel yells.

"Done and done!" Sergeant Lionel "Lion-O" Toloski says as he turns around, grabbing at the crotch of his uniform. "You need to inspect it?"

"What the fuck?" Kreigel laughs. "What's with the homoerotic humor? There're monsters in the fucking sky and you bitches are making gay jokes?"

"Nothing wrong with being gay, Sergeant," Sergeant Gary Holt says. "Right, Blumenburg?"

"Been working for me just fine," Sergeant Noah Blumenburg says as he zips up. "But if these boys want to finally throw off their repressed feelings and join the club, then I'm all for it. The more the merrier."

"You just want a cuddle buddy for your sniper hides," Ybarra says, flipping Blumenburg off. "And I don't cuddle. Get me in the sack and I'm all business."

"Out of business is more like it," Toloski laughs.

"Saddle up, bitches," Kreigel yells. "Ybarra and Holt are with me in Rover Two. Blumenburg and Toloski are with the Lieutenant in Rover One."

The men look up at the massive ash cloud far above Mountain Home Air Force Base. The base is still without power from the EMP, but the Chinooks were able to set down and refuel using the manual pumps, getting the SEAL Team that much closer to their target: Dr. Probst.

"Move!" Kreigel yells and the men double time over to the waiting helicopters and the Humvees attached underneath each one.

"Hold on!" Lieutenant Taylor shouts as the men start to run towards their respective Humvees, ready to ride inside the vehicles instead of inside the helicopters for the last leg of the trip. "Huddle up!"

The men circle their lieutenant and lean in close so they can hear him over the rotors.

"We can only go two hundred miles before the Chinooks have to drop us," Taylor says. "That way, they have enough fuel to get back here. That puts us about one hundred and fifty miles from where the last transmission came from. We do not know what we are walking into. We have no idea who is hostile and who is friendly. Do not forget that no matter what is happening in that sky, everyone we meet is still an American citizen. Martial law may be in effect, but I want you to think hard before you pull that trigger."

"Humvees will be almost out of fuel by the time we hit the target, sir," Toloski says.

"I don't know if you've noticed, but there are these things called gas stations, Toloski," Taylor smirks. "You pull up into one and get to pump your own gas. Hell, son, some even have diesel. It's an amazing world we live in."

"I know, sir," Toloski grins. "But without power the pumps won't work."

"Then we do it the old fashioned way," Taylor says. "We siphon straight from the tanks. There are hoses in each Humvee."

"Hey, Ybarra?" Blumenburg shouts. "You get to play out that cocksucking fantasy you keep having. You can practice on the syphon hose before I let you go down on me."

"You don't want the power of these lips on your little pecker, Blumenburg," Ybarra laughs. "I'd suck it right off and choke on the little thing."

"You two done?" Taylor smiles.

"They finish fast, sir," Kreigel says.

"Load up, kids," Taylor yells. "Strap in and get ready. Keep guns hot and watch the skies. Those bogeys haven't shown themselves on the trip so far, but they are bound to come at us as we get closer."

"Fun!" Holt yells. "I love duck hunting!"

"Shut up and get in the Humvee," Kreigel says. "Leave the jokes to the other guys, Holt. You suck at them."

"You know who really sucks?" Holt asks.

The whole team groans and several throw soft punches at Holt's head.

***

"We aren't going to talk about this?" Bolton asks Lu as they walk along the highway, Bolton's eyes look from the map to the CLD to the road in front of them then back down to the map. "Once we get to the coordinates, things will change. We may not have another opportunity. If there is a sat phone, then my orders may not be the same as yours. We may have to split up anyway."

"Then I go and find Kyle," Lu says.

"Lu, you're still a United States Marshal," Bolton says. "That may not be an option."

Lu shrugs.

"I'll go find him," Lowell says. "I've got nothing better to do."

"You're a convicted killer," Bolton laughs. "They'll probably execute you on the spot to save the hassle of transporting you."

"Nice," Lowell says. "That's the thanks I get for saving your asses? God bless America."

"You killed judges, killed police officers and kidnapped a little girl," Lu says. "You may think we're all in this together now, but we aren't. We aren't friends, Lowell. Not now, not ever."

"An hour ago, you were about to let me go free," Lowell snaps.

"Go for it," Lu says, pointing at the tree line by the side of the road. "Knock yourself out."

"Fuck you," Lowell says, looking over at the trees. He thinks about it for a second, but then a roar from off to their right changes his mind. "I'm good right here."

"That one was close," Bolton says. "I'm surprised we haven't run into anything since Coeur d'Alene."

"I think it's because of them," Lu says, pointing up at the flying monsters threading in and out of the ash cloud. "I don't know why, but I think the ground ones are afraid of the ones with wings."

"You don't think they're on the same side?" Bolton asks.

"There may not be sides," Lu shrugs. "Just individual groups trying to survive. Just like us."

"Yeah, I don't think you can apply this to our situation," Bolton says. "Nice try, though."

"You know why I took that girl?" Lowell says quietly.

"What?" Lu asks, turning on him. "The one you kidnapped?"

"No, the other one," Lowell snaps. "Yeah, the one I kidnapped."

"Hold on," Bolton says. "We're close."

He watches the red flashing coordinates in the CLD and starts jogging down the road.

"This way!"

Lu and Lowell jog after him and they come to a gravel road, completely weed choked and covered with ash. The ash is undisturbed, telling them no one has been on it in a while.

"The signal is stronger that way," Bolton says, pointing off to the right of the road. "But we may be able to follow this for a while."

He takes off at a fast walk and Lu and Lowell fall in behind.

"You want to hear what I have to say or not?" Lowell asks. "Like your boyfriend said, there may not be another chance later."

"Why the sudden need to unburden yourself?" Lu says. "I honestly don't give a shit why you did anything you did."

"Liar," Lowell laughs. "It's been eating you up inside ever since you read my file. That little piece of the puzzle didn't fit and you're the type of person that has to make sure everything fits, even if you have to force it to."

Lu glares at him then looks at Bolton's back.

"Fine. Tell me," she responds. "I'd love nothing more."

"My plan was never to get away," Lowell says. "I just needed to go to federal prison. Oregon State Pen wasn't for me."

"You wanted into a federal prison? Why?" Lu asks.

"I had my reasons," Lowell says. "All part of something that started a long time ago. But this isn't about that. I could have taken anyone hostage, but I specifically chose that little girl. Guess why?"

"I don't want to guess," Lu says. "Just tell me."

"No, I want to hear your theories, see if they are even close," Lowell says.

"Whatever," Lu says. "They didn't find any signs you molested her and she said you didn't force yourself on her orally, so you aren't a pedophile."

"No, but you're close," Lowell says.

Lu gives him a puzzled look. "Close? So, what? You wanted to, but didn't act on it?"

"Now you're further away," Lowell says. "Total wrong direction."

Lu thinks for a second. "Who hurt you?"

"Me?" Lowell replies and starts to argue, but then stops. "More people than I would have liked."

"Parents? Uncles? Teachers? Who?" Lu asks.

"The list is long," Lowell says. "There are groups in this world that like to share. I was one of the things they shared." He sighs. "So was that girl."

"Whoa...what?" Lu asks, stopping and grabbing Lowell by the arm. "What the fuck are you saying?"

"The people she was with may have been her parents, but they weren't tourists," Lowell says. "They were part of a group that shares little kids with others. They were in Enterprise for a delivery. The girl hadn't been touched yet. That was part of the bargain. Fresh meat."

"How the holy fuck could you even know that?" Lu asks.

"I just knew," Lowell shrugs. "There're signs. I learned them all. I spotted the pattern right off and knew the girl wasn't going to live longer than a couple of months."

"She didn't come up as missing," Lu says. "Those people were her parents."

"Right," Lowell says. "And some parents suck. They were going to sell her. So I chucked my plans and grabbed her as soon as possible, got her across state lines and up to Spokane. As soon as I knew she would be safe, I let her go and waited to get picked up. The girl dodged a bullet."

"But she was returned to her parents," Lu says. "If what you are saying is true, then she was right back in the same danger."

"Nah," Lowell smiles. "I left those fuckers a note. Told them I knew exactly what they were and that if they hurt a hair on that little girl's head I'd make sure some of my friends on the outside paid them a visit."

"Bullshit," Lu says.

"They live in Ann Arbor, Michigan now," Lowell says. "The girl is a straight A student and the parents haven't gotten so much as a speeding ticket. They went to Disney World last summer and had plans to go to Costa Rica this summer, but obviously that shit isn't happening."

Lu eyes him carefully, looking for the lies. She doesn't find any.

"Why would they do that?" Lu asks. "Sell their daughter?"

"Daddy had a hole in his arm," Lowell replies. "Or between his toes and upper thighs, since a respectable college professor can't be seen with track marks on his arms. The mom had been sucking cock for money since college. Pretty sure that's how the two met. You take people like that, let them procreate, and horrible things can happen."

"But they looked so normal," Lu says. "I saw their pictures in the files."

"They are normal, Marshal," Lowell says. "Evil is normal in this world. I'd think you'd know that by now having seen so much of it. It's the good people that are the odd ones out. Trust me."

"Hey!" Bolton shouts. "This way!"

Lu gives Lowell a quick nod then runs up to Bolton.

"What do you have?" she asks.

"Through here," Bolton says, pointing out an almost completely hidden trail. "Come on."

He takes off through the brush and Lu has to struggle to keep up with him. She looks over her shoulder and sees Lowell standing in the gravel road, his head turned up looking at the ash cloud above.

"You coming?" she yells.

"In a second," Lowell says. "Something's happening."

She's about to try to get a look through the trees, but Bolton takes off sprinting.

"Found it!" he shouts as he races up to a large crate.

"How do you open it?" Lu asks.

Bolton searches around the crate until he finds the right spot, and then he places the CLD against it.

"There we go," Bolton says as the crate starts to open. He looks over at Lu. "Last chance to talk before we both have to get back to work."

"No time to talk," Lowell says as he rushes up next to them, his hand pointing towards the air. "Check it out."

They all look up through the trees and see the ash cloud rushing by.

"What the hell?" Bolton asks. "What's it doing?"

"I don't know," Lowell says. "But the flying things aren't too happy about it."

"No shit," Lu says as she watches dozens and dozens of flying monsters flee the retreating cloud. "Whatever is going on has them spooked, that's for sure."

***

"Doctor Hall?" President Nance asks. "It's been hours and you haven't given us anything."

"Yeah, hold on," Dr. Hall snaps. "I almost have it."

He taps at his keyboard and the main monitor changes, showing the chasm as a thermal image. Deep inside is the wriggling mass and he gets up, his hand pointed at the monitor.

"What you are seeing are tails," Dr. Hall says. "Hundreds of tails."

"Tails?" President Nance says. "Tails to what?"

"*Whats*," Dr. Hall corrects. "And I don't know. The mass is so thick that I can't get readings on anything else."

"You've been sitting there for hours, placing orders like this place is a hotel and room service is unlimited, and all you can tell us is those are tails?" Admiral Quigley shouts then turns to the president. "Sir, I respectfully request permission to shoot this fucker between the eyes!"

There are several laughs, but the laughs are outnumbered by the calls of agreement.

"Hold on, Major," Dr. Hall says.

"It's Admiral!"

"Fine, *Admiral,*" Dr. Hall replies. "I may not know what the things are, but I can tell you they aren't adults. That's a brood, a nest of offspring. Whatever the creatures may be, they are not fully grown yet. If you, *Admiral*, can kill them now, then we won't have to find out what they are supposed to become."

"How do we kill them?" Admiral Quigley growls. "That's part of the reason you are here."

"I'd say nuke them from orbit," Dr. Hall smiles. "Only way to be sure."

No one responds.

"What? No *Aliens* fans in here?" Dr. Hall asks.

"Doctor Hall, be serious or you will be arrested and spend the rest of your life down here in a very tiny cell," President Nance says. "How do we kill them?"

"Nuke them," Dr. Hall says. "I wasn't kidding." He points at the monitor again. "See those black dots? Those are your MOABs. For whatever reason, they haven't gone off. Send in one nuke and those go up too. Kablooey."

"Sir, that's not an option," Borland says. "Like I said before, the thermals above the site would send radiation across the world. We launch a nuclear strike and our people will be pariahs. We lose our home and any chance of refuge."

"Hey, you guys are the politicians and know what you're doing," Dr. Hall shrugs. "I'm just the expert brought in to give you answers. The answer I've come up with is you nuke the hell out of that hole or you wait around and watch those little tails grow up to be big tails. Personally, I'd rather live in that cell you promised me, Mr. President, than see what those things become."

President Nance looks over at Joan and she shakes her head. He looks down the table at each member of his cabinet and finds faces in agreement with Dr. Hall and faces in disagreement.

"Any idea how much time we have, Dr. Hall?" President Nance asks. "That's the other reason you are here."

Dr. Hall turns and looks up at the monitor and the hundreds of tails. "It could be hours or it could be days. I doubt it's longer than a month. No animal would leave offspring exposed like that for very long. If they are anything like-"

He stops and just stands there, his eyes watching the monitor.

"Doctor?" President Nance pushes. "What were you going to say?"

"Hold on," Dr. Hall says absently. "Someone switch it to a normal view and pull out, please."

It's the first time the man has said please since arriving and the whole room notices instantly. All eyes fall on the monitor.

"Dear God, what's happening now?" President Nance asks as the whole room watches the ash cloud starts to obscure the view. "Is it erupting again?"

"It's derupting," Dr. Hall replies. "I know it's not a word, but that's the only way I can explain it. The ash is going back into the volcano. We're losing the view."

"Jesus," President Nance says. "Someone get me Dr. Bartolli! I want to know what the hell is going on now! How does a volcano derupt?"

"Sir?" a tech says. "We have another incoming transmission form one of the sat phones."

"Dr. Probst?" President Nance asks. "I thought we lost her."

"No, sir, it's from a different signal," the tech replies. "A Sergeant Connor Bolton, Army Special Operations Forces. His credentials check out, sir. He's on the ground and from what we can tell, he is only ninety miles from Dr. Probst's site."

"I'll get my boys on the line," Admiral Quigley says. "Have them meet up with the man. The more intel we can get from the ground, the better."

"Do that," President Nance says. "And I'm still waiting for Dr. Bartolli!"

***

"This is Sergeant Connor Bolton speaking, sir," Bolton says, his back suddenly ramrod straight as he listens to the president's voice. "Yes, sir. I was part of the convoy of federal prison buses heading to Everett, sir."

Lu and Lowell stand there, half listening to Bolton as they stare up at the sky.

"We need a better view," Lowell says.

"We also need to listen to Connor," Lu says.

"Soldier boy can handle himself on this one," Lowell says. "Not like we can hear the whole conversation." He reaches down and throws on one of the packs from the crate. "Come on."

"What do you need that for?" Lu asks.

"Now that I have it, I'm not letting it off my back," Lowell says. "This pack could mean the difference between life and death now. You should grab one too."

"We're only going a few yards out to the gravel road," Lu says. "What could happen?"

Lowell gives her a smirk and rolls his eyes.

"Right," Lu says and picks up a pack for herself. "Stupid question."

They walk along the trail and come out of the woods onto the ash covered gravel. The trees are far enough apart that they have a way better view of what's happening with the cloud above.

"Where are they going?" Lu asks, watching the monsters soar overhead, flying in the opposite direction from the ash cloud.

"Away, is my guess," Lowell says.

"Heading towards the coast?" Lu says. "God, they're going to find nothing but people. We have to tell Connor." She pulls on Lowell's arm and drags him back into the woods.

"I'm just glad they didn't decide to come down for a snack before their trip," Lowell says. "I haven't eaten shit in over a day. I wouldn't be much of a meal."

"There's food in the packs," Lu says. "Eat something."

"Nah, I'm good. I've gone days without eating. This ain't nothing."

They get back to the site of the crate and see Bolton sitting there, his chin in his hands.

"You're done already?" Lu asks. "Can you call them back?"

"Why?" Bolton asks.

"Because the monsters are flying towards the coast," Lu says. "It'll be a slaughter when they get there!"

"They know," Bolton says. "I also found out they think they know what's in the hole."

"The hole?" Lu asks. "What hole?"

"Wyoming and most of Montana up to Missoula," Bolton says. "It's pretty much a two hundred mile chasm in the middle of the continent. And it's filled with tails."

"Tails?" Lowell asks. "Did you say tails? Did he say tails?"

"He said tails," Lu replies. "What tails?"

"There's some nest," Bolton says. "They're trying to figure out what kind of nest." He sighs and stands up. "If they don't, then they might be going nuclear."

"They're going to drop the bomb on US soil?" Lu asks. "That's insane!"

"What about fallout?" Lowell asks. "That shit'll get in the air and spread."

Bolton points up. "They think now is the time," he replies. "If they drop a nuke on the nest now while the cloud recedes then the radiation shouldn't spread. They have experts."

"Why'd they tell you all of this?" Lu asks. "Little above your pay grade, isn't it?"

"Because they need me," Bolton says as he picks up a pack. "They need a spotter on the ground when the nuke goes off."

"Uh...what?" Lu asks, her jaw dropping. "The blast will kill you."

"There's a bunker we're supposed to get to," Bolton says. "I told them about you two and I have authorization to bring you with me. Once we get to the bunker, we seal it and wait for the blast. They have an inventory of the place and there are hot suits in there somewhere. We get there, find me a hot suit, nuke goes kaboom, and I hike it to the blast site to confirm the kill."

"All sounds good," Lowell says. "And tell the president thank you from me for letting me come along for the suicide mission. But, uh, how are we getting there?"

"Someone is coming to pick us up," Bolton says. "And we need to move ass to the rendezvous point."

"Someone? What someone?" Lu asks.

"Rogue Team. Part of SEAL Team Six," Bolton says. "Fucking Navy. I get dropped in the apocalypse and the goddamn Navy has to rescue my ass. I'd ask how the day could get worse, but that would be jinxing us."

"You feel that?" Lowell asks.

"Shut up," Lu says. "No time to fuck around."

Lowell ignores her and squats down, his hands on the ground. "No, I'm not joking. Feel the ground."

Bolton squats and places a palm to the dirt. His eyes go wide. "It's big," he says.

"Really big," Lowell responds.

They both stand up and start turning around, looking for the source.

"There!" Bolton shouts, pointing east. "Something is coming!"

The ground starts to tremor, then shudder, and finally flat out shakes, as the head of a giant monster appears from the horizon, just visible above the trees.

"It's coming this way," Lu says. "Guys? It's coming right at us."

"Run?" Lowell asks.

"Run!" Bolton shouts.

They turn perpendicular to the monster and sprint through the woods, not caring where they are going, just so long as they get out of the path of what's coming at them.

***

"This is the drop point!" Taylor yells over the com. "Get set! The Chinooks are going to cable the Humvees down to the- HOLY SHIT!"

The two Chinook helicopters hover a hundred feet above the road, but towering over them come two massive monsters. They run full out, their massive feet creating small earth quakes, sending trees crashing to the ground.

"Put us down!" Taylor yells. "Put us down now!"

The cables holding the Humvees in place to the bellies of the helicopters slacken and the vehicles slowly begin to lower.

"I SAID PUT US DOWN!" Taylor yells. "GET US DOWN ON THE GROUND!"

The whine of the helicopters' rotors is overpowered by the deafening roars of the two monsters converging on them. Taylor looks out the passenger side window and sees the earth coming up at them fast and is glad his team wasn't assigned two pussy pilots. Although, at the speed the ground is racing up at the Humvee, he wonders if maybe a pilot a hair more cautious would have been good.

Just as he thinks he's going to be slammed into the ground and turn into a SEAL pancake, the Chinook stops and he hears the bolts holding the cables being blasted free, the pilot above using the emergency release instead of the time consuming method of manually unhooking the cables.

Go!" Taylor yells at Toloski who is in the driver's seat.

The man slams the accelerator and sends the Humvee flying out from under the Chinook just as the helicopter lifts back up into the air.

"Blumenburg!" Taylor yells. "What's the status of Rover Two?"

Blumenburg tears his eyes away from the monsters the Humvee is racing towards and stands up, popping open the top hatch of the Humvee. He pulls himself up and looks back down the road, glad to see Rover Two is right in line with Rover One.

"Good to go, sir," Blumenburg says, dropping back into the vehicle.

"Thoughts, sir?" Toloski asks.

"Drive through them," Taylor orders. "And don't you dare slow down."

"Monster chicken, sir?" Toloski asks.

"Nope," Taylor says. "Monster slalom. Go right between the thing's legs."

"Let's hope they don't take offense to us looking up their skirts," Toloski says as he stares straight ahead, his knuckles pure white as he grips the steering wheel.

"Let's hope," Taylor says. "Blumenburg, let Rover Two know the plan."

"Already on it, sir," Blumenburg says, his hand to his throat, activating his com. "Should I tell them to get some pics, sir? We'll have a great view." He looks up at the open hatch above him. "Anyone bring the 35mm?"

***

The monster stomps past Lowell, Lu, and Bolton, its feet crushing over an acre of forest with each step. They watch it lumber past, safely a quarter mile away from its path. All three of them look like they are going to vomit from running so hard, but their stomachs don't have anything in them to throw up.

"It looks sick," Lu says. "Look how it's walking. It's stumbling more than anything."

"Great," Lowell says. "Hope it washes its hands before touching anything. I don't think any of us will survive a monster cold."

"Come on," Bolton says. "We have to backtrack to get to the rendezvous point. They have orders to wait for five minutes. If we are ten seconds late, they will be gone."

"Fuck," Lowell says as he pushes his fist against his side. "I'm already gone."

"Don't puss out," Lu says. "You get through this and maybe you don't go back to prison."

"You'd be surprised how good three hots and a cot sounds right now," Lowell says. "Not to mention the idea of having tons of steel and concrete around me."

"Changing your mind about freedom, Lowell?" Bolton laughs.

"Nope. Just made up my mind about not getting stepped on by that fucking thing," he replies, pointing at the monster as it leaves their view, lost behind a turn in the mountains. "How big you think that thing is?"

"A few hundred feet at least," Bolton says.

They hike for a while, then stop and look up, stunned yet again.

Sunlight.

The ash cloud has receded enough that there is actually sky again. Real sky and not just winter clouds mixed with a never ending ash fall.

"There's something I didn't think I'd see again," Lowell says. "I take everything back. We get out of this alive and I don't want to go to prison, as long as the sky stays like that. We go back to ashpocalypse? I go back to a cell."

"Good to have a plan," Bolton says.

"No shit," Lowell says. "So how long to the bunker once we meet up with the circus act?"

"Circus act?" Lu asks.

"You know, trained seals," Lowell smirks.

"God, why do I talk to you?" Lu snorts.

"A good hour of driving," Bolton says. "Then I have a feeling there's a hike in it after that."

"Great," Lowell says. "I love hiking. I love it so much I'm doing it right now."

THIRTEEN

"Mr. President, I have no idea how this is possible," Dr. Bartolli says, his pale face filling one of the side monitors as the entire situation room watches the massive ash cloud swirl down into the chasm. "I have never heard of this happening ever in all of recorded history."

"No offense, Dr. Bartolli," President Nance says. "But I've never heard of monsters coming out of the earth in all of recorded history."

"Dinosaurs," Dr. Hall says quietly then shuts up as he receives a stern look from Joan.

"All I need to know is what effect the nuclear blast will have on the volcano," President Nance says. "Answer me that. Will it make the hole bigger or will it cause it to collapse in on itself."

"It cannot say, sir," Dr. Bartolli replies. "The variables are too great."

"So you are useless then," President Nance snaps. He waves his hand and the monitor goes dead. "Where are we with the SEAL Team?"

"They have almost reached the bunker, sir," Admiral Quigley responds. "They'll try to get up the mountain as far as possible in the Humvees, but they may have to hike part of the way, which could slow them down."

"General Tulane? Status on the nuclear missiles?" President Nance asks. "Once I give the order, how soon until they reach the target?"

211

"Sir, I can't protest enough!" Borland shouts, getting to his feet. "This could have no effect on the enemy, but will have an effect on our relations with the rest of the world! You need to at least consult with the other Heads of State on this!"

"This is happening on US soil, Secretary Borland," President Nance states. "I will make the call on this and that is the end of the discussion. One more outburst and you will be removed from this room and sent outside with the rest of the refugees."

Borland sits down and promptly takes off his tie. He tosses it on the table and shakes his head.

"It's your call, Mr. President," Borland replies. "And your responsibility when it's all over."

"Yes, it is," President Nance says. "And if choosing the nuclear option means that we can get to a place where it *is* all over, then I will gladly make this choice." He turns back to General Tulane. "How soon will the missiles reach the target once I give the order?"

"Fifteen minutes tops, sir," General Tulane says, his eyes involuntarily going to Borland.

"I'm sitting here, General," President Nance snaps.

"Yes, sir. Sorry, Mr. President," General Tulane replies.

"Admiral Quigley, please inform your men that they will have forty-five minutes to get to the bunker," President Nance says, standing and looking at everyone at the table. "I will give the order to launch in thirty minutes unless the situation changes drastically. We need this within the hour."

***

"They want you to be the spotter?" Taylor asks as he looks over his shoulder at Bolton, having picked him and Lu up, letting Lowell ride in Rover Two. "Why can't they see it with the satellites?"

"They're retasking the satellites," Bolton says. "After the last EMP, they can't risk losing more. Once I confirm whatever I confirm, they'll go from there."

"Sir?" Blumenburg says. "I just received word from command. We have forty-five minutes to reach the bunker."

"We what?" Taylor snaps, looking over at Toloski. "What's our ETA?"

"Five minutes until we hit the road," Toloski says. "I have no idea how far we can take the Rovers up the mountain. We'll be cutting it close even if we get to drive up to the door."

"Fucking great," Taylor growls. "Fucking civilian presidents. They're just waiting to pull that trigger and can't even give us a decent window to do our jobs."

"Amen to that," Bolton says.

"I let Rover Two know, sir," Blumenburg says. "They aren't happy either."

"No shit they aren't," Taylor laughs. "I bet Ybarra is cursing up a storm right now."

The Humvees push on, their drivers taking the road as fast as possible.

"Here!" Blumenburg shouts. "Turn left!"

Toloski cranks the wheel hard and the Humvee bounces jarringly, its front wheels slamming up over a small log meant to keep vehicles from driving up the abandoned road. A bullet hole riddled "No Trespassing" sign hangs by one corner on a thick pine. It flaps in the wind as the Humvees race by.

They get a good quarter mile when Blumenburg shouts, "Shit! Incoming!" He jumps up and opens the top hatch. "Hand me that, will ya?"

Bolton grabs the .50 caliber machine gun locked to the rack behind the two front seats, unlatches it, and hands it up to Blumenburg.

"What you got, Sergeant?" Taylor asks.

"Hostiles coming fast, sir! Ybarra spotted them! Looks like six heading up the road after us!"

Bolton and Lu hang their heads out the back windows and can see Rover Two being pursued by six of the smaller creatures. The things trample pines and upend firs in their race after the vehicles.

"French kissers," Bolton says. "Great."

"What did you call them?" Taylor asks.

"Yeah, what the hell was that?" Lu adds.

"When you see their tongues, you'll know what I'm talking about," Bolton says.

The air is split by the sound of the .50 cal being opened up on the monsters. Loud roars and howls join the bark of the heavy gun and Bolton and Lu both instantly withdraw back into the Humvee, their hands grabbing anything to keep them from being thrown around as Toloski starts weaving between the trees, trying to shake the monsters loose.

"This could slow us down," Taylor says. "Hopefully, we make it in time."

"Missoula's a long way away, Lieutenant," Bolton says. "You don't think the blast will reach everything here, do you?"

"I don't know what to expect," Taylor replies. "You've been cutoff out in the field, Sergeant. The brass has been itching to give these things everything we've got."

There's a huge explosion from behind them.

"RPG," Toloski says, glancing in the side mirror. "Ybarra is giving those things everything *we've* got."

***

"I'm telling you that rockets aren't going to stop them!" Lowell shouts. "It just pisses them off!"

"Keep it quiet, convict!" Kreigel yells from the passenger seat. "Let the professionals do their jobs!"

"Have you fought these things? Because I fucking have! I've killed one!" Lowell shouts. "You're only going to make them mad!"

"Bam, motherfucker!" Ybarra yells from above. "That's how you do-"

The man screams as he is yanked from the vehicle. Lowell dives to the side as the man's legs whip past his head and are gone up through the hatch.

"Holy fuck," Kreigel says, looking out the side window. He ducks back in quickly as a bright blue tongue shoots out right where his head had been.

"Told ya," Lowell says. "Just fucking drive."

Kreigel looks over at Holt in the driver's seat. "Do what the convict says and fucking drive!"

***

"There!" Toloski says. "The bunker entrance should be just over that ridge and down the other side!"

"Get us there now!" Taylor yells.

Blumenburg suddenly drops back into the Humvee, falling right on top of Lu and Bolton. He looks up at the hatch, his eyes wide with fear.

"Tried to French kiss you, didn't it?" Bolton asks.

"Yeah," Blumenburg replies. "Not cool."

The Humvee hits the ridge and goes flying, hitting a good three feet of air before it slams back down to the earth. Toloski whips the wheel to the left and hits the brakes, sending the Humvee into a sideways skid.

"That wasn't on the map," Toloski says as they all look out the windows at the missing road. "Gonna be tricky getting to that."

Most of the roadway is gone, having slid down the mountain at some point, leaving only a two foot ledge going from where the Humvee is stopped and a huge, rusted steel hangar door.

The roar of the Rover Two's engines is matched by the roars of the monsters following them.

"Out!" Taylor orders and no one hesitates as they scramble from the Humvee and over to the short ledge.

Rover Two flies up over the ridge and they all sprint as fast as they can to get out of the way as the vehicle hits the ground and rams right into Rover One, sending the Humvee over the edge and plummeting down the mountainside.

Holt, Kreigel, and Lowell are out of the vehicle and sprinting towards the others before the Humvee even stops rocking.

"They are right on us!" Kreigel yells.

They all sprint to the huge hangar door and Blumenburg skids to a stop on his knees, his hands yanking a box and wires from his pack. He grabs at a small hatch by the side of the door and rips it open, immediately connecting the wires to two leads behind the hatch. There's a loud clang and then the door shudders.

But doesn't move.

"Sergeant," Taylor hisses. "Not much time."

Lowell elbows Taylor in the ribs and grabs the man's pistol from his hip. He takes aim and fires at Rover Two just as a second monster crests the ridge. There's the sound of a ricochet and everyone, except Blumenburg, look at the Humvee then at Lowell.

"You can't blow up a Humvee by shooting the gas tank!" Kreigel yells. "That's only in the movies!"

"Not trying to blow it up," Lowell says. "Just need it to start leaking."

Bolton realizes what he's doing and points at the Humvee.

"Nail the tank!" Bolton yells. "Just make it leak!"

Kreigel looks at Bolton and then at Lowell. He quickly remembers the last time he ignored the federal prisoner and raises his M-4 to his shoulder. The two monsters are stepping over the Humvee as Kreigel takes his shots. The beasts stop instantly and their massive heads look down at the vehicle below as the gas tank starts to leak.

"I hope that's diesel," Lowell says.

Two bright blue tongues dart at the liquid that begins to stain the ground. They both howl and try to get at the diesel, shoving at one another for space. More monsters hit the ridge, their bodies jammed up against the mountainside, and soon it's a massive tangle of giant limbs and tongues as the beasts all jockey for position.

Then one loses the wrestling match and stumbles backwards, its rear legs ending up over open space. It wobbles for a second, and then slips from the road, its front legs trying to find purchase in the loose mountain soil. The beast scrambles, scrambles, and is lost, tumbling end over end as it falls a thousand feet to the rocky canyon floor below. Everyone stares as the thing bursts open, sending entrails and blue/black blood everywhere.

"Blumenburg?" Taylor asks.

"Almost got it, sir," Blumenburg replies. "There!"

With the sound of protesting metal almost deafening, the door slides up a couple of feet then grinds to a stop. No one hesitates and they all hit the ground and roll under the door as fast as possible, leaving the nightmares outside to drink their fuel flavored beverage.

"It won't close," Blumenburg says. Then he's gone as a blue tongue shoots from under the door, grabs his leg, and yanks him outside the bunker.

"Move it!" Taylor yells. "Get clear of that door!"

The team cracks glow sticks and throws them as far as possible into the massive bay they find themselves in.

"Oh, shit," Lowell says as he sees two rows of dusty looking Humvees lining each wall, as well as steel drum after steel drum with the word "DIESEL" stenciled on their sides. "I think we just walked into the pantry. Great."

***

Gil sits there, tied to a folding chair, his head whipping back and forth as he shouts obscenities at the men and women huddled together across the room.

"You fucking traitors!" he yells. "You piece of shit cowards! You're nothing but gutless fucks! How the fucking hell can you believe in this shit? The boy is selling you a load of crap!"

"Shut up, Gil," Luke says, suddenly the leader of the group. "If it is Hell, and this is God's wrath, then we need to take it seriously. You know that."

Gil's mouth hangs open and he turns to look over at Kyle and Dr. Probst, both tied to folding chairs as well. "You have no idea what you've done, kid. I wasn't going to kill you. I was messing with you, scaring you enough so you'd just give up trying to get away and stay here. I was thinking we needed a doctor, is all."

"I'm not a medical doctor," Dr. Probst says. "You fucking moron."

"I know that," Gil says. "But you're more of a doctor than anyone here."

"That makes no sense," Dr. Probst says.

"If I am telling the truth," Kyle says. "Do you think God will be happy that you have tied me up? I bring His word to you and this is how you act? You should feel shame!"

"You're laying it on thick," Dr. Probst whispers out of the corner of her mouth.

"Only way to do it," Kyle says. "Trust me."

Luke looks over at the captives, his eyes going from Dr. Probst to Kyle and last to Gil.

"You," he says. "You tried to act like you knew what was going on. You tried to make us believe it was the government doing this to us, when all along it was the work of the devil. Most of us came here because we knew you were a true patriot and son of God. Why'd you hide the truth? Why the lies, Gil?"

"The Prince of Lies," a woman says from behind Luke. "That's why. Maybe he's one of Satan's agents."

"You have got to be fucking kidding me!" Gil yells. "There is no Satan here! There is no devil outside! That hole is not the gates of Hell! Stop acting like fools and let me go!"

"Fools?" Luke asks, moving closer to Gil. "You think those that believe the Lord's word are fools?"

Gil sighs and hangs his head. "I always knew you'd be a weak link, Luke. I should have locked you out of here a long time ago."

Luke stomps over to Gil and grabs the man by the chin.

"You're the weak one," he spits. "You believed the devil's lies and now his minions roam the earth looking for the righteous and just!"

He steps back and pulls a pistol from his hip, cocks the hammer and places it to Gil's temple.

"I do this in the name of God and his son, Jesus Christ," Luke calls out.

"You hear that?" one of the men in the group asks.

Luke pauses and turns his head as a low rumbling is heard.

"What is that?" Luke asks. "Someone go see."

Two men run off into the darkness, their candles sputtering and then lost from sight as they round a corner.

"Sounds like the backdoor," Gil says. "You think the devil would use the backdoor, Luke?"

"I knew there was a backdoor," Dr. Probst says.

"Shut up!" Luke shouts.

"I'm guessing the government has come to get its precious doctor," Gil continues. "And whatever this kid is to them. That's not demons coming for us, you idiot. That's the US military! Let me go and I can help get us out of here!"

"You aren't going nowhere, liar," Luke says He steps forward and pulls the trigger.

Gil's brains splatter across Dr. Probst and Kyle, causing both of them to yell. Luke wipes a spot of grey matter from his cheek and then crouches in front of the gore covered prisoners.

"Tell me the truth and you'll be set free," Luke says.

"I have been telling you the truth," Kyle says. "It is your duty to believe. You must show faith in His will. Shoot us and that faith will be lost."

Luke eyes Kyle for a second, and then nods. He looks over his shoulder at the others.

"Bring them with," Luke says. "Let's take them to meet the demons that are coming for us. When a demon sees a demon, they can't help but show it. Everyone knows that."

He looks back at Kyle and taps him on the forehead with the pistol.

"If you are filled with truth, then the demons will not know you," Luke says. "They will cower from your belief and reveal their true selves." He taps Kyle again. "But if they do know you, then that proves you are as much a liar as Gil and are here only to test my faith." He slides the pistol down Kyle's face, tracing a pattern in the blood and brains. "And you know what happens to liars."

***

"Missiles will reach the target in twenty minutes, Mr. President," General Tulane says. "They are armed and will detonate on impact."

All eyes turn to the main monitor and watch as the chasm is filled by the ash cloud, completely obscuring the view of the wriggling mass. The image is grainy and filled with static and then blinks out completely.

"Satellites are out of range, sir," a tech announces. "They will have to complete their orbit before we can retask them and regain visuals."

"Your man better be able to tell us what is going on, General," President Nance says, his eyes on General Azoul.

"He will," General Azoul replies.

"If his man can't, then my men can," Admiral Quigley states. "We will see this to the end, Mr. President."

"Yes, gentlemen, we will," President Nance says.

***

"This place is huge, sir," Kreigel says, his eyes locked onto a small tablet showing him the schematics of the bunker. "It's not just a munitions dump, sir, like we were told. This place has several levels to it." He looks up from the tablet and at the lieutenant. "Sir, I don't think the brass knows where they sent us. I can access the top two levels, we being on the upper one, but the bottom four are classified. I have no idea what's below us."

Taylor looks over at the sergeant and frowns, his face nothing but shadows and rage as the beams of the soldiers' flashlights bounce around the corridor.

"We'll deal with that later, Sergeant," Taylor says. "Just get us somewhere safe. When those nukes hit, we want to be behind several layers of steel and concrete and nowhere near that open door back there."

"This way, sir," Kreigel says and nods towards a large door at the end of the corridor.

"Holt, you're on point," Taylor orders. "Lead the way."

Holt moves to the front of the group, the flashlight on his carbine illuminating the dust filled, dank corridor. He leads them to the end and waits by the door until the team, as well as Lu, Bolton, and Lowell, are in position on each side of the door.

Holt holds up a hand and shows three fingers then two then one. He grabs the door's handle, twists it and pulls on the door, struggling against the rusty hinges. Then he waits.

Taylor nods and points for Holt to move out. The man rushes through the doorway and instantly gunfire erupts. He dives back through and rolls to the side, flattening himself against the wall.

"This is Lieutenant Mallory Taylor of the United States Navy!" Taylor yells. "Hold your fire!"

The gunfire intensifies and everyone ducks their heads away from the doorway. Kreigel cries out as a ricochet hits him in the chest, but he gives a thumbs up and slaps the spot where he's hit, indicating that his body armor kept the round from ripping open his lungs.

In seconds, the gunfire stops and the sound of magazines hitting the concrete tells the team it's their turn.

Without saying a word, Rogue Team rushes through the doorway, leaving Bolton in the corridor with an M-4 to cover Lu and Lowell. Gunshots pop in quick succession then it's quiet.

"Clear!"

"Clear!"

"Clear!"

"Come on," Taylor says, poking his head back through the door. "We've secured this section."

***

"Five minutes, Mr. President," General Tulane announces.

Everyone in the situation room still stares at the main monitor despite the fact it sits there blank, the satellite feed long gone.

"Sir, as much as I oppose this course of action, I support your strength to make the decision that needed to be made," Borland says. "And that's not a suck up, that's just the truth."

"Thank you, Jeremy," President Nance says, his face tired and haggard. "I'll take all the support I can get right now. In five minutes, we find out if I have made the right choice or the biggest mistake in history."

All eyes turn from the man as his words sink in. They too, every last one of them in the situation room, will be part of saving their country from an imminent threat or condemning the world to a slow death. Quite possibly both.

***

"Clear," Holt says as they turn a corner onto yet another concrete corridor. "Jesus, this place is nuts."

"Where to now, Sergeant?" Taylor asks Kreigel.

"There are what I think are administrative offices this way," Kreigel says. "Three more corridors ahead, close to one of the storage bays and secondary entrance."

They take a few steps when the door at the far end of the corridor is thrown open and several men and women hurry through, rifles of various types up and aimed at the team.

"Hold your fire!" Taylor calls as he sees Luke step through with a gun to Kyle's head and Tiff right behind him with a gun to Dr. Probst's head.

"State your business, demons!" Luke shouts.

"Uh...what?" Taylor asks. "Did you just call us...demons?"

"You wear the skin of soldiers, but we know you have devoured their souls and been sent by your master to try to take ours," Luke spits. "You will not take us!"

"Dr. Probst?" Taylor asks. "Is that you?"

"They know her! They recognize this one as part of their brood!" Luke hisses.

"No, they have been sent to take her," Kyle says quickly. "She is valuable to the truth and they want her for their own ends."

Luke looks at the boy, then over at Dr. Probst. "How do I know that? You have not proven yourself to me yet, boy."

Lu looks around Bolton and gasps as a beam of light hits Kyle right in the face.

"Kyle?" she whispers.

"What?" Bolton asks, looking over his shoulder at her. "Did you say Kyle?"

He looks back quickly and sees Luke's eyes go wide. The man presses his gun harder against Kyle's head just as Lu shouts, "Kyle!"

"They know you too, boy!" Luke yells.

Bolton squeezes the trigger and Luke's head rocks back. The gun in his hand goes off and Kyle falls to the floor. Rogue Team drops to their knees and opens fire as Lowell hits the ground, grabbing Lu and yanking her down with him.

The gunfire stops and the flashlights pierce the smoke that fills the corridor, showing Dr. Probst as the only person standing, her arms crossed in front of her face.

"Am I dead?" she asks.

"No, Doctor, you are not," Taylor says.

Dr. Probst lowers her arms and then looks at Kyle lying on the ground. "Oh, crap."

Lu shoves men this way and that as she sprints down the corridor to her son. She throws herself onto the ground and her hands hover just above the boy, afraid to touch him and do more damage than there already is.

"Is he okay?" Bolton asks as he hurries up to Lu. "Tell me he's alright!"

"I don't know!" Lu shouts. "Oh, God there's blood everywhere!"

"Move," Toloski says. "I'll check him."

He pushes Lu out of the way and Bolton has to grab her shoulders to keep her from going after the man. Toloski pulls out a med kit from his pack and starts wiping the blood from Kyle's face. He pours antiseptic across a deep gouge on Kyle's forehead then takes a deep breath.

"He's fine," he says, looking back at Lu and Bolton. "The bullet grazed his forehead. He's unconscious, but his pulse is strong." He looks up at Dr. Probst. "Is there someplace we can take him a little more comfortable than this hallway?"

Dr. Probst just keeps staring at Kyle.

"Doctor?" Taylor barks, getting Dr. Probst's attention quickly. "Where can we take him?"

"Uh, this way," she says. "There's some administrative offices they've turned into lounges. We can put him on one of the couches."

"Will that be deep enough for us, Sergeant?" Taylor asks Kreigel.

The man pulls out his tablet and checks the schematic. "Should be. Let's just hope this place holds up when the blasts hit."

"It looks like it held up during the first eruption," Bolton says. "Should be good for what's coming."

"Blasts?" Dr. Probst asks. "What's coming?"

"The president has ordered a nuclear strike on ground zero," Taylor states. "In less than a minute, we're going to be standing here or we aren't."

"Nuclear strike?" Dr. Probst gasps. "Dear God…"

"No shit, lady," Lowell says. "Welcome to the apocalypse."

***

The situation room is silent then, "Sir, the warheads have detonated."

President Nance takes a deep breath and stands up. "Right now, we are witness to the first nuclear strike on United States soil. And it was ordered by me, the person trusted to prevent such an occurrence. In the next few hours, we will know whether or not it was the right choice. Until then, I ask that you bow your heads for a moment and pray that all will be well and we have ended this nightmare for good."

FOURTEEN

"Secondary entrance is demolished," Kreigel says as he walks into the lounge and plops down into a chair. "That leaves the way we came in."

"Which has either caved in or is still blocked by those things," Taylor says. He stands up and sighs. "Only one way to find out. You coming?"

"Yeah," Bolton says as he zips up the front of his hot suit. "Let's do this."

"How are we going to get past the monsters if the entrance is still intact?" Holt asks.

"I told you I know how to kill the things," Lowell says, standing up and grabbing a hot suit from Toloski's hands. "I'm coming with you."

"Just tell us," Taylor says. "No need for you to tag along."

"Yeah, well, if I'm wrong and it doesn't work, I think I may go for a stroll outside," Lowell says. "Radiation may kill me, monsters might eat me, or I could fall off the mountain and break my neck." He shrugs. "Better than staying in here. I've lived behind concrete walls enough in my life and made a promise to myself to enjoy the sunshine more."

"You okay with this?" Bolton asks Lu as the woman crouches next to her unconscious son who is laid out on one of the couches.

"With Lowell leaving or with you leaving?" Lu asks, her eyes locking onto Bolton's.

"Both," Bolton replies.

"Yeah," Lu says. "Just be sure to come back."

"You mean him, right?" Lowell says, pointing at Bolton.

"Yes, I mean him," Lu says. "But if you want to come back too, that's cool."

"I'm touched," Lowell says. "But not making any promises."

"Suit up and let's move," Taylor says. "I'll make the call."

***

"Sir?" Admiral Quigley says, smiling at the president. "Just received word from Lieutenant Taylor. They survived the blasts and are attempting to leave the bunker."

"Attempting?" President Nance asks. "What does that mean?"

The smile leaves Admiral Quigley's face. "Their way out is blocked by hostiles, sir. Taylor says they have a plan, but won't elaborate until he knows it will work."

"It better," President Nance says. "If I don't have confirmation that this strike worked then I will have to call in another to be sure."

Everyone seated at the table stops what they are doing and looks to the president.

"You don't mean that, Mr. President," Borland states. "I know you don't."

"I do mean it, Jeremy," President Nance says. "We cannot take the chance that more of those monsters will be unleashed on our country. I will order another strike unless I hear positive results from our men on the ground."

***

"You're joking, right?" Taylor says, his voice muffled by the face mask in his hot suit. "You want to feed people to them?"

"No," Lowell says, his voice muffled as well. "I want to soak the body parts in diesel, strap some ammo to the parts, and then let the things chow down. Trust me on this. I've watched it work."

"You think it's the diesel and the gunpowder that caused that reaction?" Bolton asks, looking at Lowell. "Like that thing at the gas station? It drank a ton of diesel then ate my carbine."

"I don't think the diesel has anything to do with it," Lowell says. "The flying thing ate that arm with the pistol and in seconds it burst open with that foam."

"Then why bother with the diesel?" Holt asks.

"Bait," Kreigel says. "The things like diesel."

"Yep," Lowell nods. "We toss them the treats and they do all the work."

Taylor watches Lowell for a moment then looks over at Bolton. "You know this guy better than we do. Can we trust him?"

"No," Bolton says. "I don't trust him at all, but I know he wants to stay alive and get out of here. That I can trust."

"And here I thought we'd bonded," Lowell laughs. "Team ready? Let's move out!"

No one moves.

Taylor sighs and turns to his men.

"Find fire axes," he says. "We have some corpses to dismember."

***

"Mom?" Kyle whispers as his eyes flutter open and he sees Lu's head resting on the couch cushion next to his as she sits on the floor. "Mom, is that you?"

"Oh, God, Kyle," Lu exclaims and starts covering his face in kisses.

"Ow. Stop," he says and pushes her away weakly. "My head hurts."

"You took a bullet across the forehead, kid," Dr. Probst says, getting up from her chair and walking over to the couch. "Your dad shot Luke and saved your life."

"What?" Kyle says, trying to shove himself up from the couch. "Linder is here? He's alive?"

"You said Linder wasn't your dad," Dr. Probst says, looking at Lu. "I give up."

"Wait, why do you think Linder is your father?" Lu asks.

"Grandma told me," Kyle says.

"Did she?" Lu frowns. "I'll have to speak to her about that crap." Then she sees the look on Kyle's face. "Oh...no."

"Linder killed her," Kyle says. "When he found us, he shot her. I tried to get away, but he caught up to me." He breaks down into heavy sobs and Lu wraps him in her arms.

"It's okay, baby," she soothes. "Let it out."

Kyle wails for a couple of minutes, and then pulls himself together enough to tell his mother what happened. Lu sits there quietly, listening to every word; every description of the violence and horror Kyle went through. When he's finally done, she is crying with him.

"So who's the real dad then? Linder or Bolton?" Dr. Probst asks then shrinks back at the look of anger she receives from Lu. "Oh, sorry. I probably should have let you say that."

"What?" Kyle says. "Bolton? You mean Connor? He's my dad?"

"Yes," Lu says. "He is. I never told you because it would have put him in danger and I just couldn't afford that."

"Holy crap," Kyle whispers.

"He's here, you know," Dr. Probst says. "Well, sort of."

"Do you mind?" Lu snaps.

"He's here? Where?" Kyle asks and looks around then winces from the movement.

"He's busy right now," Lu says. "He'll be back in a while. You need to rest some more anyway."

"Yeah...okay," Kyle says, his eyelids already drooping. "Don't let him leave when he gets back."

"I don't plan on it," Lu says. "I'll make sure he stays with us from now on."

***

"There are five of the things out there," Lowell says. "And we each have two bundles. We have twelve chances to make this work."

"Good math," Kreigel says as the men stand by the door that leads into the hangar entrance. "Let's just get this over with."

Lowell holds up a bundle, which happens to be a man's thigh with two magazines of live ammunition taped around it. "This should be enough gunpowder to do the trick. Once we get through, we find a drum of diesel, get with the dunking of our treats, and toss them towards the door. Pretty sure the fucking things will smell them and snatch 'em up. Got it?"

Taylor nods at Holt who rips open the door so the men can rush into the hangar. They hurry across the concrete towards the entrance and the monsters that wait on the other side.

Except they aren't just waiting. All the men stop in their tracks as they see parts of five heads wedged against the opening in the massive hangar door, their blue tongues lashing out at the diesel drums that had been stacked against the wall, but are now strewn everywhere, their metal sides pierced and leaking.

"Oh shit," Lowell says. "I hope they didn't ruin their appetites."

All tongues stop and zip back across the floor to their respective mouths. Cold black eyes watch the men as they stand there with their bloody bundles in hand.

"What now?" Toloski whispers.

"We'll never get to the drums before they nail us," Holt says.

"Then we bowl," Bolton replies.

He draws his arm back and hurls one of his bundles at the drums. It bangs against the metal and lands right in a large puddle of fuel. None of the beasts go for it.

"Toss them all," Taylor says. "Maybe they need volume for it to be worth the effort."

A blue tongue shoots out towards them and they all dive to the side. But Lowell isn't fast enough and it snags him around the ankle, pulling him towards the entrance and the hundreds of waiting teeth.

"Oh fuck!" Lowell yells as the plastic suit he's in slides across the concrete.

Just as he passes the diesel drums, he reaches out and drags his bundles through the large pool of diesel, soaking them completely. He rolls onto his back and lifts his head so he can watch the tongue take him to his death.

"Fuck you!" he yells and tosses the bundles into the open mouth.

The monster shrieks and the tongue lets go. He slides another foot or so and then stops. He hears the thing chomp down on the fuel soaked body parts and ammo. Lowell scuttles backwards, his eyes never leaving the gap under the hangar door. He watches as another of the creatures focuses its attention on him and he quickly realizes he doesn't have anything left to bribe this one with.

"Here!" Bolton yells and tosses a bundle towards the entrance.

More and more bundles of dead flesh and ammo land with it and tongues go flying, snatching up the snacks. The bundles are nothing but quick bites for the enormous monsters, and in seconds, the mouths stop chomping and the black eyes once again return to the opening, focusing on the men before them.

"Shit," Taylor says, taking his M-4 from his back and putting it to his shoulder.

A tongue darts out at him and he leaps out of the way. More tongues follow and the men dive this way and that, dodging the deadly blue appendages. Then the attacks stop and a low moaning can be heard.

The single moaning is joined by more sounds and the heads quickly withdraw from the hangar door. The men pick themselves up off the ground and walk slowly forward, except for Lowell, who stays right where he is.

"Have you never watched a horror movie?" Lowell snaps. "Dudes! They're coming back!"

A head appears at the hangar door and a tongue starts to shoot out, causing the men to jump back and open fire. But the tongue only makes it a couple feet before it slows and lies there limp and useless. Then a gush of grey foam shoots out of the monster's mouth and begins to harden. The thing hisses, groans, then goes silent. And still.

No one moves, even when they hear more hisses and groans from outside, followed by the sounds of large things falling and liquids gushing.

"Sir?" Kreigel asks, looking over at Taylor. "Should I check it out?"

"Yes, Sergeant," Taylor says.

Kreigel nods, adjusts his carbine against his shoulder, and steps cautiously towards the hangar door. He reaches the opening, takes a deep breath, then crouches down. He peers through the two foot space, his M-4 sweeping from side to side and then sits down on his ass.

"Holy shit, sir. It worked," Kreigel says. "The things are dead. Like seriously dead."

The rest of the men rush over to the entrance and crouch down, their eyes wide as they see the burst open bodies and hardened grey foam that surrounds those bodies.

"I only see two," Taylor says, looking at the beasts that lay still on the ground by the torn apart Humvee. "Where are the others?"

"Down there," Kreigel says as he crawls under the door and moves to the edge of the short ledge. "They must have lost their grips. Take a look."

Everyone joins him and they peer over the side and look down at the broken and mangled monster corpses below.

"Nice," Lowell says, joining the rest. "It worked."

"That tone makes it sound like you weren't sure," Taylor says, looking at Lowell.

Lowell shrugs and smiles through the face mask. "I wasn't. Just had a hunch."

"Good hunch," Bolton says.

"No shit," Kreigel agrees.

"Okay, let's get moving," Taylor orders. "We have a long walk ahead of us."

***

They can see for miles from the high ridge and the view is breathtaking.

"It'd be kinda pretty if it wasn't for the destroyed city," Holt says as the men stand in a row, their eyes focused on the spot where the massive hole should be.

But it's not there. Instead, there is a huge depression in the land, like a two hundred mile wide divot has been carved out of the earth. Yet, there is no sign of an ash cloud or wriggling mass of monsters.

"Want me to call this in?" Kreigel asks.

"Job isn't done yet," Bolton says, tapping at the wide radiation strip on his wrist. The color is bright green, indicating that no radiation has made it to the ridge yet. "We have to get close enough to see how bad the contamination is."

"Good thing I wore my good boots today," Holt says and the men turn and start to make their way down to the ground below.

It's a good couple of hours before they reach Missoula and another couple more hours before they get as close to the divot as they feel comfortable getting. Despite there being no sign of monsters coming up from the divot, there are still the monsters that emerged previously to worry about. Not to mention the very good possibility that the ground within a mile of the divot is highly unstable.

"I don't get it," Bolton says, looking at the green strip around his wrist. "We should be picking up something, but I don't see any signs of radiation at all."

"The hole could have collapsed and covered it," Taylor says. "Like nuclear waste buried in the Nevada Mountains."

"Could have," Bolton says. "But do you really believe that?"

"I'll believe almost anything after these last few days," Taylor says. "Now call it in."

***

"Thank you, Sergeant Bolton," President Nance says. "Your service has been invaluable. Your country is proud of you and I am proud of what you and Rogue Team have accomplished."

"Thank you, Mr. President," Bolton replies over the com. "When can we expect extraction, sir?"

President Nance looks down the table at General Azoul.

"We'll be sending a Chinook in to get you within twenty-four hours, Sergeant," General Azoul says. "I wish we could get you sooner, but our resources are thin at the moment, as I'm sure you can understand."

"Yes, General, I can," Bolton responds. "We'll be waiting here for your word. We'll also be keeping an eye out for the monsters that are still on the loose. I hope we don't see any, but we know they are out there."

"Yes and thank you for your information on how to kill these beasts, Sergeant," President Nance says. "You have gone over and above your call of duty."

"I don't know if that's possible, sir, but thank you again," Bolton says. "Uh, on that subject, I do have a request, sir."

"I think you can save your requests for a more formal setting, Sergeant," General Azoul interrupts.

"Nonsense," President Nance responds. "What's your request, Sergeant?"

"The man that figured out how to kill the monsters, sir," Bolton begins. "Anson Lowell. He is technically still a federal prisoner. I'd like to request his sentence be commuted, sir. I wouldn't be here if it wasn't for him."

Joan slaps a file on the table in front of President Nance. He opens it and scans the contents quickly.

"The man killed two judges, as well as police officers, Sergeant," President Nance says. "I don't know if I can honor that request."

"I understand, sir," Bolton says. "Just wanted to ask. It's the least I can do for the guy."

"Understood, Sergeant," President Nance says. "You men be sure to take care of yourselves until we can get you safely home. I'd hate to lose this nation's newest heroes."

He waves his hand and the connection is cut.

"Where are we?" he asks the table.

"Power is slowly being restored to areas affected by the EMP, sir," Joan responds. "We have had sightings of the large and small ground monsters. All commanders have been informed on the theory on how to kill them."

"What about the flying monsters?" President Nance asks. "Where are we with those?"

"Jets have been pursuing them, sir," General Tulane states. "We have had some success with engagement, but mostly, we are following them."

"Following?" President Nance asks.

"They are all moving out to sea, sir," Admiral Quigley says. "I have ships off the Pacific coast reporting they are just flying out across the ocean by the hundreds. They aren't stopping and they aren't attacking, just flying, sir."

"That is what I am hearing as well," General Tulane agrees. "They are all just flying out over the water."

"Well, better than trying to attack our people," President Nance says. "How soon until we have satellites over ground zero?"

"Four hours, sir," Borland says. "I am coordinating with several organizations and institutions to put together research teams. We'll want to get them on the ground ASAP and start studying the area. The more information we have the better prepared we will be if this happens again."

"Do you think it will?" President Nance asks. "Dr. Hall? What can you tell us?"

"That I'm exhausted," Dr. Hall responds. "And hungry again. Other than that, not much. Everything I've told you has been based on educated guesses. Until we have hard facts, we can't really know if more of those things will come up from the ground or if the destruction of ground zero has sealed them off once and for all."

"Then we stay vigilant," President Nance says. "Now, let's talk about the continuing relocation of our citizens. Since we cannot be sure this is entirely over, I believe we should proceed as planned."

"Yes, sir," Joan nods. "I have the numbers right here."

***

"What is this?" Kyle asks as he dips his spoon in the Mylar pouch once again and lets the orange goop drip from the end. "Tastes like puke."

"It's carrot puke," Lu smiles. "You like carrot puke."

"No one likes carrot puke," Kyle smiles.

"I'm so hungry I'll eat anything," Dr. Probst says, greedily slurping the orange paste from her own spoon. "Mmmm, yummy."

They all take a few more bites, grimace and then set the half empty pouches to the side.

"Let's fill up on water," Lu says, handing Kyle a bottle and tossing one to Dr. Probst. "We can all use the hydration anyway."

Dr. Probst takes a long drink then looks at Kyle. "Can I ask you a question?"

"Uh, sure," Kyle shrugs. "What's up?"

"How'd you know that Luke guy would react that way?" she asks.

"Moss gave me the idea in Missoula," Kyle says. "He said Luke was raised on the crazy side of religion. I guess I figured he would latch onto the whole end of day's thing. The guy seemed like he wanted to believe in a divine struggle more than a terrestrial one."

"Terrestrial?" Lu laughs. "Where'd you hear that word?"

"Champion may have been small, but it did have a high school, Mom," Kyle replies. "Grandma wouldn't accept anything less than a B, remember?"

The thought of Terrie makes the two Morgans frown and then grasp hands.

"Hey," Kyle says suddenly, making Lu and Dr. Probst jump. "What was the info you wouldn't tell the president? The guy sent a SEAL Team to get you, so it has to be good."

"Yeah, well, I'm going to pay for it," Dr. Probst says, "because there isn't any info. I saw a big, huge hole in the ground, that's it. Well, and a lot of monsters coming out of the hole, but nothing they don't already know."

"You lied to the President of the United States?" Lu asks, shocked. "You could go to prison for that."

"I could," Dr. Probst says, "but I'm betting that the man has bigger things to deal with."

"So you risked men's lives just so they would rescue you?" Kyle asks. "They may have been needed somewhere else, you know."

"I did know," Dr. Probst nods. "I also knew *I* needed to be somewhere else. I was forced to jump from a plane that had lost power, landed right next to a hole full of monsters, had to hide and run from those monsters, watched men get killed, watched monsters chase us while I was on horseback, which I'll never ride again, and then got stuck in a bunker with crazy people. Cheryl needed to go home."

"Who?" Kyle asks.

"Cheryl. That's me. I'm Cheryl."

"Hey, Cheryl," Lu says. "Thank you for making that call and lying. Otherwise, I wouldn't be here and I wouldn't have found my son."

"Anytime," Dr. Probst says then stretches. "I think I'm going to find a quiet place and crash out. Wake me up when the cavalry gets here. Or if we need to run from monsters."

"Let's hope for the former," Lu smiles.

She watches Dr. Probst grab a candle then nod her head as she leaves to find a private room.

"Nice lady," Lu says.

"Yeah, she is," Kyle says then sighs. "You think he's dead?"

Lu looks at her son and nods. "Linder? Yeah."

"So no more running?" Kyle asks.

"No more running," Lu nods. "Time to come out in the open. Or at least once we know we won't get eaten."

"You ever going to tell me the real story?" Kyle says. "Why you never told me about my real dad? Why Grandma thought Linder was?"

"I will, I promise, just not right now. Let me get my strength back and sort it all out."

"Okay," Kyle says. "But make sure you sort *everything* out. I don't want to live with lies anymore, Mom."

Lu leans in and kisses the bandage on his forehead. "I don't either, baby. I don't either."

The ground shakes slightly and Kyle and Lu look at each other.

"What's that?" Kyle asks.

"I don't know," Lu says. "Hold on."

She gets up, takes a candle, and walks out into the hallway, surprised to see Bolton running towards her.

"Connor! You're back!" she shouts. "What's happening?"

"I don't know," he says, and then they both stumble to the side as the entire mountain is shaken to its foundation.

"Is it erupting again?" Lu shouts.

"I don't know!" Bolton shouts back as they clutch at each other and try to stay on their feet.

***

The long, black sedan pulls away from the curb as Dr. Hall turns around and looks up at his boring apartment complex. Having spent most of the last twenty-four hours deep below the White House, he's not sure how he can go back to being boring old Dr. Blane Hall. He sighs and walks up the stone steps to the entrance.

He fumbles around in his pockets, but quickly realizes, he doesn't have his keys. He looks at the row of buttons on the wall and tries to figure out who will be home and who has already evacuated. He then realizes he doesn't really know his neighbors well enough to have the answers he needs, so he just starts pressing buttons, hoping someone will be home.

"What?" someone snaps.

"Hey, sorry, it's uh, Blane Hall in 3C," Dr. Hall says as a wind whips up and he pulls his coat tighter around him. "I forgot my keys. Can you buzz me in?"

"You the guy that got mad that time my girlfriend was making kimchi? Kept saying it smelled like Korean farts?"

"Uh...no. Must have been some other guy," Dr. Hall replies, hoping the guy buys the lie.

"Whatever."

There's a loud buzzing and Dr. Hall opens the front door as fast as he can. He makes his way up the two flights of steps and sighs again when he realizes he can't get into his apartment either. He puts his back to his door and slides to the ground. He closes his eyes and is asleep in seconds.

The radiators in the hallway tick and clank. Dr. Hall wakes up, drenched in sweat, and groggily takes his winter coat off. He slides the sleeves of his sweater up and looks down as static electricity causes his arm hair to rise.

Then he jumps to his feet, his eyes glued to his arm. He smoothens down the hair, but it stands back up instantly. He looks around and kneels next to his bag, tossing stuff out onto the floor until he finds a small, plastic water bottle with the presidential seal on the side. He thought he was stealing it for a memento, but now knows it could be the most important water bottle ever.

He pours some water on his arm and watches as the hair slicks down and clumps up. He swirls it with his finger and then gasps at what he sees.

"Oh no," he mutters. "No, no, no. I fucked up. Oh, shit, I fucked up big time."

He grabs his cell phone and dials a number he was given.

"Yes, this is Dr. Blane Hall," the man almost shouts into the phone. "I need to speak to the president immediately!" He listens for a second. "Yes, it's an emergency! I'll hold, but we may not have much time!"

He starts to pace the hallway, getting frustrated with every second that passes.

Finally, "Dr. Hall, this is President Nance. I was told it was urgent. What do you need?"

"Sir, I was wrong," Dr. Hall says. "The hole, it didn't have tails in it, sir."

"What are you talking about? What changed your mind?"

"It doesn't matter," Dr. Hall says, rushing his words. "But those things weren't tails, sir."

"Then what were they? We all saw them."

"They were cilia, sir." He waits, but doesn't get a response and figures the man doesn't know what cilia are. "Like hairs on some organisms. We have them in our tracheas and other mucosal areas. They are usually microscopic, because of their size ratio to the organism they are on. That means, sir, that if I'm right, the organism in that hole is beyond the size of anything we have ever seen."

He waits some more, but still no response.

"Mr. President, did you hear me? Whatever is in that hole could be thousands of feet tall. And considering your men didn't find traces of nuclear radiation, I'm thinking the nukes may not have killed it, sir, but fed it! Hello? Mr. President?"

He looks down at his phone and realizes the signal has been lost. He's about to dial again when he feels a buzzing in his head and a cramping in his stomach.

Then the lights go out.

He runs to the window at the end of the hall and looks out on the city around him. For blocks and blocks he sees nothing but darkness.

"Oh, no, not again," he whispers. "Oh, shit, it's coming."

**

"Dr. Hall?" President Nance shouts. "Did we lose him? Someone call him back!"

"Sir, we can't," Joan says. "We've lost all communication with the outside world."

"We've what?" President Nance asks. "How?"

Joan looks over at one of the techs.

"Another EMP, Mr. President," the tech says. "As far as we can tell it's affected the entire country."

"It what?" President Nance asks. "How is that possible? Unless..."

"Unless the supervolcano erupted again," Joan says.

"Dear, God," President Nance says, his features looking ancient and haggard. "If the EMP was big enough to cover the whole country, then what is coming up out of that hole this time?"

No one in the situation room answers his question. They all just let it hang there, lost in their individual fears. The world as they know it, gone forever.

THE END

Author's Note:

Why, yes, this will be another series! Thank you for asking.

Seriously, *Kaiju Winter* has been conceived as a four book series from the beginning. Some may think I cliffhangered y'all, but I didn't. This is the first part to a much longer narrative. It does end suddenly, but only after the major conflict is resolved, i.e. shit gets nuked.

What now? You'll have to wait and see! And don't worry, if you didn't get enough Kaiju in this one then rest assured that the next novel, *Kaiju Storm*, will have uber amounts of Kaiju. It'll be a veritable Kaiju buffet!

So thanks for reading and hanging with me during my entrée into a new genre. It has been a blast writing about giant monsters and I can't wait to share the next chapter in this saga!

Cheers!

Jake Bible lives in Asheville, NC with his wife and two kids.

A professional writer since 2009, Jake has a record of innovation, invention and creativity. Novelist, short story writer, independent screenwriter, podcaster, and inventor of the Drabble Novel, Jake is able to switch between or mash-up genres with ease to create new and exciting storyscapes that have captivated and built an audience of thousands.

He is the author of the bestselling Z-Burbia series for Severed Press as well as the Apex Trilogy (DEAD MECH, The Americans, Metal and Ash).

Find him at jakebible.com. Join him on Twitter and Facebook.

9428413R00136

Printed in Great Britain
by Amazon.co.uk, Ltd.,
Marston Gate.